Dan knew he was stating the obvious, but he had to explain to her.

"Of course it's about more than just the review," she yelled, throwing her arms in the air. Then she looked over her shoulder at the door as if waiting for one of her employees to come in and see what was wrong. "You're a restaurant reviewer, it's your *job* to write reviews and sometimes you have to write bad ones. Maybe you're even one of those sick bastards that gets enjoyment from skewering chefs from your position of power. I don't know and I don't care."

Her breasts lifted the buttons on her chef's jacket as she took a deep breath and her hands returned to their enraged position on her hips. Despite himself, the action momentarily distracted him.

"What really pisses me off is that you panned my restaurant and then *courted—*" she said the word like it was rotten food at the bottom of a garbage can "—me. Did you get some sick thrill knowing you were kissing the woman whose career you tried to destroy?"

Dear Reader,

Years ago I read a romance novel where the heroine was a cook at her family's restaurant and the hero wrote a terrible review. The hero wasn't a restaurant critic by career; he was covering the beat for a sick coworker. I liked the book (the name of which I've long forgotten), but I wished the hero had loved food as much as the heroine. Through that wish, and many years later, Tilly and Dan were born.

I set the novel in Chicago because it is my favorite city. Chicago is a city of neighborhoods, with delicious restaurants reflecting its strong immigrant communities. Tilly's Babka grew out of her experience in her parents' Polish restaurant and from her grandparents, who immigrated to Chicago. Like Dan, many Chicagoans are immigrants from other places in the United States. They're drawn to the city by diverse neighborhoods, good food and magical summers full of festivals (making up for the terrible winters). No matter their previous home, people find community in Chicago. I know I did.

The best part about setting a novel in my favorite city was I got to revisit some of my favorite places, this time through Dan and Tilly's eyes. I have fond memories of the long trek from the South Side of Chicago up to the Ravinia Festival to make use of the free tickets for students and I have a Chicago-style hot dog every time I visit friends in Chicago.

If you've never been to Chicago, I hope you may come to love the city as Dan and Tilly do. If you love Chicago the way I do, I hope they take you to some of your favorite haunts. If my novel makes you hungry for Polish cooking, Tilly and I rely on the encyclopedic *Polish Heritage Cookery*, by Robert and Maria Strybel.

Enjoy!

Jennifer Lohmann

Reservations
for Two

JENNIFER LOHMANN

HARLEQUIN® SUPER ROMANCE®

Recycling programs
for this product may
not exist in your area.

ISBN-13: 978-0-373-71834-4

RESERVATIONS FOR TWO

Copyright © 2013 by Jennifer Lohmann

Printed in U.S.A.

ABOUT THE AUTHOR

Jennifer Lohmann is a Rocky Mountain girl at heart, having grown up in southern Idaho and Salt Lake City. After graduating with a degree in Economics from the University of Chicago, she moved to Shanghai to teach English. Back in the United States, she earned a master's in library science and now works as a public librarian. She was the Romance Writers of America's librarian of the year in 2010. She lives in the Southeast with a dog, three chickens, four cats and a husband who gamely eats everything she cooks. She's an adventurous eater, having celebrated the sale of her first book with an invertebrate dinner at a museum, followed a few days later by an offal dinner at a favorite restaurant.

Thank you, Mom, for teaching me how to cook.

We boss each other around and argue about technique too much to be in the kitchen together anymore, but the love of food stays with me.

CHAPTER ONE

FOR THE FIRST time since her junior prom, Tilly Milek's main goal was not to be featured in *Saveur*. Her new goal: to hunt down the identity of *CarpeChicago*'s The Eater and shake him until he told her why in the name of Mary the Blessed Virgin he had written that review.

Her day had started out innocuously enough. She had gotten to Babka at nine, spent an hour and a half doing the restaurant's bookkeeping and answering emails, planning today's menu, creating prep lists for AM Carlos and confirming several reservations. All the reservations through OpenTable had real phone numbers. Not a single person had entered 312-123-4567. Guaranteed to be a good day.

Until all the staff had sat down for the family meal, without their hostess, Tilly would have placed serious money on tonight being a big night at Babka.

Clearly, she hadn't said enough rosaries in her lifetime because God was laughing at her.

"We don't have the whole day to waste waiting for Karen. We're going to get started." Tilly looked around at the staff eating their dinner. "Now, about the menu tonight…"

"Our first review!" Karen, hyperactive as usual, slammed through the silver swinging doors between the kitchen and the dining room, holding her iPad in front of her as an offering to the kitchen gods. "It's The Eater, on

CarpeChicago." She was loud enough they could probably hear her at the bookstore next door. "It's a great place for it, right? I mean, that blog is one of the most widely read in the city and their opinions on everything from food to music are trusted by anyone who can use a mouse. That's what you want, right?"

Right now what she wanted was for Karen to arrive to work on time, Tilly thought, as her hostess skidded to a halt beside the table. Karen should have been at Babka about a half an hour ago finishing up the last of the reservations instead of Candace having to call with confirmations.

"The review seems a little early," Tilly commented.

As far as her records indicated, no one who'd eaten at Babka more than once had ordered enough for a review or taken photos, so she hadn't expected a review out of the *Sun-Times* or *Tribune* for at least another month. *CarpeChicago* might be a blog, but their restaurant reviewer adhered as strictly to professional standards as any newspaper, whether writing about the experimental and constantly-topping-restaurant-lists Alinea or a new hole-in-the-wall noodle shop in Chinatown. The Eater's honesty and willingness to eat anything was what made his reviews so popular. That, and the constant guessing game about who he was. Tilly wasn't even sure The Eater was a man. If her records on their customers were right, The Eater might be a group writing together. Those who knew weren't telling. He (they?) were the best kept secret in Chicago.

Whoever it was, Babka *needed* a good review.

"Karen, you're late."

"I know, I know. But you'll forgive me because I come bearing such wonderful gifts. We should open a bottle of champagne. Candace—" Karen motioned to the bartender, a short, attractive African-American woman "—get some glasses and we'll pop a bottle."

Tilly put her arm on Candace's shoulders to stall her. "We'll hold off on the champagne. It's four-thirty in the afternoon. Bubbly can wait until later, when we know what he said. I'd hate to waste a bottle of the best on a crummy review."

"Omigod! I didn't even read it. It popped up on my RSS feed while I was on the bus and I ran here from the bus stop as fast as I could." Karen panted as if to emphasize her mad dash. "How could the review be bad? I mean, look around. No restaurant in Chicago is better."

Babka was everything Tilly had ever wanted in a restaurant of her own, even though the place had cost more to get up and running than she'd planned. Babka was homey and calming, but sophisticated without being snotty. Every time she walked through the door, she got a jolt of pride; the place was all hers. Well, hers and the bank's.

"Don't keep us in suspense any longer," Candace said from her left, looking up from the wine list and tonight's menu. "Read the review already."

Karen tapped her finger on the tablet's screen until she pulled up the review. "'Babka and Polish Cuisine in Chicago Serves World War III.'" Uncharacteristically, Karen was still for a moment. "The headline doesn't sound good." She turned the tablet around to face Tilly. "Do you want to read it, Tilly, before the rest of us do?"

"No, I don't think so. We worked on Babka together and we'll read the reviews together."

Everyone around the table waited.

Karen still didn't start reading so Tilly waved her hand. "Read the stupid thing, will you, before the suspense kills me."

"Okay, here goes." Karen lowered her head to read from the screen. "'Tila Milek's first restaurant, Babka, is one of the most visually pleasing restaurants in Chicago.'" Karen's voice brightened. "Hey, that's good. I'm sure it only gets better. 'While non-Chicagoans will wonder at a fancy Polish restaurant, Milek winks at both her Polish heritage and the city itself. Painted outlines of Chicagoland's Polish landmarks, including her mother's restaurant, are barely one shade lighter than the cream walls. Combined with dark wood and beet-red accent colors, the interior is subtle, without being boring.'"

Tilly took a couple more deep breaths to calm herself, the hummingbird in her stomach settling down. No matter how fabulous the food, customers judged a restaurant based on how it looked when they walked in the door. Every moment of the experience had to meet their expectations if she wanted them to come back on a regular basis.

"'Our reservation was handled swiftly, and we were seated with no wait.'" Karen looked up from the review and giggled. "See. You always knew I was worth the tardiness."

"You're worth every penny, but don't let it go to your head."

Despite Karen's general bounciness and habit of being late, she was well organized and kept details about each customer in her head until she had time to make notes at the end of service. She had a global view of the dining room and, if she were more punctual, Tilly would make her general manager.

Karen beamed at the compliment and returned to her tablet. "'Once seated, the service was flawless. The waitress was at our table quickly and efficiently told us the specials and gave recommendations. I asked her several questions and her knowledge of the menu was extensive. We intended to start with the summer beet soup and mushroom pâté, but unfortunately, our meal was rudely interrupted. When we finally sat down to eat, my food was badly oversalted.'"

"Wait," Tilly interrupted. "Why was his meal interrupted?"

"He might say later. Maybe he came back?" Karen's voice jumped an octave with hope. "'Our meal at Babka started with a slightly bitter rye bread and eggy flatbread matched with a tangy smoked fish spread made with a fresh cheese. Every bite of our bread was heartily enjoyable and we might have continued dinner the same way, if not for the cat that snuck in the front door.'"

Mother Mary, he was here *that* night. A customer's Yorkshire terrier had escaped a woman's purse and another customer let a stray cat slip in through the front door. An epic battle between feline and canine had been fought in *her* dining room, with customers serving as tactical points of attack. As she'd handed her credit card over to the emergency vet when she picked up the cat the next morning, Tilly had been grateful the only costs seemed to be a dry-cleaning bill, a vet bill and free drinks and desserts for every customer. Surprisingly, not many plates had been broken, especially considering how many tables were turned over before the battle was won.

Tilly flopped her head down onto the table and buried her face on her crossed arms.

Then the other pan dropped. "I do not serve oversalted food," she murmured into her arms.

Even the night of the disaster, the food leaving her kitchen had been impeccable. Just her luck Mother Nature—could a stray cat and spoiled terrier be considered Mother Nature?—had crashed the party.

"Should I read on?" Karen asked, her voice shying away from its usual exuberance. "We know what happened next."

Tilly lifted her head with all the pep of a wet noodle. "Yes, I want to hear what he says." Her heart was slowly sliding down to her toes. "Maybe he has some constructive comments about…oh, I don't even know what about."

"I don't know if I should. You're a little pale."

Candace reached over and laid her hand on Tilly's. "You're like ice."

Tilly jerked her head up, pulled her hands away and looked at them. Her hands were how she made her money. Her nails were short and a bit ragged. The backs of her hands were dotted with small burn scars from banging her hand on a hot oven eleven too many times. She had a callus along the forefinger of her left hand where she held her knife and one fantastic scar across her palm from a cut at Culinary.

Chef's hands. They weren't useful for anything else. All she'd ever wanted to do was cook, and the end of her career might be on Karen's hateful iPad. She wished her first review had been in the *Tribune* so she could at least throw the damn thing without owing her employee several hundred dollars.

"If The Eater and his review are going to be the end of my career, I want to hear every word," she said, still studying her hands.

That stupid cat and dog, or some anonymous man hiding behind a ridiculous pseudonym, couldn't be the end of her career. Her hands—what would she do with her hands if she wasn't cooking?

"Um, okay." Karen's voice dropped to a mumble as she read the dreadful tale everyone around the table had witnessed. Customers were said to be helping right tables when

Karen interrupted the review with a small voice. "Do I have to go on?"

"How long did he stay?" Tilly strained to keep her voice steady. The effort made her hands shake, but those were now under the table so no one could see them. "What did he eat?"

"Um…" Karen skimmed ahead and read off The Eater's order. "He says his tablecloth got snagged on the cat's claws and their butter and fish spread ended up in his lap. He wasn't amused, though he does mention some of the customers laughing so hard they could barely stand. He writes you got the chaos under control and he might have overlooked the accident, but each dish he had ordered was like a salt lick. They left before finishing their dinner."

"Okay, so one lesson we've learned is that big purses are banned from Babka." Tilly tried to laugh a little. If she could control her emotions and learn from this calamity, then everything would be okay. Her life and her dream would all be fine. Babka and her grandmother's legacy would survive. No problem. She could turn this mess around. "What other lessons can we learn?"

"Can you work backward from what he ate to see who oversalted the food?" Karen asked.

Tilly shook her head. "I can't pin everything he ate on one cook. His dishes came from different stations, so the only way everything got oversalted was if *I* added salt at the pass. And I didn't do that."

"The reviewer—which customer was he?" Candace glanced from Karen to Steve, the runner. "Steve, do you know who got that combination of food? Karen, you're normally so good at remembering customers. Do you remember him?"

"What I want to know is," Steve slipped in, "why he

wrote the review when the cat incident was obviously a fluke."

"The Eater is a jerk," Karen said. "No reviewer writes on one visit. Everyone knows this. He should have come back."

Tilly took another deep breath. "Karen's right. No reader would believe a review written about one night, even from The Eater." Her heartbeat slowed to a more normal speed. "Don't worry, Babka will be fine."

Faces at the table just looked at her. Her staff didn't believe her, either.

"Um, Tilly?" Karen's voice was still missing its pre-review cheer and Tilly knew instantly what she was going to say. "You're demonstrating at the Taste of Chicago on Monday. What are you going to do?"

Poof. The tiny feeling of calm she had been clinging to flashed brightly before her eyes and disappeared in a cloud of smoke. Tilly groaned.

The Taste of Chicago was a huge food festival, spanning the week of July Fourth. Thousands of Chicagoans and tourists converged on Grant and Millennium parks to try bites of every kind of food Chicago had to offer, to watch chefs demonstrate their signature dishes and to celebrate warmth in a city famous for its cold.

"How many people at your demonstration will have read the review?" asked one of the waiters.

Something in her stomach bubbled, but he kept talking. "Will you be chopping onions for the birds or will the seats be filled with hecklers?"

Whatever had been bubbling in her stomach was moving up her throat.

"Do you think they'll have stuffed cats to throw?" Karen joined in with a giggle.

No one seemed to notice Tilly's stomach was rebelling, even though her face was surely green.

"What do you think is worse, a tent full of empty chairs or everyone bringing their pets to Tilly's demonstration?" Candace asked with a slight smile on her face.

Could no one see that she was about to be sick? How could they find anything about this situation funny?

Whatever was gurgling was ready.

Tilly jumped up, covered her mouth and ran to the bathroom. Her dream was about to go down the toilet.

CHAPTER TWO

DAN MEIER RELAXED against the wall, swinging his racket between his thumb and forefinger, waiting outside the racquetball court for Mike and feeling pretty good about himself. After hitting Enter and scheduling his next blog post for *CarpeChicago,* this one on a small taqueria in Cicero, Dan had rushed over to the gym for his weekly match. He wanted to make sure he was here and waiting so he could gloat in person. His blog post was ready two days early. Even Mike couldn't deny that Dan had beaten him this week. Lunch at Dan's favorite German bar on the Northside would serve as a good payment on their weekly bet. The kielbasa at Babka had been too salty to eat and Dan had been craving sausages ever since. He swung the racket up and smacked his other hand before letting it fall back into rhythm. Brats and sauerkraut weren't kielbasa and pierogi, but they were close enough for lunch.

He closed his eyes and enjoyed the satisfaction of knowing he would win a bet.

"You even relax like a jerk."

"Ah, Mike." He didn't need to open his eyes to see the contemptuously lowered eyebrows on his friend's face. "I was just thinking about the brats you now owe me."

"You should have eaten the kielbasa at that Polish restaurant. I scheduled my post four hours ago and I want Thai."

"What?" Dan's racket clattered on the floor. He picked

it up and followed his friend into the court. "Not possible. You've never been this early."

Mike's weekly column on sports was posted to the blog every Thursday. Another friend from college, Shane, had a weekly post on the local music scene, which went live on Fridays. All other content on the blog, and the general management of the site, was handled by Rich, the fourth of Dan's close college friends.

Dan had barely gotten his feet set when Mike served and the hard blue ball made its characteristic *thwap* off the front wall before flying toward Dan. So this was how they were going to play. Fine, two could play dirty.

Mike grunted as he swung his racket to answer Dan's hit and laughed when Dan missed and the ball bounced along the floor. "I've never been so motivated to smack my dumbass friend upside the head as I was when I read your review of that Polish place. But I'm not a fool. You'd probably wrestle me to the ground and hold my arm in some unnatural position until I cried uncle. I'm settling for winning the weekly bet and I think we should up the stakes next week."

"What did I ever do to you?" Dan tossed the ball up in the air once before throwing it at his friend's head. Mike caught it and laughed.

"It's not what you did to me—" Mike bounced the ball on the floor before swinging his racket and launching the ball back into play "—it's your poor grasp of journalistic ethics that bothers me so much."

Dan darted to the right, missing the ball again. "What the hell are you talking about?" He panted. "My journalistic ethics are better than yours." When Mike served again, he swung his racket a little too hard, straining his shoulder, but he hit the ball before it bounced twice on the floor. "You're a sports agent, which falls somewhere between a cockroach and a turd. Do agents even have ethics?" The ball careened around the court, hitting both side walls before striking the back wall and shooting back to Mike.

Mike waited until the ball was in just the right spot before he thwacked it with a hard swing. "I don't know why Rich posted that piece of junk. I thought he had more sense."

Dan tried to play the ball off the back wall and missed. "What the hell?" Dan asked, aggrieved. Rich had published the review because it was good, no matter what crap-ass side of the bed Mike had woken up on.

The next rally lasted longer, until Mike's ball slammed against the front wall and shot back to Dan. He swung hard and missed, the court echoing with the brunt of his curse. The noise of the curse soon gave way to the lonely sound of the ball plopping its way down the court. "Do you want to share your problem with me or is this some bizarre guessing game?"

"He's mad about your review of Babka." Rich, the brains and brawn behind *CarpeChicago,* walked into the court. He stooped to pick up the ball, tossing it in the air as he spoke. "Shane called to say he can't make it this morning. Wanna play a cutthroat?"

"As long as it's us against Mike," Dan said.

"No," Mike said, "I think it should be Rich and me against *you.*"

"Fine." Dan shrugged. Moral outrage was fueling Mike's play so much so that he wouldn't even wait for Dan to set his feet before serving. Dan was going to lose anyway. Might as well go down in a giant ball of fire. "If this is about my review of Babka, you can eat there next time. That was the worst experience I've ever had at a restaurant, including the place in Shanghai with rats at my feet. My mom's birthday dinner was ruined and I ended up with fish spread in my lap. Should I have nominated Babka for a Michelin star?"

"Rich, the review was unjust and you know it." Mike was indignant enough about the review that he almost lost control of the ball when he bounced it against the floor to begin the serve. "Even if his first experience was terrible, he should've gone back at least twice."

Dan answered the serve and waited for Rich's return. Mike could rely on Rich to be a steady player, reliable in a fast-moving game, even if he never seemed to move very quickly. Dan would like to believe Rich's composed style meant he wasn't nearly as angry about the review as Mike, but Rich was always even-tempered. *Hell, Rich published it,* Dan reminded himself. *If he hated it, he has only himself to blame.* Besides, Dan's review of Babka had been harsh, but not worth Mike's moral alpine ground.

The ball zoomed around the court, the loud bounces against the walls and floor killing any hopes at conversation. Dan just tried to stay on his feet and keep his head in the game as two of his closest friends plotted his death by exhaustion. Once, Dan wondered if Mike had aimed the ball at his nuts.

Mike smacked the ball low against the front wall. The perfect kill shot dropped and bounced twice against the floor before Dan had a chance to think about saving it.

"That's fifteen," Mike said as he left the court, his face as smug as an angel in the choir. The jerk didn't even look winded. Jerk also had a partner. Dan was playing on his own.

After following Mike and Rich off the court, Dan bent over and rested his hands on his knees as he huffed in air. *This game is going to kill me.* Mike was the better racquet-ball player, but Dan could usually count on at least holding his own in the first game. He didn't have a chance against a pissed-off Mike, much less a pissed-off Mike aided and abetted by Rich.

"We got more hits on that one review than we do on anything other than the big political scoops. It's worth the negative comments and Mike's little temper tantrum," Rich said simply.

"We're *The Enquirer* now, sacrificing truth for sales?" Mike took a long drink from a water bottle and wiped his forehead with a towel. "Oops," he said, handing Dan the sweaty towel. "It seems that one was yours."

"What is this passive-aggressive shit?"

"What's passive about it? I'm actively handing you your towel and I actively beat your ass into a sniveling turd hiding in the corner."

"Mike…" Rich sighed, ever the voice of reason. "We want the blog to be read. Dan's a nationally known food writer who enjoys trends before they make the *New York Times*. I'm lucky he still slums it to write for this dinky outfit when he could be writing his next feature for *Bon Appetit*. If he prematurely ejaculates out a review and I know it will be liked on Facebook up and down Lakeshore Drive, who am I to turn it down?"

"Ah, Rich, you say the sweetest things. If we had that kind of relationship, I'd give you a fat kiss on the lips."

Mike rolled his eyes at them, but what Rich said was true. Dan was a sought-after freelance food writer and had been wooed by the *New York Times* and much-missed *Gourmet* as a staff writer, though he had turned both publications down in favor of the independence of freelance. He was lucky enough not to need the money, and most writers, even the good ones, couldn't say that. He kept writing as The Eater for *CarpeChicago* out of loyalty for Rich and, well, blogging anonymously was fun.

Rich had started the blog in college as a part of an assignment on alternative forms of voter education. At first, it was little more than city government updates and summaries of the news found in different city papers. It had gained popularity during a presidential election and it hadn't taken long for Rich to envision a project bigger than a political blog. He recruited Dan, Shane and Mike to write weekly columns or reviews on their areas of expertise and supplied most of the rest of the content himself. The heart of the blog was still citizen education, and Rich's position as a professor of political science at DePaul allowed him both the freedom of schedule to track down public review documents and a willing army of student volunteers interested in padding their résumés. Now the former school assignment got more visits from Chicagoland IP addresses than either the *Tribune* or the *Sun-Times,* though neither paper would admit it. Rich didn't touch nationwide or worldwide news, but no better website existed for basic information important to Chicagoans.

Dan was proud to work on a website his adopted home city relied on. There may be more prestige in writing articles for *The New Yorker* on a breeder of heirloom tomatoes in Iowa and his fight against Big Ag, but *CarpeChicago* gave Dan a chance to explore the city's constantly evolving food scene. Rich didn't care whether Dan did reviews or columns, as long as he provided engaging writing and attention to detail. Dan wasn't stupid. Rich had asked him to write for the blog because they were friends, but there were any number of Chicago foodies who would poison his Italian Beef for the chance to be The Eater. Rich expected good work and would boot Dan's freelance butt to the door if the quality of the blog suffered.

Authenticity kept readers coming back to *CarpeChicago* day after day.

"I expect, like your belief in the chocolate and bacon

craze from several years ago, which I still think sounds nasty, that you will prove to be correct about Babka," Rich said. "And I'll give you a chance to prove it. Tila Milek is demonstrating at the Taste of Chicago today."

Dan groaned. Rich wasn't his boss and couldn't force him to go, but Rich's words implied a challenge and Dan wouldn't back down. He hated to be wrong, and the Taste would be a good opportunity to prove to both Rich and Mike that his review was spot on. Rich had published Babka's review because he trusted Dan's instincts and knew the review would garner a lot of hits. Now Dan had to prove he was justified; his pride was on the line.

Dan turned to his scoffing friend. "Your Thai lunch will have to wait until tomorrow. I'm having a smorgasbord for lunch today."

"I can wait. That review will come back to bite you in the ass and I'm going to enjoy that more than any Thai lunch."

"Care to bet it?"

"You're on."

Rich sighed. "Are we going to finish the racquetball game or stand here? I have a class to teach."

"Dan won't make it another round…" Mike smirked. "Besides, we need you to be a witness to the bet and determine who wins. Since you also lose when the review makes a meal out of Dan, you get to decide the winner."

"Fair enough," Dan agreed. "What do I win when I'm right?"

Mike looked up at the ceiling while he pondered his answer, which meant he'd probably had this bet planned since the review published, the rat bastard. "I foresee…" He stalled for suspense and Dan was tempted to head to the lockers so he could deny Mike the satisfaction of dragging out the bet. "A White Sox game in your future, complete with a black-and-white jersey, purchased by you for you. There's a Crosstown Classic game at the beginning of August. Get out your markers, because some signage about the Cubs' curse and the dominance of the White Sox will be required."

"Fine. The Cubs are playing the Cards in late August. I hope you're prepared to sit in the Wrigley Field bleachers in a Cardinals uniform." Dan arranged the proper level of concern on his face, making both Rich and Mike laugh. "I'll try to prevent Cubs fans from inflicting permanent bodily harm, but please remind your mother that no one ever died from a shiner."

"You're on." Mike stuck his hand out and they shook.

"Great. We can get back to the game now." Rich turned to walk back into the court.

"Dan," Mike said quietly as he turned to follow Rich, "I'm not just angry about the quality of your review. The whole thing stank a bit of your father, and your father is a douche. Think about that before you judge Tila Milek and her restaurant." Point made, Mike pushed past Dan through the door into the court.

Mike was right about one thing; Dan's father was a douche. But Dan had had one goal after graduating high school, to be the very opposite of his father. It was impossible for the review to "stink a bit" of the old man.

Even though his mom had accused him of being judgmental and unfair, which was pretty much the same thing.

Dan shook the miserable thought out of his head and followed Mike into the court. Mike was trying to get under his skin and affect his game. What was usually a low-key racquetball game turned into a blood match, dirty tricks and insults included.

CHAPTER THREE

GOOSE ISLAND LAGER in hand, Dan Meier followed his nose to the Vienna Beef line. Twenty people were in line ahead of him, but the hot dog was worth waiting for. He had even indulged and gotten extra food tickets so he could have two. He could have a Vienna Beef anytime, but it was a requirement at the Taste.

As he waited, the crowds got thicker, with sleeves and summer dresses brushing against him as people walked past the line to other food booths. He smiled. The crowds were part of the fun and he was determined to enjoy himself, even if he had been manipulated into coming. His mom's insinuation stung worse than Mike's moralistic taunting. His father was a manipulative and hypercritical asshole. Dan was a critic who had written a bad review of a restaurant that deserved it.

Maybe he had been oversensitive because his mom's birthday dinner had been ruined. Or because his mom had blindsided him with Beth's ridiculous plan to get pregnant, and his father had chosen that moment to offer him the company again. Or because when he complained about his oversalted soup, his mother had flinched in expectation that he would demand an apology, telling every employee how they were a waste of space until they lost a bit of their soul and bent to his will. It's what his father would have done. But even after the cat-and-dog fight in the restaurant, and his oversalted soup and his oversalted kielbasa, Dan had been perfectly polite. By the time he'd sent his entrée back to the kitchen, his mother had looked so nervous and uncomfortable he'd left cash on the table and taken her somewhere else for dinner.

So he was here at the Taste to watch Tila Milek's cooking demonstration and prove his review was justified. Distasteful, and not a venture he was looking forward to, but he wasn't going to let unpleasantness get in the way of a perfect summer day.

Tasty food, crowds, street performers and jazz. Even the normally stifling summer Chicago weather had eased with a light breeze. He had spied some craft tents with doodads for his sister. One of the tables had a garishly flowered, knitted scarf Beth would hate, but feel the need to gush with pleasure over before repurposing it into a dog bed. Getting each other truly inappropriate and unwanted presents was a time-honored tradition between the Meier siblings.

The line inched forward and people with hot dogs, deep-dish pizza, pierogi, beer, Italian beef and all the other treats Chicago offered a hungry man wove through the crowds. When Dan scooted back to make room for a family with ice cream to go through the line in front of him, he backed into something solid. His beer sloshed over the rim of the plastic cup and spilled onto his shirt.

He grimaced. The beer was going to get sticky as it dried and he'd have a big stain on his white shirt. Annoying, but plenty of people would be hawking T-shirts, so he could always buy himself a new one. He wouldn't let this ruin his day.

"Oh." The something solid had a sweet, soft voice, much more interesting than his wet shirt. "I'm sorry. I went forward and, well, you went back."

He turned, his eyes cast downward at the large wet

stain on his shirt. The nice voice had well-shaped feet with blue polish on the toes and a toe ring. They were wearing Roman-looking sandals. He moved his gaze up. She had a flowy white skirt with a large beaded belt, nice curvy hips, a pink strappy tank top, firm, round breasts, a chunky wooden necklace, cute round face, deep brown eyes and...blue hair?

Even with the strange hair, she was attractive. Artificially colored hair wasn't normally his thing, but the hair wasn't just blue. It was like an ocean wave in the Caribbean, a cascade of every color blue he could imagine. Catching him staring, she lifted her hand self-consciously and fluffed its ends. The wave of blues flowing through her fingers was mesmerizing. It made her whole appearance more interesting, and today he was in the mood for interesting. He wanted to take his mind off the upcoming demo, and she looked like the woman to distract him.

"The hair's because of a bet," the blue-haired woman offered in explanation. "I'm not sure if I won or lost." She rolled her eyes extravagantly before seeing the enormous wet stain on his shirt. "Oh, I'm sorry." She reached out to touch the stain, then pulled her hand back, her cheeks tinged a light pink.

Dan looked back at the stain on his shirt. He'd forgotten about the wet spot as soon as she began to speak.

A gut instinct told him to invite her to spend the day at the Taste with him. He'd been following his gut all his life and never been disappointed yet. It was the reason he told the city of Chicago to try the Vosges bacon and chocolate bar and the reason he'd written his post on Babka. His gut and his mom's ruined birthday dinner.

He could take this woman to the demo, which would make the distasteful business more fun, walk around the Taste with her, then take her out for a fabulous meal. Up on Chicago was a great sushi place. His shoulders relaxed. The day was looking even better than it had ten minutes ago. Before the moon rose, he would know for himself if her hair felt as silky between his fingers as it looked.

"Don't worry about it." He flashed his best smile. No one turned down the smile. "You should always wear clothes you are willing to lose to the Taste anyway. You never know when someone's pizza is going to land on your front."

She smiled back at him, a gentle smile at odds with her fanciful hair. "Still, can I buy you another beer, or shirt? I feel awful. Not only did you lose half your beer, but you're going to have to walk around with a wet shirt."

"If you're offering me alcohol to dull the pain of a hot summer day, I'll bite. A cold beer will help cool me down."

They talked a bit as they moved up the line. At the counter, Dan turned back to the intriguing blue-haired woman. "Do you like your dogs with everything?"

She raised her brows. "Of course."

"Great." He turned to the hot dog trailer and pushed food tickets through the window. "Two dogs with everything." He turned back. "I'm bribing you. I've never met a woman with blue hair younger than my grandmother." He flashed another smile. "Walk around the Taste with me."

"Why do you need company? Surely you could've brought a date if you wanted one."

"I didn't want a date until I got my beer spilled all over my front."

"Low blow." She laughed. "You might not get much for your money. I can only wander around for about an hour. I have an appointment."

"Deal." When she took her hot dog, he lifted his dog up like a flute of champagne. "A toast, to blue-haired women and Vienna Beef."

She laughed and lifted her hot dog to match his. "To free hot dogs," she said and took a bite.

Her mouth was nicely shaped, with lush but not overly pouty lips. She ate her hot dogs with everything. He was definitely interested, in both her shapely lips and clear enjoyment of food. Judging by the roundness of her hips, whoever this woman was, she could eat.

She closed her eyes and moaned with pleasure as she took her first bite.

"Good, huh?" He took a bite and the spicy peppers hit his tongue, followed by the taste of the sweet, alien-green relish and acidic tomato. "I've eaten delicacies from all over the world and I think the Chicago dog beats them all."

"I know." She laughed again. She had a throaty laugh at odds with her sweet voice. The combination was intoxicating. As a package, the blue-haired woman was entrancing and, from the way she fluffed her hair and pursed her lips, she probably had no idea. "No French-trained chef could come up with this mix of flavors. The pickle is my favorite. Why have a pickle on the side of your meal when you can have it on top?"

"I like to think all the vegetables make this a complete meal."

"An American one-upping of the Earl of Sandwich."

"Exactly."

She savored her last bite of hot dog and when she licked the celery salt off her lips, his jeans got uncomfortable. If the day continued this way, he would need to throw himself into Lake Michigan to cool off. "So, mystery woman..." He popped his last bite of hot dog in his mouth. "Do you have a name?"

"My friends call me Tilly." She stuck out her free hand and Dan took it.

"Dan."

His hand brushed scars and calluses as it slid out of her grip. Tilly did something with her hands for a living, which made him more curious about her. "Some street performers are over by the fountain. Shall we?" He offered her his elbow.

She took his outstretched elbow and they walked toward the lake. She smelled fresh, like lemons. Like her sweet voice and seductive laugh, the clean scent was unexpected with her vibrant hair.

They stopped at the street show. An aerial dance team had set up scaffolding and used black silk ribbons to propel themselves through the air in a dance, moving as naturally vertically as they did horizontally. They flipped upside down and did splits three feet above the ground with only the ribbons tied around their ankles keeping them from falling, all choreographed to Sam Cooke singing "Summertime."

"I've never seen anything like it," Tilly said with awe. "I could watch them all day."

Dan looked at the spellbound woman at his side. "You can," he said to tempt her. "Cancel your appointment."

A grand total of maybe twenty minutes in her presence and he wanted—*needed*—more. Dan didn't believe in love at first sight, but he believed in desire at first sight. The woman at his side fit perfectly against him. A pairing as unexpected and perfect as French fries and champagne or, he smiled wryly, bacon and chocolate.

The way Tilly looked at him, she must think him a serpent offering her an apple from the tree of knowledge. Desire heated her rich, cocoa eyes, but something else lurked deep in their depths. Wistfulness, a need to live in the present and not think about the future. Not quite fear, but apprehension.

What about her appointment scared her?

"Oh, I couldn't," she said with all the force of an addict turning down another hit. "I'd be ruined. Please don't ask again. I might take you up on it." She turned back to watch the dancers, but pressed herself more tightly against him, as if he was the only thing keeping her standing.

Tilly had a secret. A secret she was trying to pretend didn't exist, if only for the next hour. Was she married to an abusive, scary man? She didn't wear a ring. An appointment with a doctor? Was the hair a wig covering up the bald head of a cancer patient?

Maybe it wasn't any of his business, but he had to know before the day was over. Every cell in his body wanted him to stick to this woman as if she were honey. How could she not feel the same way?

Time for a new tactic. "I'm sorry. We can change the subject. Did you catch the Cubs game last night?"

"I'm a White Sox fan," she said, still not looking at him.

Well, hell. Meeting Tilly was a magic moment, but apparently he was the only person here who felt that way.

She turned to face him, her back to the dancers and her attention completely focused on him. "I'm being rude. It's just…" She sighed and all the warmth left her eyes, replaced by tension. "I'm a little nervous about what I have to do in forty minutes. I don't want to talk or think about it, but I can't miss it, no matter how tempting you are."

"I won't ask you to cancel your appointment, but I won't promise not to get you to spend more time with me. Dinner?"

"Maybe. Depends on how the afternoon goes. I might want to crawl under the DuSable Bridge and never come out. If you hear reports of a troll, it could be me."

"That bad?"

"Yes." She bit her bottom lip and nodded. "That bad."

He smiled at her. "Then my job for the next forty minutes is to keep your mind off whatever you are abandoning me to do. Baseball's out, so how about I tell you a story?"

"A story? Like I'm a little kid?" she asked with amusement lifting the corner of her lips and left eyebrow.

Dan smiled his best devious and inviting smile. "It's not appropriate for a little kid, but let me tell you about the noodle restaurant I was assured had the best noodles in all of Thailand. I was traveling on a research trip and several Bangkok cabdrivers told me I *must* visit this place." He looked at the children also watching the aerial dancers. "No, I can't tell this story here. Too many innocent minds around and I don't want to disturb the show. Let's walk," he said as he threaded his fingers in hers and pulled her along.

"Is the story going to be better than the dancers?"

"I don't know about better than the dancers, but it will distract you."

Once they were far enough away from any mothers likely to overhear him, Dan continued his story. "I'd been in Bangkok for over a week, subsisting only on noodles. Street vendors, little storefronts, fancy restaurants catering to tourists—if they sold noodles I tried them. Only the noodle shop the cabbies recommended wasn't on any restaurant list I could find. My hotel told me they catered mostly to tourists. 'If that was the type of place I wanted to try,' they'd say in a hushed voice. Implying, of course, they thought I was different. I'd said I was trying to hunt down the best Thai noodles, but they wondered if maybe I was in Bangkok for some shadier reason."

Dan chuckled at the foolishness of it all. "I decided the hotel was a stuffy lot and I would eat on the cabbies' recommendations. The place looked like almost any other storefront noodle shop, only the cabbies had said to ask for 'plus' on anything I ordered. I stuck to the basics and ordered pad Thai, plus."

"And was it the best noodle shop in Bangkok?"

"The noodles themselves were terrible. Mushy and drowning in fish sauce. One piece of chicken, one measly peanut. I wondered if the rubbery chicken and one stale peanut were the plus, and what a minus meal would be. But as soon as I put my fork and spoon down I found out why the cabdrivers told all their Western tourists it was the best."

Dan looked over at Tilly to make sure she was paying attention. Her eyes were wide and dancing with curiosity. The tension had eased out of her body and been replaced with an eager lightness that brightened her skin. If she looked like that while he was telling her a story, how would she look as he stripped off her clothes? Would her skin flush and her eyes deepen with desire?

Any thoughts in that direction were stopped with a gentle elbow to his ribs.

"You can't stop now. I *have* to know."

"As an older woman picked up my half-full plate and empty beer bottle, this younger woman came up to me and asked if I ordered 'the plus.' When I nodded, she told me to follow her. Curious now, I followed her into a back room."

"I think I know where this is going," she said with pursed lips and raised eyebrows. "I can't believe you're telling this story on a first date."

"In my defense, I was too creeped out to do anything more than scuttle out of the room. The pad Thai had killed my appetite for anything the brothel had to offer me. As for it being a first date story…" He waved her comment away. "You wanted to be distracted. You can't tell me you are thinking about your appointment now."

"No." She snorted before her face got serious. "But please tell me the woman was over eighteen."

"The story wouldn't be funny if she were a child," Dan

said with enough gravity in his voice that she would know he found the situation as distasteful as she did. And he knew it could have been much worse. "I guess it's lucky that while I looked like a man willing to have sex with a woman in the back of a noodle shop, I don't look like a pedophile. I got two articles out of the trip, the one on noodles in Bangkok and the other on sex tourism and the sexual exploitation of children in the United States."

The second article had landed one prominent Seattle restaurateur in jail for sex trafficking and been instrumental in closing down a trafficking route into Vancouver. Dan had flown to Seattle to be in the courtroom for the restaurateur's sentencing, one of the proudest moments of his life. He wrote engrossing, thought-provoking articles on food, cooking, farming and how what people ate defined who they were. They were important articles—food was at the heart of every culture—but that was the first and only time his research on food had landed someone in jail.

"You're a writer?"

"Mostly freelance, but my articles aren't generally as weighty as sex trafficking."

"Do you enjoy it?"

"I can't imagine doing anything else. I get paid to create, and the final product, good or bad, is my responsibility. The control is both ridiculously scary and the most freeing thing imaginable."

"I understand. I would have never associated the feeling with writing, but I get what you're saying." Tilly put her hand on his arm, the contact burning through the light cotton of his sleeve. "The control is why my job is important to me."

Dan reached out and tucked a short strand of hair behind her ear, her dangling earrings ringing like tiny bells with the movement. The crazy blue hair slid through his fingers, slippery and smooth. It was like trying to hold on to the creek behind his parents' house. He anchored one hand at the back of her head and used the other on the small of her back to pull her against him. The slight touch wasn't enough. He wanted more. "I want to hear about your job. I want to hear everything you have to tell me." He angled her face up to him and lowered his mouth until a breeze wouldn't fit in the space between their lips. "But first, I want to kiss you."

It wasn't supposed to be a long kiss. A peck was all he'd had in mind. Then he noticed how soft her lush lips were against his and how they opened willingly under gentle pressure. He could taste celery salt when he ran his tongue along the inside of her bottom lip.

She made a noise in the back of her throat and he slid his hand down to cup her round butt, pulling her body close to him. Her arms came around his neck and her fingers pulled through his hair. God, she felt good.

Then the moment was nearly ruined when, through his haze of desire, he heard a catcall. He pulled back and looked at Tilly's upturned face. Her eyes were half-closed and her mouth was partway open. She looked like a woman who still wanted to be kissed and he still wanted to kiss her.

He pressed his forehead against hers and chuckled. "I guess I got a little carried away. I promised I wouldn't ask you to cancel your appointment, but maybe you can at least agree to meet me for dinner, no matter how the appointment goes. I want to see you again. Soon."

"Okay," Tilly said as she took a deep breath. "But I might not be good company for dinner."

"I can't imagine how you wouldn't be."

"It's embarrassing. I'm giving a cooking demonstration here today."

CHAPTER FOUR

AH, SHIT. That would make her...

Dan winced, but Tilly was too caught up in her story to notice his reaction. "And in the most recent review on *CarpeChicago,* my restaurant got slammed by The Eater. I'm afraid no one will be in the audience, or worse, they'll show up to watch the woman whose career is over because of a series of ridiculous events." She took another deep breath, the force of this one shuddering through her entire body.

"I mean, Chicagoans can be so brutal sometimes. They can get such pleasure out of watching someone fail spectacularly. I have a feeling the whole thing will be awful and when you asked, I was afraid to tell you. I'm embarrassed to be the woman at the butt of a whole city's joke. What if people toss cats or something?" Her eyes were big and rimmed with tears. She sniffed and her laugh came out as a hiccup. "Oh, God, I'm crying in front of a stranger. This might be more embarrassing than the cats."

He was here to watch a woman whose career he had ruined. He wasn't planning on throwing any cats, but he had planned on her failing spectacularly. His mom had questioned his review, Mike had challenged him to a bet and Rich had all but ordered him to watch the demo. He was here to watch her fail so he could be right.

What if my mom and Mike were right and I am turning into my father?

And now she was crying. Did women know crying was an unfair tactic?

Dan put his hand under her chin and lifted her face to inspect her. God, she was pretty. On most people, the hair would look ridiculous, but instead it deepened the brown of her eyes and brightened her skin. On her, the hair almost looked natural.

His role in her tears didn't dampen Dan's desire to take her out to dinner after the demo. He didn't want to think about what the yearning said about his sanity or the journalistic ethics Mike was already questioning. Was he a sadist because he was unwilling to let her go?

Unless Tilly could pull a rabbit out of her chef's hat, he gave her restaurant six months at the most. The doomsday prediction bothered him. Some critics loved to brag about the restaurants they'd brought down or tried to out-insult big-name chefs, both things Dan found disgusting. He gave honest reviews, wasn't afraid to criticize a chef he believed was overhyped, but he'd rather talk about restaurants he loved. Any idiot could write a review of a restaurant they hated. It took training and practice to write an intelligent, positive, *critical* review that was more than "dude, the food was tasty so I ate it."

Unfortunately, he had to accept the fact that his attendance at her demo was not far off the distasteful scale from the critics he generally dismissed.

Even with her failure of a career, he wanted to spend the evening with her. In a big city with lots of women, he had never met one he liked so much so soon. Cute, interesting, funny. If he told her who he was, she would probably respond with more tears. Besides not getting to spend the rest of the day with her, the truth would make her feel worse about her cooking demonstration. He couldn't do that.

And, he rationalized, if he were here to honestly judge

her skills, telling her now would affect her performance. Any opinion he formed of her ability would be tainted. He could make sure he won the bet, but that would ruin his chances of seeing Tilly again. Not even to mention it was a shady way to win.

He would tell her after dinner.

"Tilly, I…" Her eyes turned down to focus on his shoes. He could watch her demo, give her some support before she went onstage, report back to Rich that his review was spot on, as usual, and reassure his mother that he wasn't turning into his father. "I'd like to spend some more time with you. How about I come watch your cooking demo? That way, at least you know you have one person in the audience to support you."

TILLY APPRECIATED DAN'S OFFER to go with her to the demo. Normally she wouldn't let some stranger pick her up at the Taste. Or kiss her. *What were you thinking, Tilly?* Chicago was a big city and her mother was constantly emailing her stories about women being abducted by strangers in broad daylight. But she connected to Dan in some way. When he had turned around, a big beer stain on his shirt, she'd felt… well, she wasn't sure what it was, but she did feel as though she had known him longer than just twenty minutes. Being with him felt a bit like being home. Comfortable. Probably why she'd nearly burst into tears in front of him.

Plus, he was attractive. Not just notice-out-of-the-corner-of-your-eye good-looking, but giggle-with-your-girlfriends-over-a-cocktail gorgeous. Before the hair and the restaurant and her complete lack of time to do anything but work, he would have been the kind of man who interested her. Thick blond hair, bright blue eyes, a strong chin and nose slightly too big for his face. Broad shoulders and taller than she was, without towering over her absolutely average height.

The kind of corn-fed, Midwestern man who had wrestled and played football in high school and now played softball for the company team every summer and went boating in Wisconsin on long weekends.

They usually thought blue hair was weird. They were right.

She was still surprised he had asked her to join him. Despite his easygoing, nonchalant manner, he carried with him the air of someone who expected everything he touched to turn to gold. The dark blue of his jeans and bright white of his shirt—minus the beer stain—suggested a man with an eye for perfection.

Though she had stopped being self-conscious about her hair all the time, she had attracted a different type of male attention since the change to blue—the two-eyebrow-piercings-tongue-stud-with-a-tattooist-named-Butter type of men who expected her to buy fetish shoes at the Alley. Men seemed to think she was wild, when in reality she was a thirty-year-old woman stuck with a bet she had made when she was eighteen.

"I would appreciate the support at my demo. Thank you." She raised her gaze to meet his again and saw a mix of sympathy and unease. Almost as if he wasn't sure she would say yes. If the look had been pity, she would have said no. Babka was her life. Her work. The review, the cat, the oversalted food were all hers to own and figure out what to do with. She wasn't interested in a sympathy date.

"You've still got twenty minutes. Let's go back to the aerial dancers, then head over to the cooking tent. In the meantime, we'll just talk about meaningless things." He held out his hand to her and she placed hers in it. He led the two of them back to watch the performers and she listened while he entertained her with silly stories meant to do nothing but distract her.

THEY TALKED ABOUT THE WEATHER and the chances of either baseball team making the playoffs, nothing they needed to focus on. As they chatted, Dan could see Tilly relax. She wasn't thinking about the demonstration anymore.

He admired her. Many people, forced to face an audience after a bad review, would have backed out of the commitment. The best head chefs were control freaks and perfectionists; bad reviews were not easily laughed off. He knew some who would have gone on a wild bender, then come to the demonstration hungover—if not still blitzed—after a bad review. Not only was Tilly here, she was sober and there were no signs of a bender from the night before. More than sobriety, she was mostly holding herself together. He could support her through this demo without undermining his view of Babka and her abilities as the chef and owner.

The hair was deceiving. She wasn't just some wild woman his parents would hate, though they would hate her, his father especially. The unnatural hair complemented a determination he admired. With her callused hand in his, Dan found himself feeling more content than he had in years. Too bad this relationship could never be.

He looked at his watch and straightened. Time for her to prepare for the demonstration. "Come on. You can get ready and I'll get a seat right up front."

Her feelings ran through her eyes as clearly as a movie on a screen. Nerves and resignation, followed by a fixed resolve.

He gave her another quick peck on the lips. "For luck."

CHAPTER FIVE

TILLY GRABBED THE bag she had left in the changing room
of the demonstration tent and pulled out her clothes. She
changed into her chef's jacket and checks, then sat down
on the nearby folding chair and rubbed her forehead. She
felt a headache coming on and her stomach did jumping
jacks. Nerves.

Not only nerves, but she had been kissed by a stranger.
Soundly kissed by a stranger. And she had kissed him
soundly back. She didn't remember the last time she had
been kissed like that. Kissed so her toes tingled.

Her last boyfriend had been when she was still in New
York, which seemed like decades ago, even if it had been
less than two years, and a great kisser he wasn't. He hadn't
wanted to move to Chicago with her. "Why move when I'll
see you even less?" had been his response to her invitation.

Since Babunia had died and left her money to get a restaurant started, with tons of help from the bank, she hadn't
wanted to waste any time kissing frogs hoping to find a
prince. She didn't have time for frogs or princes.

The nerves were responsible for the headache, but Dan
was responsible for the jumping jacks.

At least she was cooking familiar dishes. She had contemplated trying a new dish, but you never knew how a recipe
would work out until you'd made it several times under different conditions. A guaranteed success was even more important now, in the aftermath of the *CarpeChicago* review.

She had the added distraction of a kissable stranger in the audience. She had wanted Dan's company for a distraction before the demo, but she couldn't let anything preoccupy her during. Today was as good an example as any for why she shouldn't go around kissing attractive men.

The tent flap opened and her sister walked in, calm and sedate as usual. Unlike Tilly, who let every emotion echo on her face, her older sister, Renia, was always serene. No matter the situation, tall, thin Renia was walking elegance. All it took was her presence and people responded as if given a drink. Their shoulders fell when the tension left their body and they took deep, relaxing breaths.

The cost to Renia was staggering. Tilly wondered about the last time Renia had allowed herself to feel an emotion. No, she corrected, she didn't have to wonder. Renia hadn't displayed any emotion since she was fifteen and busy discovering the many opportunities Chicago offered to a teenager who wanted trouble.

"I'm sorry I couldn't come see you over the weekend. I was out of town at a wedding. Just got back today." Renia bent down to kiss Tilly's cheek, then sat, putting her camera bag on the floor. "I read the review. The Eater is a moron."

"Oh, Renia," Tilly said, resting her head against her sister. "I'm glad you're here. I'm so nervous." Renia began to stroke her hair and with each stroke Tilly's headache eased. The jumping jacks in her stomach remained.

"You'll be fine. Better than fine, you'll be perfect." As she talked, Renia combed her fingers through her hair. "The other chefs will have nothing on you."

"Are there any people out there?"

"The chairs are filling. It's a good crowd for a Monday demonstration." Tilly stiffened. "Don't worry—I didn't see any tomatoes for throwing. They're here to see you. Mom's in the audience, too." Renia laughed. "I think she's trying to be incognito, but she hasn't realized she's the only woman in Chicago who thinks sunglasses and a scarf over her hair in July would be a disguise. She said she didn't want her presence to pressure you."

"At least there will be three people in the audience for me."

"Three?" Renia's hands stilled for two counts before they continued their combing.

"There's this man I met at the Vienna Beef stand. His name is Dan, and he bought me a hot dog even though I spilled his beer."

"And? There's something else. I can hear it in your voice." Renia's fingers again slowed their progress through her hair.

"He kissed me." The fingers stopped. It was the only sign of surprise her sister would show.

"And? I'm your sister. I get details."

"There aren't many details to give. He gave me a kiss, saying it was 'for luck.'" She left out the first kiss, not for luck, with open lips and the little sound of desire she'd made.

"There's still more. I know there is." The fingers had started pulling through her hair again. Whatever shock Renia had felt was tucked away. Tilly didn't know how her sister managed such control.

"There isn't more to the kiss."

"No, there's more to your reaction. Come on, Tilly, you don't get kissed by random strangers every day."

"I'd like to think I never get kissed by *random* strangers." She let out a big sigh. "It was just a kiss. But it was the first kiss I've gotten in over two years and the first *good* kiss I've gotten since, I don't know, Culinary maybe. And so I was sitting here getting a headache from my nerves and waiting for my stomach to leap out of my skin and do a little dance on the floor from the kiss.

"And then—" Her words sped up, running together and threatening to crash in a heap on the floor. "I wonder if I'm being silly about a kiss on the lips from a handsome stranger, like I'm some starry-eyed teenager again. And I have to cook for God knows how many people, who have all read a review of my restaurant where the place was almost destroyed because of a stupid stray cat and oversalted food I can't explain."

"Good." The word was no less emphatic for being said in Renia's serene voice.

"What do you mean *good?*" She pulled her head out from under her sister's hands and turned to gaze up at her. "I barely know this man and my nerves are a tightrope. How is this good?"

"Tilly, I don't think you've looked at a man, seriously looked, since your prom date ten years ago. That boyfriend in New York doesn't count. He was a tool. Since you decided you wanted to own your own restaurant, men are only visible to you if they are head chefs."

"I look at pastry chefs, too."

"Tilly, I'm not joking. I'm not saying you have to have a boyfriend, but it's as if you turned off any sexual or romantic part of you in your determination to own a four-star restaurant before you're thirty-five. It's not healthy."

"I may not date, but *you* only date men you can push around." Hurt crept into Renia's eyes before she could blink it away and Tilly felt bad about striking back. Renia was right and the truth was painful. Her sister dated, but she wasn't interested in the men she was dating. Tilly didn't date at all.

"I'm sorry, Rey. I didn't mean it."

"Yes, you did." Renia grabbed Tilly's head, forced it

back around and resumed her calming rub. "And maybe you're right about me. Fortunately, this conversation is about you. Shall I scope him out for you? Make sure he's as riveted by your demonstration as he should be?"

Tilly chuckled and enjoyed the comfort of her sister. "No, you'll meet him after the demonstration. I assume you'll be sticking around."

"Of course. I'm here as long as you need me. Now, point him out to me before you get onstage."

They stood and walked out together. Before Tilly climbed on the stage, she looked out into the crowd, then closed her eyes and wished she hadn't seen the rows of full chairs. Picturing people naked would only distract her.

Dan was easily found in the crowd. She leaned into her sister and whispered, "He's the man with the blond hair and stained shirt three rows back, on the aisle."

Renia looked. Then she shoved Tilly in the side.

"Ouch! Why did you elbow me?" Tilly leaned over in pain and rubbed her ribs with overacted outrage, but Renia didn't even notice.

"You must be nervous to describe that man as handsome. He's gorgeous. It's too bad you caught him first." Renia looked at Tilly with a wide grin on her face. "You can't be nervous now. A man like that picking you up while you're in line for a hot dog has got to be good luck." A last kiss on the cheek and Renia was off, threading her way through the crowd before finally finding a seat close to the front.

Tilly could easily pick out her mother, sitting in the back, her head bent over a magazine. Renia was right. She was wearing a checkered scarf over her hair, probably thinking Tilly wouldn't notice the one woman in the audience wearing a babushka like some caricature in a Russian movie.

She could do this. Even if everyone else in the audience jeered, she could talk to the three people there not out of curiosity, but out of support. They would be enough. Tilly climbed into the kitchen and a techy-type guy fitted her for a mike.

"I'll be introducing you." Tilly looked up to see an older, smartly dressed African-American woman with glorious salt-and-pepper curls standing in front of her. "I'm Patricia Humphries. We talked on the phone to arrange your menu. I'm sorry I wasn't here when you dropped off your supplies."

"Yes, I remember. I assume you got the bio I emailed to you."

"Yes. It was perfect. Are you ready?"

Tilly nodded and followed Patricia onto the stage.

"Welcome, fellow Chicagoans and visitors." Patricia's voice boomed over the crowd. "Today, the Taste of Chicago is honored to present Tila Milek. Tila started her cooking career in the kitchen of her family's Polish restaurant on 45th Street. Healthy Food is a Chicago institution and you can still find her mother in the restaurant's kitchen, cooking up traditional Polish dishes. After graduating from the Culinary Institute of America, Miss Milek worked in several New York restaurants before moving back to Chicago to start her own restaurant, Babka, in Bucktown. Please welcome a truly local talent, Miss Tila Milek."

The audience clapped and Tilly saw her sister taking pictures. Tilly's heart warmed at the sight of her mother giving her a standing ovation and Dan's thumbs-up.

She took a deep breath and stepped forward. "Thank you. First, I'm going to tell you about Babka. Then I'll demonstrate some of the traditional Polish food we serve. To give you something to nosh on while I talk and chop, we're going to pass around *podpłomyczki,* which is an unleavened bread with a history going back to the ancient Slavic tribes roaming around Eastern Europe. We've kept the bread warm from the oven and are serving it with a little *pasta rybno-twarogowa,* or fresh farmer's cheese and smoked fish spread."

Tilly turned to the waitstaff, surprised to see Steve, her runner, with Karen and Candace. When the three stepped forward with encouraging smiles and trays of nibbles, she didn't wonder where her missing waiter was. She could do this demonstration. She *would* do this demonstration. How could she fail with such wonderful support?

She smiled back at them and turned to the audience. "Please give a warm welcome to some of my staff from Babka." Tilly waited for the applause to die down before she continued. "Today is their day off and they are here to give me moral support. As you might have heard, we've had a rocky couple of weeks." The audience laughed and tension left the tent in a whoosh as her wonderful, fantastic, better-than-she-deserved staff headed off the stage bearing food.

"In Polish, *babka* means two important things. A *babka* is a tall, yeasted cake and, more important, a grandmother. My restaurant is an homage to both meanings. My grandmother was my favorite person when I was a child. When I told my mom I wasn't going to work at Healthy Food, but was going to culinary school and start my own restaurant, it was my grandmother who helped me fill out the applications."

DAN TOOK A BITE of the eggy, chewy bread with its creamy, smoky spread and listened while Tilly talked about her grandmother and her restaurant.

"Babka highlights the traditional Polish foods lost amongst kielbasa and pierogi. Of course, we serve handmade pierogi and house-smoked kielbasa, but we serve some of the lesser-known dumplings, sausages, stews and soups while using fresh, seasonal ingredients."

When Dan first heard about Babka, he had hoped to eat there on a regular basis and try many of those forgotten Polish dishes. Then the cat, dog and oversalted food had turned him off Polish for a week.

"The nibble you are enjoying is an excellent example of what we serve. *Podpłomyczki* is as traditional as rye bread in Poland and the farmer's cheese in the spread is made using milk from a family-owned Wisconsin dairy that raises only Jersey cows."

He licked some of the spread off his fingers and let it sit on his tongue while he enjoyed the subtle flavors. The cheese had a definite richness to it from the butterfat in the Jersey milk, highlighted by the smoked fish and the bite of the chives. Simple and delicious.

"It's summer, and summer in Chicago is hot. Like most of you, I want to eat something cooling and traditional Polish food is just what my Babunia ordered. Cold dishes are an important part of any Polish meal and we serve many cold summer soups. *Chłodnik litewski,* which I'm preparing now, is a beet soup, similar to *barszcz* or borscht, served cold with crisp summer vegetables and, if you're feeling fancy, a little chopped shrimp or crawfish."

Dan ducked his head to get out of the way of a woman snapping photos as if this was a presidential debate and settled in to watch Tilly chop, mix and talk. She was skillful. He couldn't deny her proficiency, and the demo wouldn't be enough for him to feel confident in his review. He'd have to see her again at Babka. He was still certain his review was right. All the things that had gone wrong that night couldn't have been a fluke. Something was rotten in the Polish kitchen. Tilly might be mastering the demo, but she was responsible for the entire restaurant. Whatever the problem was, it was her responsibility. No matter how good a cook she was, she'd failed somewhere as a chef.

She handled the crowd well. First, he could see her gaze lock on him and a few other people in the seats. As she got more confident, she engaged more of the audience. By the time the cooked beets had been blended with sour cream and shredded cucumber, Tilly had gotten comfortable with herself and the audience and watching her cook and teach was like watching a seasoned actress manage the orchestra seats. He'd wager money half the people in the audience who had grimaced at a cold beet soup were licking their lips and thinking about how refreshing the soup would be right now, especially with the cooling crispness of the cucumber.

Tilly dipped a spoon into the soup and slurped down a taste. Her plump lips puckered around the spoon and her entire face relaxed with pleasure before she pronounced the soup perfect. "Or nearly perfect. *Chłodnik litewski* is better if left to sit in the fridge overnight and served with hard-boiled eggs, but I don't think we want to wait that long." The audience laughed and she smiled, her lips stained a deep, sexy red from the beets. More alluring than any saucy red lipstick, especially to a man who thought about food for a living.

"Do you want some soup, sir?" His eyes shifted from Tilly's red lips to a small wax cup with an even smaller tasting spoon held out to him by a short African-American woman with cropped hair and gliding movements. The bartender. If he remembered correctly, Babka had a good wine list. Not impressive, not outstanding, but good. What had been outstanding was their beer list, which included Northern and Eastern European beers, many he'd never heard of.

She raised her eyebrow at him and he accepted the cup.

Sweet from the beets, rich from the sour cream, tart from a little vinegar and with a crunch from the cucumber and radish. No one flavor dominated and it would be the perfect cooling soup to pierce through the heat of a Chicago summer, if he didn't look back up at the stage to Tilly's stained lips and wonder if they would still have the salty taste from the hot dog on them or if they would now taste like the beet soup.

He'd kissed her and he wanted to kiss her again. Drinking an entire barrelful of whatever she called this soup wasn't going to cool him of his desire. Her passion while they kissed had been arousing.

Just as arousing as those red lips.

And with that image Dan knew he had to leave directly after the demonstration. His fledgling personal relationship with Tilly compromised his ability to judge her professionally. His review compromised any personal relationship he might have with her. The best thing he could do right now would be to cut his losses. Make up some excuse not to take her to dinner—*aren't you even more of a jerk now, Danny boy?*—and wash his hands of Babka. If the night of the review had been a fluke, eventually she would gain more customers and another review. Unless she truly deserved it, his review wouldn't kill Babka.

He'd at least leave this situation with some of his morality intact. If he were the douche Mike accused him of being, he would wait until *after* taking the pretty chef home to bed. If he were turning into his father, as his mother had accused him of doing, he would manipulate Tilly until *she* apologized to *him,* all while collecting on his bet and sleeping with her.

Whatever was rotting in Tilly's kitchen would come to pass—and he would win his bet—or it wouldn't and he could forget this whole episode ever happened. Involvement would only put his reputation at risk.

Dan discarded his worries and decided to concentrate on lips he was never going to kiss again.

So far, the demonstration was running smoothly. Tilly was enjoying cooking and teaching. She'd chosen simple, familiar recipes packing a punch and easily made at home by anyone in the audience. She wasn't going to get people excited by her recipes, only to have them get to the grocery store and realize the key ingredient was only available by mail order.

"Many of you may now be wondering if you came to a demonstration of Polish food only to leave without any pierogi." The audience chuckled as she reached under the counter and brought out some precut rounds of dumpling dough. "Don't worry. I've got the dough and filling ready, so I have time to demonstrate rolling and stuffing the dumplings. I will need some help from the audience to fold enough of the pierogi for everyone while I fry them."

Tilly smiled as she passed over her mom's upstretched hand and picked two women and one man to help her. While they washed their hands and were outfitted with aprons, she explained the filling. "There are as many different fillings for pierogi as there are Poles, and fillings range from savory cheese or cabbage to sweet apple or plum. I've made a fresh mushroom filling. After I boil the dumplings, I'll fry them in butter and we'll serve them with cold sour cream."

Her new helpers introduced themselves and she set pierogi dough and filling in front of them. "While you should watch how much you stuff into the pierogi, it's a beginner's mistake not to put enough filling in," she said as she spooned mushrooms onto one side of a dough circle and folded it into a half-moon. "Pierogi should look like a man's hat cut in half, with a small brim and a fat crown. Get a tight seal on the pierogi or they'll burst as I cook them. You can use either the fork or your hands, but get the seal good and tight."

Together they stuffed and folded, while premade pierogi boiled away until she had enough to fill the four frying pans. The practiced motions of folding over the dough and crimping the seams closed with her fingers calmed her. She loved to cook, had known her whole life she would work in a kitchen. Her grandmother had joked she was born with a wooden spoon in her mouth. She had gotten in trouble as a child for skipping out on her homework so she could help in the restaurant. She would sacrifice anything for Babka.

The hand of one of the women slipped and mushroom filling spit out onto the counter while she swore loudly enough for Tilly's mike to transmit her words through the tent. The audience tittered as the woman blushed. Tilly left the pierogi sputtering and frying in the butter while she went over to the woman and helped her clean up the mushroom filling.

"Now is a good time for everyone to learn a little Polish." Tilly gave the counter one more wipe and the woman a reassuring smile before returning to her sizzling pierogi. "Everyone repeat after me, *Święty Jacek z pierogami.*"

The audience stumbled gamely along as the Polish twisted their tongues in knots. "One more time, with feeling, *Święty Jacek z pierogami.*" The audience tried again and got a little closer.

"I'll bet you want to know what you said." Heads nodded and the audience chuckled nervously. "*Święty Jacek z pierogami* is a Polish version of 'good grief' or 'St. Hyacinth and his pierogi.'" Tilly laughed along with the audience at the silliness of the phrase. "You didn't think I was going to teach you to swear in Polish with my mom sitting in the audience, did you? Stand up and give a bow, Mom. This is your recipe for mushroom pierogi."

Her mother stood and bobbed with embarrassment and pride as the audience clapped and cheered until Karen, Steve and Candace whisked the first plates of pierogi into the crowds. The cheering stopped immediately, replaced by chewing and jealous looks.

Tilly turned back to her fry pans and slid more pierogi into hot butter. "Cooking pierogi is easy, but I want to emphasize that they shouldn't be rushed. Too much high heat will toughen the dough. Take your time and your patience will be rewarded."

Completely into her rhythm, Tilly fried and plated pierogi until everyone in the audience got a taste, then she cooked up a few extra for her helpers. By the time she turned off the gas to the stove, she was exhausted and starving. It wasn't standing on her feet and cooking that drained her—she was used to that from years of restaurant work—but the emotion of the day. Nerves from the review and the demonstration. Desire from the kiss from Dan. More nerves, also caused by Dan's kiss. Holding herself together and keeping up a stream of light chatter while she cooked and waited for jeers. Relief when all she got was cheers. Tilly couldn't recall the last time she had been so happy to see the blue flame flicker and die.

She'd agreed to have dinner with Dan, but all she wanted to do was clean up and take a long nap on the couch. Perhaps Dan could fan her and feed her grapes. Wasn't that every man's fantasy? Checking Twitter for comments about this demonstration and any kissing could wait until *after* her nap.

The demonstration wasn't over yet. She had planned one more sample for the audience. Tilly washed her hands and got out a clean cutting board and knife as Steve, Karen and Candace brought three babkas forward on trays. The audience gasped in anticipation at the sight of the tall cakes dusted with powdered sugar.

"For your last treat, I baked three *babka podolska,* or babka baked with the Italian prune plums that are now showing up at the markets." Tilly cut into the desserts and laid pieces of the fluffy yellow cake with glistening purple plums onto paper plates to be handed out to the audience.

She breathed a sigh of relief when the last slice left the counter for the audience's eager hands. The demonstration was almost over. Patricia had warned her that the audience was encouraged to come up to the stage and talk with the chef after the demonstration. Before the review had been posted, Tilly had been looking forward to talking with the audience about Babka and Polish food. Now, even after a successful demo, the crowds that had been laughing and clapping along with her cooking suddenly seemed to loom down the aisle.

A fashionably dressed blonde hurried up to the stage with confrontation on her face. Tilly braced herself and plastered on a smile.

"I read the review."

How to respond? It wasn't a question about the food, more an accusation that Tilly didn't belong here. She tried to be nonchalant. "Yes," she said, waving her hand lightly in the air as if brushing away some bothersome flies. "It was quite a night a Babka. Doubly unfortunate a food writer was there. I'm sure people will overlook a review written after only one visit, and I hope The Eater will return to my restaurant and try us on a normal night."

"I think it shows bad management and I'd be afraid to find cat on the menu." The woman chuckled at her own joke and took a bite of the babka on her plate.

The audience crowded around the counter, waiting for Tilly to respond. Some were trying to pretend their babka was so engaging they dare not glance up from it, others were busy memorizing the recipes Tilly had provided, while others didn't even bother to hide the fact they were eavesdropping. One man even stood with his fork poised halfway to his open mouth.

"If there is something we can do to change your mind, please let me know," she replied calmly. It was an effort to keep her voice steady, but she didn't want to risk losing the business of other people crowded around eating her food.

"It's sad to see how many restaurant hopefuls fail in the first year. Besides all those fancy dishes, the cooking schools really ought to teach some classes in the reality of the business. Do you know how many restaurants close in their first year?" The woman took another bite of the cake and chewed appreciatively.

Don't give in to temptation. Don't give in to temptation. Don't give in to temptation. Tilly knew her face was red and tight with irritation, but she forced a pleasant smile when all she wanted to do was pace or sit on her hands in the corner.

No, all she wanted to do was shove the nasty woman and her comments in the oven and shut the door. Unless she wanted to be arrested for Hansel-and-Gretel crimes, she would have to grin and bear it. Maybe someone in the audience would notice her self-control and reward her for it by spending money at Babka.

A muscular arm threaded around her waist and she smelled spicy bay rum.

Dan.

She leaned into him and allowed his presence to comfort her. It was nice to have someone else stand with her as this woman attacked her restaurant and everything she had worked for.

Before she could respond, she heard Dan say, "It sure does look like you enjoyed the babka. I know it's some of the best cake I've ever had."

Her stomach got all tingly and she wanted to shake like a puppy. *Best he's ever had?* Tilly had a vision for her restaurant and love of food that transcended any review. But she still liked compliments.

The woman finished her cake, sniffed and walked away. Almost immediately the void around her was filled with people talking to Tilly from all directions.

"Best I've ever had, too," said a Hispanic woman with a black leather purse.

"Eat at your mother's restaurant at least once a month and I'm looking forward to trying what you can do," said an older man with a round Polish face Tilly vaguely recognized from the neighborhood.

"Never thought I'd like a cold beet soup, but I'm going to make some for my next cookout."

"I've always wanted to make pierogi at home, but they seemed too scary. I'm going to make some this weekend."

"Do you think Babka would be a good place for a date?"

Dan bent his head and whispered in her ear. "Nothing to worry about. I was paying attention to the audience. They were riveted and you won all of them over. That woman is the only one who remembers the review." He gave her a peck on the cheek and slipped his arm away. "You look exhausted, so I won't hold you to your promise of dinner. Nice to meet you, Tilly Milek. See you around."

As she responded to all the people clamoring for her attention, she watched Dan weave his way to the back of the tent. Her date, the perfect kisser, was gone.

CHAPTER SIX

TILLY WOKE UP Tuesday morning with a giant smile on her face. She snuggled deeper into her sheets, content to doze in her post-demonstration high until her alarm went off. A post-demonstration high and the wonderful fuzziness of being attracted to a man and having him be attracted back *at the same time*. She'd pump her fist in the air, but that was too much action for first thing in the morning. Better to pull the sheets closer to her face and continue to sleep.

So she didn't know his last name. She had no idea how to contact him again. The cards were completely in his hands. Normally that would make her nervous, but, in this case, it took some of the pressure off.

She didn't need a boyfriend. As her ex had informed her while she packed up to move to Chicago, sixteen-hour workdays didn't give her time for a boyfriend. Until Dan contacted her, she had the memory of a perfect kiss to sustain her through long hours on her feet at Babka. And when she was ready for a man in her life, she would have a memory of a perfect kiss to help her sift the wheat from the chaff.

Her large orange cat, looking more like a pet and less like the devil animal who had ruined a dinner service now that he'd been to the vet and been eating regular meals, settled on her stomach and began purring. As for Dan contacting her again, well, she'd deal with that problem when and if he appeared. Right now, Imbir, Polish for ginger, was all the man she needed.

"Another perfect summer day for those of you headed to the Taste of Chicago." When her radio clicked on to the chatter of a morning show, Tilly popped the sheets off her face and blinked at the sun streaming in through the slats of her blinds.

"Speaking of the Taste, Sam, do you remember the review of the new Polish place on *CarpeChicago?*"

She swung her legs over the side of her bed and stretched, tugging her T-shirt down over her panties. A good demonstration yesterday and now the most popular morning show in Chicagoland was talking about her restaurant. This had to be an auspicious sign. Babka would have a Tuesday to remember.

"How could I forget, Marty? That article must have been forwarded to me from twenty different people and we got more comments on our Facebook page about that than any story we posted in the past several months. Viral is not a word you want associated with a restaurant, but that review went viral. It was sick, man."

Tilly padded across her small studio apartment to the bathroom and started brushing her teeth.

"Well, the Twitterverse is full of a new development. Apparently The Eater, the writer of the review and wrecker of Tila Milek's career, was at the demonstration. A friend of mine snapped a picture and it's posted on our Facebook page."

"His identity is supposed to be a secret, like the identities of The Musician and The Sports Nut. Only The Politician's identity is known for certain."

Tilly spit toothpaste into the sink and turned to glare at her radio. *Stop talking, Sam. I want to know what Marty has to say about The Eater.*

"It may be a secret, but it's not a nuclear passcode. I have it on good authority one of the men in the photo is The Eater."

Tilly rinsed her toothbrush. *The Eater was at the demonstration?* Which one was he? Did he enjoy her food? Would he write an apology?

Which one was he?

She set her toothbrush on the sink, rinsed her mouth out and went to her small desk. Now, of course, was the moment when browser needed to update for security reasons. Tilly clicked No—the laptop could update tomorrow, or next week. Right now, she needed to see the picture.

She entered her password and a couple of clicks later, Tilly was on the station's Facebook page, staring at the thumbnail picture hiding The Eater's identity.

"It's not a very good picture, Marty," the other morning host chided.

No, it's not, Marty. If you're going to freak me out, the least you could do is post a good picture.

The DJ laughed. "My friend's not a very good photographer. I won't tell you which one is The Eater, but for those people who know, they will have a good laugh."

Tilly clicked on the picture to enlarge it, but it was no help. The image was blurry and even if it had been clear as Julia Child's consommé, there were at least twenty different people in the photo, not including her sister, her mother and her. She examined the men. One portly gentleman who clearly enjoyed his food. Maybe, but she'd heard The Eater was a college friend of the blog's founder, so he was too old. Two younger men laughing together. They were the right age, could it be one of them? Dan, with his arm around her, was giving her a peck on the cheek. Maybe? Tilly shook her head and dismissed the thought immediately. No one, *no one,* could be that cruel.

She skimmed the comments, looking for clues, but if anyone else in Chicagoland knew what The Eater looked like, they weren't telling. A couple of comments expressed amusement, several said The Eater was a jerk—*yeah, jerk!*—and one person said she'd been to Babka and had a delicious meal.

Wasn't all publicity supposed to be good publicity? She'd take some pity customers right now. Her food would convince them to come back.

Tilly signed in to Twitter and scanned #babkacatfight for more news and, hopefully, more photos. No luck. There were several comments on the demonstration, mostly positive, some lingering jokes and comments about The Eater's appearance at the demonstration, but no other photos. Only one lone photo drawing all the attention. One person helpfully pointed out The Eater was wearing a white shirt, but so were at least five of the men in the picture, including Dan. *You couldn't have described his shirt better? Logos or anything more specific than white?*

Imbir mewed loudly as he threaded his body between her legs. Breakfast. She didn't have time to hunt around the internet for a photograph of The Eater. Again. The photo on the blog was a headshot of a guy in a Cubs hat and sunglasses stuffing an oozing Italian Beef in his mouth. A Google search had revealed the faces of many different men, including the frustrating blog picture, but nothing she could conclusively pinpoint as the right Eater living in Chicago and currently ruining her life.

"Meeeoooow!" Imbir bit her ankle.

"All right, I get it. It's breakfast time and if I don't get a move on, I will be late for work. Then who will bring you home bits of sausage for your late-night snack?" She picked up her cat and groaned. "You are one heavy kitty, Imbir. It's a wonder I need to feed you at all."

His only response was a squirm as they neared his dish. She poured out some food and he began to chow down, purring contentedly. "What do you think, Imby? Should I look at the image search for The Eater again and see if my Dan is one of the pictures?"

He ignored her, which was all the answer she would get until his bowl was empty and every last taste of kibble licked off the crockery.

"You're right. I don't have the time, nor do I have the inclination. The Eater may be a jerk for writing the review, but no person could be so cruel as to write that review and then kiss the woman whose career he tried to ruin."

HER SOFT SKIN REACTED to his fingers, her rosy nipples puckering as his hand caressed her perfect, white breasts. Her body was as wonderful as he had imagined. *She* was as wonderful as he had imagined. The English language did not contain enough superlatives to describe how he felt right now.

Blue hair spread across the white pillowcase was hotter, her voice sexier, and the way she squirmed and stretched at his touch was enough to keep him aroused all night. For days. Weeks maybe. His hand traveled down her stomach and she laughed her husky laugh as he tickled her sides. A dirty gleam came into her eyes, her bottom lip lowering, inviting…

"Dan!" A heavy hand pounded on the small table of the coffee shop where Dan was desperately trying to finish his edits for a *Vanity Fair* article. "Wake up. You're supposed to be editing your next column, remember? Slamming another upstart restaurant."

Some people had voices fitting for their personalities. Shane wasn't one of them. If the world were just, Shane would have a voice for print media instead of the deep

baritone that made his evening radio show the most popular in its time slot. Most of the time, Dan didn't mind him,
but today he wasn't in the mood. He had been happily en-
grossed in an erotic fantasy about a blue-haired chef and
Shane had killed it. He couldn't even return to that fantasy
for at least an hour. He wasn't going to risk Tilly saying
something in Shane's voice again. He shivered. The idea
was too disturbing to even joke about.

"What do you need, Shane?"

"I was walking by when I saw you in the window."
Shane lowered his booming voice, but half the coffee shop
heard what came out of his mouth next. "Sex with the hot
Polish chick whose restaurant you tried to destroy? Way
to go!"

Dan pinched the flesh between his left thumb and forefinger with his right hand and willed the pain to keep him
from exploding at Shane. "What are you talking about?"

Shane knew the local music scene, was a good writer
and—Dan hated to admit this—an excellent DJ. His personality was also stuck in middle school where all the boys
could talk about was which girls filled out their bras first
and who would let you touch their butt at the school dances.
The man couldn't have an adult conversation if he needed
to talk his way out of being bounced from a club. At least
after Shane left Dan could get back to work. The upside to
Shane's visit was he could get back to making his Wednesday productive.

Noticing Dan wasn't going to ask about the rumor,
Shane decided to pull up a chair and share what he knew.
"My girl went to the Taste on Monday and decided to check
out the cooking demonstration of the poor woman whose
career you ruined. Lo and behold, who does she see with
his arm around the blue-haired lady, but The Eater. The
charming food writer who never gets drunk at parties and

still manages to be the most entertaining person there, who always seems to have a beautiful date, was making pretty with the chef owner of Babka."

Dan marveled at the generosity of the female sex. It never ceased to amaze him Shane could have a girlfriend. He understood the attraction of the voice, but how did women manage to ignore the crap pouring out of Shane's mouth most of the time he opened it? Then the full force of Shane's story hit home. If Shane knew about Tilly, he would tell the whole world. He might have already told the whole world on his radio show and decided to make sure he had the pleasure of telling Dan the story himself because he knew Dan didn't listen to his station.

This was a disaster.

Shane was still talking. "I got to know—how does a man get to screw a woman twice? Sheer class, man."

Dan had been feeling guilty enough about Monday and the Taste, without the lowest man on earth implying he was a dung beetle. Despite how much he liked Tilly and how hard his libido was trying to convince him that withholding the truth was okay, he knew it wasn't and he couldn't go through with taking Tilly on a date under false pretenses. He couldn't "screw a woman twice," as Shane had nicely put it.

Dan had been a douche for not telling Tilly, or even for going to her demo after meeting her, and it was possible the whole of Shane's audience knew. He wanted to be mad at Shane, but his humiliation—Tilly's humiliation—was his fault. He had made the mistake and, no matter how hard he looked, he couldn't find anyone to blame it on. His father always told him people had to own up to their mistakes. Realizing in his junior year of high school that he'd never heard his father admit to a mistake or apologize had tempered that particular parental lesson. If Dan Sr. couldn't convince someone they were wrong with honeyed words, he used vinegar, but the injured party always admitted they were at fault.

Saying goodbye to Tilly had led to a photo that embarrassed her, but apologizing would only make the situation worse. It was better for both of them, Tilly especially, if Dan stayed away from her. The punishment didn't quite fit the crime, but every time he wanted fresh pierogi and had to eat frozen ones, he'd know it was his own damn fault.

"This is a story to go down into the triumph of testosterone tales. What did you tell her to make up for your review? Did you say the editor was riding your tail? Did you feed her some line that you could make her restaurant great again with the right incentive? I got to know."

Shane wasn't going to leave. He had made up his mind to torture Dan and he was going to stay until state secrets had been revealed. Dan could leave, but he had a message to deliver first. Shane needed to learn he couldn't talk about Tilly. If he'd already mentioned Tilly on his radio show, Dan would have to deal with the fallout later, but he could stop any talk from now on. He reached over and grabbed Shane's wrist. "Don't ever talk about Tilly again."

Then he squeezed.

Dan dug his fingers into the tendons and veins in Shane's wrist as the man yanked his arm, trying to get it away from the pressure. Dan's grasp was far stronger than Shane's ability to pull his arm away and Dan held on until Shane finally gave up.

Message delivered, Dan grabbed his laptop and left the coffee shop and Shane, who was sitting in the chair rubbing his now-tender wrist. Like a middle-school boy, Shane understood threats. Especially since he knew Dan had the ability to carry them out.

Mike found him later, sitting in a German bar off Irving

Park, an undrunk beer in his hand, and brats and kraut un-eaten on his plate. The lunch crowd had thinned, leaving a barstool beside Dan for Mike to slide onto.

"You heard the rumor," Dan said.

Mike took the beer from his hand and took a swig. "The whole city knows."

Dan scowled as Mike confirmed his fears, probably rel-ishing being right.

"Haven't you been paying attention to the news? Face-book? Twitter?" Mike asked.

"I assumed Shane announced something on his radio show. I don't know anything about the others. Twitter an-noys me more than Shane ever could and I check my Face-book page once a week, no matter how many stupid emails they send me about birthdays and events."

"Shane wasn't the one who announced anything. One of the morning shows has a picture of you with your arm around Tila after the demo and someone at the station knows it's you." Mike pulled his phone out of his pocket and Dan peered at the tiny, blurry photo of him giving Tilly a peck on the cheek while the audience crowded around her counter.

"I'll bet you a hundred dollars Shane's girlfriend took that photo. Doesn't she also work at a radio station?"

"Did you tell her who you were?"

"No." Before Mike could start in on him, Dan held up his hand. "It's not the way Shane made it sound. I didn't know who she was when I started talking to her and I cer-tainly didn't take her home with me. We had a nice con-versation and I watched her demo. Then I left."

"Didn't want to tell her, huh?"

"You make it sound like I did something dirty. I didn't know who she was. When she told me, it was too late."

I'd already kissed her. "I couldn't tell her right before her demo. I'm not that much of an asshole."

"She looks cute." Mike took another drink of Dan's beer and smiled. "And the hair sure is blue. Why didn't you recognize her from the night of the review?"

"She was wearing a bandanna over her hair. From the chaos, I remember this woman with a bandanna who got control over the customers, the dog, the cat, everything. Mom said Tilly came by the table to greet everyone after the place was cleaned up. I was in the bathroom cleaning smoked fish spread and butter off my lap. I would have remembered the hair."

"Just the hair?" Mike had finished the beer and pulled Dan's plate of brats over. Dan watched his lunch disappear and tried to work up irritation as Mike ate his food, but he was too angry with himself to be angry at Mike.

"Okay, dammit. She's very pretty, even with the hair."

"And there was no moment, not even a second, when you had the time to tell this particular cute chef that you were not just another Dan enjoying a day at the Taste, but The Eater from *CarpeChicago?*"

"When was I supposed to tell her, oh great and wise sage? When she told me who she was, while she was blushing furiously? Hell, I could practically see her nerves. What about when the woman was attacking her business and accusing her of being another restaurant casualty? Now that would have been great." The volume of his voice was rising. People were starting to stare at them. He calmed himself. His problem wasn't Mike's fault. "Not only would she be nervous about all the people there to watch the demo, but she'd have to worry about the asshole critic in the audience. It was for her own good and I'm not going to apologize for it!" He slammed his fist down on the bar, making the plates jump and drawing a nasty look from the bartender.

"Why'd you write the review?"

"We've already had this conversation. We have a bet on this, remember?"

"You seem to be feeling rather guilty about something. Since it's not keeping your identity from the cutie-pie chef, I have to assume you feel guilty about the review."

"I've got nothing to feel guilty about." Dan regained control of his voice. He didn't want the bartender to toss him out of one of his favorite lunch spots. "The review was legitimate. Being a restaurateur is about creating the perfect meal, consistently. No mistakes. No overcooked steaks, no undercooked chicken, no chipped plates and no cats. Not everyone gets to eat out at an expensive restaurant every night. There should be no question about the quality of the experience. The apologies, free drinks and free desserts don't matter. Tilly failed her customers that night. She failed badly enough that she doesn't get another chance."

"You let me know how comfortable that knowledge is while you're sleeping by yourself at night."

"Dammit, Mike. I don't feel guilty about the review and I don't need to apologize for it."

"Hey, friend, no one was saying you have to apologize. I'm just here for the gossip. Think about what you said and thanks for lunch." Mike pushed back his plate and walked out of the restaurant.

Dan looked down at his now-empty plate, sitting next to his empty beer glass. If Mike hadn't been one of his closest friends, he'd say the guy was a complete jerk.

CHAPTER SEVEN

DAN CURSED HIS ringing phone as he rolled over in bed. The screen was lit with Mike's phone number. Why the hell was Mike calling him at four-thirty in the morning?

"I hope you need bail."

"Good morning, sunshine. I scheduled my next post. I believe I beat you and you owe me two lunches."

"Couldn't this wait until a reasonable hour?" Dan growled into the phone. This was Mike's second win in a row.

"I figured you would want to know as soon as possible, so you didn't have to rush. I mean, you're not going to beat me anyway. Why hurry?"

Dan threw his head back into his pillow, wincing when his skull glanced off the headboard. "What I want is to go back to sleep."

"Since you owe me two lunches, I'll cut you a deal and we can make it one dinner."

"Whatever. Text me where you want to go and I'll meet you there." How was Mike chipper at four-thirty in the morning? "Don't expect a response until at least ten."

"We have a deal? We'll eat dinner wherever I want tonight?"

"If it will make you shut up."

Mike laughed. "Sleep tight, Goldilocks. Bring your appetite."

His phone faded to black after Mike disconnected, but

Dan still didn't trust it. He turned the damn thing off entirely and shoved it into his bedside table drawer for good measure. Then he pulled his blankets over his head and hoped for a couple more hours of sleep before whatever torture Mike had in store for him tonight.

THE RESTAURANT WAS EMPTY. Again. Sure, there were a couple of full tables, but it was eight o'clock on a Thursday night and any successful restaurant would be more than half full. The money her grandmother had left her was powering lighting for her and her staff. No customers. What a waste. This couldn't continue. She had to have some customers or her restaurant would fail. More important, somewhere in heaven, Babunia would be disappointed.

Her more immediate problem was that the staff was out of sync. AM Carlos had put all the prepped ingredients in the wrong places in the sandwich units and PM Carlos was threatening AM Carlos's entire family and all future generations every time he reached for softened butter and got breadcrumbs instead. He refused to move the ingredients, defended them against Tilly's attempt to put everything back in its proper place, because the prep work should be right. If it was wrong, everyone should suffer the consequences. And suffer they did. He was impervious to threats of being canned. PM Carlos was a solid line cook and could get a job at another restaurant easily. Right now, Tilly needed him more than he needed her.

The upcoming soccer game between Mexico and Guatemala was making the tension in the kitchen worse. Enrique would normally side with PM Carlos against the bad prep, but Enrique was rooting against Mexico and using the prep mistake to further nettle PM Carlos.

As a consequence, the kitchen was behind. And so dinner service was behind. The servers were flustered by the strain in the kitchen and making little mistakes. Customers left disgruntled, but couldn't identify why. Karen was busy keeping the waitstaff together and she didn't have time to make her usual careful notes on customers for Babka's records.

What should have been an easy night was speeding its way into disasterland because AM Carlos had put the breadcrumbs where the butter went. Something he had never done before. When she had called him to ask about it, AM Carlos claimed he had put everything in the right place. Which meant Tilly was left blaming a poltergeist. Did poltergeists haunt restaurants?

Tilly sighed and walked back through the swinging doors into the kitchen. Bright white plates sat on the metal shelving, waiting for food to be elegantly arranged on them. Enrique was sautéing trout and Tilly could see the salamander glowing as it browned a *babka kartoflana z pieczarkami,* a potato-mushroom cake and one of Babka's few vegetarian dishes. The smell of butter and onions filled the kitchen. Everything was ready for the food to come off the heat. No tickets were printed out, so she stood at the pass with nothing to do but ban any mention of soccer for the rest of the night.

To emphasize her ban, she repeated it in Spanish.

Hoping that looking busy would make her busy, she walked into the closet she called an office to review possible menus for next week. Babka was serving some great dishes, if only there were customers to enjoy them. Tomato season was here and they had a starring role. Tomatoes stuffed with a green pea salad could work as a starter or as a vegetarian entrée, and tomato soup with a few puff pastry squares floating delicately in the bowl would be a nice change from the beet soup. But tomatoes were perishable and she didn't want to buy too many if her restaurant was going to be this empty every night. If she was going to fail, she wanted to fail with as little debt as possible. On the other hand, if her business picked up, she didn't want the servers telling customers they were out of the green-pea-stuffed tomatoes.

She looked back at the staff preparing the food. Jon, her sous chef, had taken over calling out the few tickets. She would rather be in the kitchen hollering out orders and yelling at PM Carlos to get his meat entrée done than in her office staring at paperwork. The sounds of the kitchen—knives hitting wood cutting boards, the click of the lids on pans and the hiss of food as it hit hot butter—those sounds were her music. The smells, good ones like garlic and onions, and bad ones like the gas stove, both soothed and energized her at the same time.

Some of the audience from the Taste demonstration needed to come in. She needed their business. It had been three days since all those people had told her they loved her food. Was she being impatient? Maybe they needed to find a babysitter before they could have a night out. Maybe their grandmother died. Maybe they just forgot.

Or maybe they remembered the review and decided it wasn't worth their trouble to come to a restaurant that was going to fail.

And Dan. Would he show up? She had promised herself she wouldn't think about him, but if she was being honest about the future of Babka, she could be honest about Dan. He had provided much-needed support when she was barely in control of her nerves and she was grateful. He'd been a kind face, and then he had left. She was a little disappointed he hadn't taken her out to dinner after the demo, but the honesty parade forced her to admit she had been too tired to be much of a dinner companion. One glass of wine and she would have put her head down on the table and snored her way through the meal.

And maybe she didn't have time for a serious relationship and maybe she didn't want one. Tony, the ex-boyfriend she'd left behind in New York, had complained about the hours she'd worked until thinking about the pain in her feet from being in front of a stove for sixteen hours a day, five or six days a week, had been easier than listening to him. And she hadn't owned a restaurant or been a head chef in New York. Between the long hours at Babka, the stress of being a struggling small business owner, the long hours at Babka and more long hours at Babka, thinking about a relationship with anyone, even Dan with his inspiring smile and broad shoulders, seemed fruitless.

But maybe she should. Those broad shoulders looked as if they would support her weary head nicely. His kiss had made her stomach flutter and forget her troubles for a few wonderful moments. Could a man who made her skin tingle, her knees weak and every other cliché schoolgirls giggled over really just kiss her and leave?

Even if he was a man she was willing to risk heartache for, who was she kidding? When she wasn't at Babka, she was visiting farms within driving distance of Chicago. And when she wasn't visiting farms, she was researching Polish food and culture. All in pursuit of a dream.

Men required time and energy, which were sparse ingredients in her busy life. Babunia had left her money so she could start her own restaurant and make a success of it. Right now, she was spending that inheritance on staff with no one to cook for and repairmen for kitchen equipment that wouldn't stay working, but success could happen if she worked hard enough. She had no other choice. If she didn't put everything she had into Babka, she would be betraying all her grandmother had meant to her.

Tilly knew it was better that Dan had walked off after her demonstration than for him to have stuck around and gotten her hopes up. Better she didn't have that excess worry. She didn't even need to consider what had made him leave the Taste with a peck on the cheek and generic "see you around."

Dan had helped make the demo a nice memory and that was all he should ever be.

She needed to have this conversation with herself about ten more times before she would believe it. Then pigs would fly into her restaurant and volunteer for her fry pans, and twelve dancing princesses would waltz in to order appetizers, entrées, dessert and drinks. And tip twenty-five percent.

She put away the menus. She wasn't thinking about tomatoes anyway. She was feeling sorry for herself and her little business. She needed something besides ads, her website and the crummy review. What she needed was something big to publicize her restaurant. Word of mouth was important, but needed a jump start.

Until Babka was the restaurant it could and should be, she wouldn't have time to think about Dan, or any man for that matter.

"Tilly?" Steve stood at her door, his thin frame like a long grain of rice standing at attention.

"Yeah? What is it?" She swallowed her groan. Steve, like all runners, was always busy, no matter how many people were in the restaurant. The energy needed to be a runner was why many people had turned a blind eye to his drug habit for years, until he started forgetting important details. She'd called several past employers before hiring him and they all said he was great—when he wasn't using. He was clean now and she hadn't had a single complaint about him.

If he had time to linger outside her office door, something was wrong.

"There are two men out here, both dressed nicely. They're asking for you."

Dan.

She shook her head. Now she was being ridiculous. Given the past week, she should prepare for the worst. Representatives from the bank to see where their money was. A surprise health inspection during dinner service. Maybe the old man sitting at the bar was a twenty-year-old with a good fake ID and better makeup and she was going to have her liquor license revoked.

Don't be ridiculous, Tilly.

"Did he ask to speak to the owner or the chef?"

"He asked to speak to Tilly. Kinda strange, if you ask me, since you're not dating anyone. He looks nothing like your brother. Anyway—" Steve's smile broadened his narrow face "—the front-of-house gossip is that he's handsome in a wholesome, Midwestern boy way. Karen said that before saying she'll take him if you don't want him. Apparently, she wants to take him home to her parents."

His news passed on, Steve left.

Midwestern. Wholesome. Definitely Dan. Even with a beer stain on his shirt, Dan looked as if he had been a football quarterback, growing up practicing his passes with his dad on their farm. Maybe a little too short to be the quarterback, but a wrestler was still a good guess. Strong and lean. Also, carefree and sure of himself.

But who was he here with?

Tilly looked down at her white chef's jacket and houndstooth pants, then shrugged. The uniform wasn't stylish, but it was practical and she couldn't change anyway. She settled for dusting off the little bits of pepper and flour that had settled on her jacket. The beet stain on the front made her look as if she'd been shot in the gut, but it would have to remain where it was.

Tucking some flyaway strands of hair back under her bandanna, she took a deep, relaxing breath and walked into the dining room.

The restaurant looked more barren than ever. The two men waiting for her in the far corner couldn't make up for the ten desolate tables eating up the dining room. For the second time that night, she reminded herself not to worry. As she walked closer, one of the men smiled, his white teeth reflecting the light from the candle on his table. It was the slow, confident smile she had seen before and she forgot all her promises to focus on her business and put relationships out of her mind.

"Hi, Tilly." Dan had a clear, calming voice. It warmed her and smoothed away her nerves, like a verbal cup of strong tea. It was almost enough to make her forget about how attractive he was.

Almost.

"Dan, it's nice to see you again." She didn't even try to keep the smile out her voice. To sound as if she didn't remember the kiss and how it had heated her body. She hoped she sounded like a confident businesswoman instead of a silly schoolgirl.

Dan stood and pulled out a chair for her. "Please sit with me for a moment, unless you're needed in the kitchen." He looked around at the empty restaurant. He knew she wasn't needed in the kitchen. "We just ordered. Mike and I need company."

"You should start going places with dates, since you always seem to want company." Tilly crossed her arms over her chest, remembering how he'd left her right after the demo and she hadn't got the dinner he'd promised.

"I never seem to be missing company until I see you,"

he replied. His smile was less confident, but just as alluring, and his eyes were hopeful.

The compliment caught her off guard, but she quickly recovered. "An obvious line if I've ever heard one, but I'll bite."

She sat and Dan returned to his chair.

"Tilly, this is my friend Mike. We work together and he was dying to come here for dinner tonight."

Mike gave Dan a wry smile that turned warm as he shook Tilly's hand. "Dan's said so much about Babka I had to try your restaurant for myself."

"I wish I could say I'm too busy and can't stay long but…" She looked around at the nearly empty restaurant. "We would all know I was lying."

"Is this how it is every night?" Dan asked.

"Yes, since the review in *CarpeChicago*. I had hoped after the cooking demonstration…" She wanted to ask why he'd left with a vague reference to the future but nothing she could hang on to (or throw away) and, more importantly, why he had come back to the restaurant. She didn't have the courage, not yet.

Besides, she didn't want him in her life. Dan or any man. *You're too busy, Tilly.*

"I hadn't planned on coming to your restaurant tonight, or even seeing you again. I thought that day at the Taste would be a fun date with a stranger, one to tell your children about. Like the movie *Before Sunrise.* Where the man meets a beautiful woman he's half in love with, even though he knows he'll never see her again."

Her heart caught on *that* word—love—but her brain thought it was a line, part of his charm, like the smile. It didn't feel as if he was telling the whole truth. Maybe he had another reason not to see her again. He didn't look directly at her when he talked.

If she didn't know better, she would have thought he had a secret.

"But?"

"But I owed Mike dinner and he mentioned Babka. So here I am…"

He hadn't come here to see her, but because he owed his buddy dinner, and he'd asked for her because it would be awkward if she walked into the dining room to see him sitting here.

"…and I realized there is no place I'd rather be."

Well, that shut up her cranky mind.

He'd probably known what to say to a woman from the womb, but she didn't buy it. It had her looking at the goods, though. She wasn't sure if she was a sucker for looking or a skeptic for not buying it right off. *You're too busy to window-shop.*

"Dan, why are you here?"

Mike snickered and Dan looked abashed, but Tilly just raised her eyebrow.

"I told you. I owed Mike dinner and he wanted to come here. I'm looking forward to my dinner. Last time, I only tried a couple of bites."

Tilly cocked her head a little. "What last time?" And why had he talked about Babka to Mike?

"At the Taste." His gaze dropped from her face and again the thought he was hiding something struck her. "The beet soup was so good I had to come to your restaurant." He was looking back into her eyes, confident again.

A waitress came out with his salad and placed it in front of him. She turned to Tilly and said, "Tilly, something in the kitchen needs your attention."

Tilly caught her breath and the memory of that stupid cat held on to every last bit of air in her body until she had to cough out, "What is it?"

"It's the pot sink."

Tilly let out a great puff of breath. *Now the pot sink, on top of everything else.* "I'll be there in a minute. Turn off the water to the sink and we'll see what we can do." She turned her face back to the two men at the table. "Dan, Mike, enjoy your dinner. I'm sorry, but I have to take care of this."

A SWOOSH OF HOT AIR hit Dan as he came through the swinging doors in the kitchen. He found Tilly in the back, sitting cross-legged on the floor, fumbling with some pipes under the large metal three-basin pot sink that was piled with dirty pots and pans. Even a nearly empty restaurant produced a lot of dirty dishes. If he had a chance to eat his dinner, his plate would be one of the stack.

What should have been a busy, noisy kitchen with rich smells and people rushing from stove to plate was calm. Cooking for the three full tables out in the dining room didn't stress Tilly's kitchen. But, he noticed, they also weren't goofing off with their free time. Tilly had managed to make sure they had something to do, and, from the looks of it, not just busy work. Ignoring the dog-and-cat fiasco, Tilly might be better manager than he thought.

By the cursing coming from the direction of the sink, whatever was wrong with the pot sink wasn't easily fixed. He walked back to where Tilly sat. The floor was wet and a toolbox lay open on a folding chair next to her. The wrench she had in her hand was definitely not the right size.

"Want some help?"

Tilly jerked and hit her head on the sink. "Ouch." She rubbed the spot and crinkled her nose up at him. "What are you doing here?"

The crinkled nose was adorable. Her expressiveness was one of the things he liked about her. She blushed, groaned, grimaced and laughed. Every emotion she felt was clear on her face, but she never let them get in the way of her life. Tilly grabbed on to life and lived it. It was wonderful to watch.

"I came to see if you want some help." He gestured to the water on the floor. "You look like you need it."

Tilly slumped her shoulders and put her wrench down. "I've called a plumber and they won't be here for another three hours. The drain can't stay this way for three hours. Even as empty as we are, we need the pot sink."

Dan crouched next to her and looked over the pipes. "You don't need a plumber. I can fix this."

Tilly straightened and looked at him, her eyes bright with hope. "You can?" She shook her head. "I mean, I can't ask you to do that. You're a customer. I can't have paying customers fixing my messy plumbing problems."

"Let's call it a trade, then. Don't charge us for dinner and I'll fix your sink for you."

"I can't ask you to do this. I really can't." Her voice, heavy with gratitude, betrayed her.

"You're not asking. I'm volunteering. Come on." He stood and offered her his hand. She took it and he pulled her to her feet. "I have some tools at my house I need to get. My place is nearby and it will take me much less time than it would take a plumber to get here."

Tilly looked at the mess on the floor, then at Dan. Then she touched her pants. They were soggy with dirty water. The wet fabric appeared to make the decision for her. "Thank you. You're getting the best meal Babka has to offer. While you're gone, I'll change into my spare clothes and plan your dinner."

"Can your employees manage without you for a half an hour?"

She blinked, obviously affronted. "Of course. Why?"

"Why don't you come with me? You can use my shower to rinse off that nasty water and put on your clean clothes there."

Despite all his valid reasons for staying away from Tilly, Dan wanted to help her. She needed help and he could provide it, plus it would be a good way to apologize for the embarrassment of her photograph ending up on Facebook. The urge wasn't because he felt guilty about the review. And it wasn't because he had lied to her. Those were decisions he didn't have to feel guilty for, no matter how much Mike chided him.

Tilly gingerly patted her wet backside again. "Yes," she said wistfully. "I would like to rinse off. But what about Mike?"

"He won't mind," Dan lied. Mike would mind—not about their lost dinner, but he would have plenty of objections about Dan spending more time with Tilly. "And your employees can manage without you…"

"Yes."

"Good. I'll drive my car around back and pick you up so none of your customers will see you soggy."

"Okay." She took a deep breath. "Thank you. Let me call Karen and tell her where I'll be going." She looked at him and narrowed her eyes a bit. "You're sure it will only be for half an hour."

"Yes. I live off Milwaukee, not far from Damen. You'll be back in no time. On my way out, I'll even leave my address and number with the bartender in case they need to get in touch with you in the meantime."

"Okay." She nodded once. "I'll meet you at the delivery entrance. I'll get some towels so you don't have to suffer my wet, dirty butt on your car seat."

Dan wouldn't mind her butt anywhere in his life, but he only smiled. "I have some beach towels in the back from my last trip to Wisconsin. You can sit on those. I'll explain things to Mike, get my car and send Karen to you. The sooner we leave, the sooner we can get your sink fixed."

When he told Tilly he wouldn't be long, Dan hadn't anticipated the time it would take for Mike to lecture him in hushed tones that fell to a whisper every time Tilly's staff walked past them.

"You really are an asshole," Mike said.

"What? I'm helping her. Don't you want me to?" Dan asked, wincing inwardly. His motives were pure; he didn't have to sound as if he was asking permission.

"It's not the help you're an asshole for. It's why you're doing it."

"'Cause I'm a nice guy and I want to?"

"Then you should probably come clean with who you are and do something about that review you wrote."

But if I come clean about who I am, she won't talk to me again. I want her to keep talking to me. Let her see that I'm a nice guy. "I will tell her, but not tonight. Tonight she needs my help. Hell, you're the one who suggested we come here for dinner."

"If you're helping her because you think her restaurant deserves a second chance, come back here several more times to eat pierogi. Then eat crow by telling Chicago you were wrong. If you're helping her because you want to get in her pants, I don't want to be your friend anymore."

"The two things aren't related. And I'll tell her," Dan said, unable to hide his wince at the pleading whine in his voice. Babka's review and his desire to get into Tilly's pants were unconnected, though he could no longer pretend that fixing her sink was a silent apology for the photograph.

If he were being honest with himself, Tilly had handled her destroyed restaurant as well as anyone could have, though the oversalted food was inexcusable and unexplainable. He'd written the review while angry at his messed-up family. When he'd excused his actions to his mother by saying her birthday dinner had been ruined, she'd been appalled.

As for Tilly's pants…

"Most women I want to have sex with," Mike continued, "at least those I want to see naked more than once, know my last name before we fall into bed. Does she even know yours? Maybe start by being honest about that."

Dan held up his hands to stop whatever Mike was going to say next. "Let me help her with her restaurant so that when I finally do tell her, she's not as angry with me and I have a *chance* at her pants."

This entire sorry episode would be easier if that was all he wanted. He could keep lying, take her clothes off and disappear from her life after a roll in the hay. The greater problem was that he wanted to be with her before *and* after the pants came off. As a goal, it was hard to reconcile with his current predicament. Continuing to lie worked as a short-term strategy. He had no long-term strategy, and the more time he spent with Tilly, the more he needed one—at least, longer term than it would take to fix her plumbing.

"Are you sure you're not being some poor little rich kid with a chance to piss off his father by dating a blue-haired woman with an interest in locally sourced food?"

"Hey!" Dan drew back, insulted. "You're supposed to be my friend, and this is what you think of me?"

"Dan, at heart, you are a good person and I don't think you would intentionally hurt anyone. But you make stupid decisions in reaction to your old man and I've known you to want something just because it will piss him off. Your sister is slaving away, running a company your father will never let her have. You won't touch it, even though he'd hand it over to you in a heartbeat."

Dan Sr. had cited Hugh Hefner's decision to pass over his daughter—who was running the company—in favor of his infant son as his inspiration. Hurricane-force winds whipped through Wisconsin when Dan Sr. started talking about the importance of heritage passed from father to son to grandson, etc. As if Meier Dairy was the crown of England and Dan Sr. was Henry VIII—though even the English had been better off with their queen.

Dan didn't believe his father really wanted him to run the company; he just wanted Dan within reach of his manipulations. Living in Chicago, Dan could delete emails and refuse to answer the phone. He would move farther away, but that would leave Beth in the lurch when she needed to escape.

Mike wasn't done with his lecture. "You began a career as a journalist after your father said writing was the most wasteful way a person could spend their time. And, while you don't draw on your trust fund for your everyday expenses, you do make a point of making sure your father knows when you've done something he would consider a waste of money, time or his gene pool. And it's no secret how he feels about the movement towards locally sourced food."

Dan Sr. had no love for family farms or small businesses. He valued mass production over craft, efficiency over care, and he wasn't shy about saying so. Television interviews led to public relations disasters for Meier Dairy because professional interviewers weren't so easily manipulated into following Dan Sr. neatly down his self-righteous path. The more Dan Sr. felt his platform slipping away, the more manic he became, leaving Dan's sister working behind the scenes to smooth over the "Meier message." Meier family relations gave a whole new meaning to "the big cheese."

In another life, Dan Sr. would have tried to become a cult leader.

Dan sighed. "You're right. My dad would hate this restaurant. He would scoff at every mention of the local farms supplying her produce, farmer's cheese and meats. He would also think Tilly got exactly the review she deserved, because mistakes are not to be tolerated and God helps those who help themselves. And by that he means playing fair is for chumps and dirty play is part of life. But that's not the reason I'm doing any of this."

Dan didn't want Tilly because he couldn't or shouldn't have her. When he made decisions to piss off his father, his inner teenager jumped up and down, egging him on. When he looked at Tilly, his inner teenager was strangely silent, as if he knew she was out of his league.

Instead of his inner teenager reacting to Tilly, Dan found his inner retired old man waving his arms at the chance of visiting the grandkids he could have with a passionate, warm woman who already knew how to dye her hair blue.

Quickly followed by astonishment when he realized he was the kind of weirdo who thought about grandkids when he'd only interacted with the woman twice. Three times, if he considered the review currently ruining her career.

Mike gave Dan a long, hard stare before nodding once in understanding. "I'm going to hold you to this."

"I know."

"When you get back in the kitchen, ask them to pack up my dinner and I'll take it home. There's a Sox game on tonight."

KAREN'S BLOND HAIR BOUNCED as she nodded over the minimal instructions Tilly left. Every employee knew what he or she was supposed to do. If the restaurant was busier, they would miss her, but with few people in the dining room, she could be gone for hours and it would be fine. Her management professor at Culinary had told her the sign of a good manager was one with nothing to manage and, if that was true, she was the best manager ever. Having experienced, dedicated employees helped.

But if she didn't get business soon, even her most loyal employees would leave her. No waitstaff could afford to work in an empty restaurant. Normally, it was the kitchen staff who got the shaft in hourly compensation, especially when waiters were walking away with hundreds of dollars in tips after a busy Saturday. In a slow restaurant, the kitchen staff had a solid wage while the waitstaff was working for nonexistent tips. She would be facing a strike soon.

She closed and rubbed her eyes. The problems plaguing her were unfixable, at least right now. Now she needed to focus on her pot sink, which she could fix. Or hoped Dan could fix. So long as it got fixed, she didn't care if Julia Child rose from the dead with a tool belt and her pants dropping plumber-style over her zombie butt. She needed that sink to drain.

With a short prayer that there wouldn't be any problems while she was gone, Tilly left through the delivery entrance and climbed into a waiting green Subaru with her bag of spare clothes. Dan had already spread towels over the passenger seat.

She turned to face Dan as he drove out of the alley and onto the street. "Are you sure you don't mind?" She hated imposing on people. She'd gotten this far in her life on her own, and accepting help, even such a small thing, was hard.

"I am definitely sure. You make me want to play the white knight." He smiled at her and all her objections flew out the open car window.

They turned off Milwaukee and down a few streets before parking in front of a row of town houses. He led her into the corner town house. In the dark, it was hard for her to see any detail beyond that it was a modern glass-and-steel structure.

"I didn't expect a wreath and pots of flowers." The flowers and wreath were very feminine. Did he have a girlfriend? No, he'd asked her out on a date. Had he just broken up with someone? This was all none of her business. She was here to shower and get her sink fixed.

"Those are from my sister. They were housewarming presents when I bought this place a couple of years ago."

"I'm impressed the flowers are still alive. I didn't picture you as much of a green thumb."

Dan chuckled as he unlocked the door. "I'm not—killed them the first year. It pissed off my sister, Beth, enough that she hired a high school kid to water them and replant the pots every year."

Entering the house, Tilly was struck by a decorating scheme she decided to call modern male messy. All the walls were painted white and the only warmth came from some dark wooden furniture. There were no pictures on the wall and no pillows, just debris scattered around. By the front door was a pile of shoes, and a matching pile of mail sat unopened on a table. "It's a little stark, except for the mess."

His smile was sheepish. "I would've cleaned up if I'd known I was having company. I spend most of my time in the kitchen or my office. The other rooms came with the kitchen and office."

"We should trade houses, then. My kitchen, office, bedroom, living room and dining room are all the same thing. You take my apartment and I'll paint your walls."

Dan laughed and gestured up the stairs. "The guest bathroom is upstairs and to your right. Towels are under the sink. I'll get my tools and wait by the front door."

Tilly walked up the stairs, a little embarrassed she was getting ready to shower in a strange man's house. But she was desperate to rinse the nasty water off. It had dried and the remnants of whatever had been in the sink were beginning to get sticky.

Gross.

She shuddered. Grease traps, clogged toilets and foul sink water were part of the job, but she didn't have to like them.

She found the bathroom, also with white walls. Thick lavender towels were where Dan said they would be. She smiled at their fluffy softness and absurdly girlie color as she undressed. The towels must be from his sister, who was probably also responsible for the dish of potpourri on the back of the toilet.

Turning on the water, she stepped into the shower and let it beat down on her shoulders. The water was hot, and after she toweled off and stepped into her clean clothes, Tilly felt as if she could conquer the world. Amazing what a shower could do for a girl.

She was clean and Dan was going to fix her pot sink. Life was great. She even found a hair dryer and quickly dried her hair so she wouldn't get her kerchief wet.

Come on, world, I'm ready for anything.

Dan was waiting by the front door when she came down the stairs, a large toolbox in his hand. He was dressed in a pair of old cargo shorts and an olive T-shirt, and she could see he had an athletic shape, with strong arms, powerful legs and a muscled chest. Tilly didn't need any imagination to picture the flat stomach or the ridges of muscle hidden under his clothing.

She stopped on the stairs and swallowed. Dan looked like a page out of a man-of-the-month calendar—large, masculine and ready to come to a woman's aid.

Is he going to kiss me again?

Hell, I'm a modern woman. Am I going to kiss him?

The thought of another kiss—and the possibility of more—made her feel as if she were standing in front of the hot stove on the sauté line in July in Miami.

She was staring, openly, blatantly staring. How embarrassing. For all she knew, she was drooling, too. It would be the perfect story to tell Renia—a gorgeous man agreed to help her repair her sink and she rewarded him with drool. She shut her gaping mouth and searched her brain for something clever.

"You look better than my plumber." Not clever at all. Didn't cover up the drooling. *Shoot.*

"You look better than my plumber, too." He smiled the confident smile he always had ready, the one where it looked as though he was so sure he was saying the right thing and would get the results he wanted. It worked, sucker that she was.

She blushed. Her whole body was hot, and not from the shower. She needed to have her head examined. Surely she should be able to look at a man without conjuring up images of him without his shirt on.

He checked his watch, apparently unaffected by the lust coating every muscle of her body in a glaze of longing. "You're not due back for another ten minutes. We'll have you back to Babka with time to spare."

Dan offered his hand and Tilly took it. The contact tingled through her whole body and she wondered if Dan would want to date a woman who worked every Friday and Saturday night and most holidays.

Just thinking about the possibility he might understand made the shadows cast by the streetlights fade. Past failures were not an excuse not to try; they were simply a lesson in being more careful, even if reminding herself to take care didn't lessen the bounce in her step.

CHAPTER EIGHT

DAN SPENT THE quiet car ride back to Babka wondering what
Tilly's blue hair looked like wet. Was it a deeper blue or
did it keep its bright character? While he had gathered his
tools, he'd tortured himself imagining her in the shower,
then soothed his nerves by promising himself he'd at least
know what her hair looked like wet. Instead, she'd put her
hair under her white bandanna again and he was left to
continue to ponder the hair question, which sent his mind
back to how she looked in the shower.

Her damp chef's pants had been nicely revealing. He
now knew that her butt was firm and round, her legs nicely
shaped. And that she wore white underwear with red polka
dots.

When she walked down the stairs, it had taken all of
his self-control not to drop the toolbox and kiss her. He'd
already kissed her twice under less-than-perfect circumstances. He wasn't aiming for three poorly timed kisses
out of three. He could wait until he'd begun to make things
right. But he could no longer pretend he could avoid her and
everything would be fine. He needed a new plan.

His inner geriatric did cartwheels over the woman sitting next to him in the car and his inner teenager was
plotting how to engineer physical contact, any physical
contact. His inner teenager was horny and not interested in
any move that didn't get him to at least second base. Mike
would be disappointed by all the voices in Dan's head. Even

Dan's inner geriatric was telling him not to come clean yet, but to wait until Tilly was ready to forgive him.

Fixing the sink would be a good first step.

"How do you know how to fix a sink?" For a moment, Dan wondered if Tilly could read his mind. How terrible it would be if she could.

"My father has peculiar ideas about things, including what a 'real man' knows. A real man can do his own home repairs. Not that *he* actually does his own home repairs," Dan scoffed, "but he made sure I learned. I also know how to milk a cow, even though the last person in my family to run a dairy was my grandfather."

His father had also taught him people got punished for their mistakes and would have said the pot sink and the cat fiasco were Tilly's punishment for her failings. Dan thought he had abandoned all the judgmental tendencies he had inherited from his father and only ever wrote reviews he could justify without pejorative clichés. What did that mean about his review of Babka? His dinner had been terrible, but with Tilly sitting next to him in the car, he wanted to go back in time. To go to Babka on a different night, where there wouldn't be a cat and dog, or oversalted food.

"I'm glad he taught you, even if he doesn't do repairs himself. Maybe I should send him a free dinner, too."

At the approving look Tilly had given him earlier, Dan would be forever grateful his old man made sure he had basic plumbing skills. He didn't need a free dinner. Her eyes were filled with enough heat to ignite a building, not to mention what they did to the fit of his shorts. The lust in Tilly's eyes did nothing to discourage his mind from wandering over her body as she sat in his passenger seat.

"I don't think he'd appreciate Babka."

"He doesn't like Polish food?"

"He's suspicious of the locavore trend in food."

"Oh."

A car pulled out of the first spot in front of the restaurant and he pulled into the space easily.

"Do you always get princess parking?" she asked.

"Princess parking?"

"A spot right in front of where you want it to be. The closest one that's not the handicap spot."

"I prefer the term 'rock star parking,' but yes, I guess so. Why?"

"Do you always get everything you want?"

"Usually." A strange turn of the conversation.

"What do you want tonight?"

His mind flashed to the scene he'd created of her in his shower, water running over her naked body. That image was quickly replaced with the betrayed look that would be on her face the moment she found out he was The Eater, and his lust calmed a bit. "To fix your sink and get dinner."

"Oh." Her voice rang with disappointment. "We'd best get started, then."

Dan got out of his car and followed Tilly around to the back of the restaurant and through the service entrance. Pots and pans had piled up at the pot sink, though the dishwasher was running the smaller ones through the dish machine. Someone had attempted to mop up most of the worst of the mess on the floor. With the pipe broken and the drain clogged, it was hard to make much of a dent in the chunky dishwater surrounding the three metal sinks. He gave Tilly back her toolbox, set his own on the chair in its place, sat down and got to work.

TILLY WATCHED DAN plop down in the water and take her restaurant into his hands. She hoped he knew what he was doing. If not, the plumber would have to come anyway. At least she had seen his strong, muscular legs in those shorts, even if all he wanted to do was fix her sink. He didn't notice she'd turned to jelly at the sight of him in a T-shirt with a toolbox.

Before she got lost in her plumber fantasy—who would have guessed she even *had* a plumber fantasy—Tilly turned away to find Karen and fix Dan's dinner.

From the corner of her eye, Tilly saw Dan finally stand up and stretch. She'd been trying not to be obvious as she watched him, telling herself she watched him out of concern for Babka, not out of interest in his body. Several times he had looked at the pipe and shaken his head at whatever he found.

When he bent down again to turn on the water at the base of the sink, then stood, stretching out his back, she decided to investigate.

"How is the sink?"

He turned to her, a bit of sweat gleaming on his forehead under his blond hair. "It should be fine." He reached over and turned on the faucet. Out came water, which flowed nicely into the sink, down the drain and through the pipes. At the sight, Tilly instructed Karen to cancel the plumber.

Relief lifted the worry off her shoulders. "Thank you."

Dan stepped back and looked over his work. "And even though you came home with me to shower, I still beat the plumber."

"I don't think I can ever thank you enough, but dinner should be ready."

"What's dinner?"

"A noble dish for a noble deed. Fresh Babka-made kiel-basa cooked in beer with saffron, raisins and boiled new potatoes. The dish has many names, but one of them is *wereszczaka,* for a court chef to the Saxon kings of Poland in the late 1600s."

"Maybe we should get you a cooking show and you can

do for Polish cooking in Chicago what Rick Bayless did for Mexican. Have a show on PBS and everything."

Tilly gazed wistfully over his shoulder. "I'd get to go to Poland," she said.

"You've never been?"

"I've never had the money or the time. All my extra money went into school, then into Babka. And, while I'd like to be the Rick Bayless of Polish cuisine, I'm not yet, which means I have to be at my restaurant rather than traveling." She gestured to the plate of sausage and potatoes. "Everything you see here is the result of an attentive Polish grandmother and lots of reading."

He flashed his confident smile. "The food smells delicious. Is there someplace I can eat other than the dining room?" He gestured to his shorts, which were now soaked. They clung to his thighs and Tilly was forced to remind herself he was here to fix her sink, not be her sex object. *You don't have time for a relationship. You have a restaurant to run.*

Her inner admonishments couldn't compete with the feeling Dan had her back. Or she wanted to see his naked back.

He smiled at her and she didn't care about her restaurant or her pot sink.

"Oh, I didn't even think to remind you to pack extra clothes. Do you want to go back to your house and change? Dinner will keep."

"No worries." Dan waved her concern away. "I'll change later. I'd like to talk with you while I eat."

Her heart skipped. No customers had packed into her restaurant since her sink had broken. They had time to discover the meaning of life together, solve the secrets of the universe and create a budget for the federal government.

She gestured to her office/closet. "Have a seat at my desk and I'll get your dinner."

Dan looked directly at her as he responded. "Perfect."

Tilly shivered.

BY THE TIME TILLY RETURNED with his food, Dan had washed his hands and arms and found a towel to sit on in the folding chair. She placed the food in front of him, ignored her desk chair and sat down on a second folding chair.

"This looks amazing." He grabbed a fork and knife and took his first taste of sausage. "This *is* amazing," he said after he'd swallowed. The sausage popped in his mouth as he bit through the casing, releasing a flood of garlicky juices. Vinegar in the sauce cut through the richness of the meat, and the sweetness of the raisins paired perfectly with the spicy luxury of saffron and black pepper. "If this isn't on your menu every night, it should be."

"Thank you."

Dan took another bite. "Is there marjoram and paprika in here as well?"

"How did you know?"

"I have a great palate. Let's chat a little before we talk about your drain. The subject would ruin my meal." Dan took another bite and chewed the savory sausage. Tilly Milek was an excellent cook. Her food was passionate and intense, just like the chef herself.

More people needed to come into the restaurant and try her food. Doubting a review was a bad position for a critic to be in, but he hoped what he'd written would inspire people to come to Babka, even if only out of curiosity. For the first time in his writing career, he hoped people ignored him. As a reviewer, he had to hold firm to his position. Stick to his guns.

Except sticking to his guns seemed a sure way to blow

himself to bits right now. One: he didn't think Tilly was the failure he'd supposed her to be earlier. Two: when it wasn't oversalted, her food was delicious. Babka could have culinary staying power in Chicago.

This was why he didn't make friends with chefs. He was supposed to remain objective in his reviews. Mixing business and pleasure also ended poorly—don't get your bread where you get your butter and all that. He kept The Eater firmly separate from his image as Dan Meier, food writer, so no one questioned any conflicting motivations. Keeping The Eater anonymous helped. But now he didn't just have conflicting motivations. He'd poured all his motivations into a cocktail shaker and was trying to mask cheap gin with olive brine.

He swallowed and mashed a tiny, boiled potato into the sauce before enjoying its fluffy earthiness. "Why did you get into cooking?"

Tilly blinked in surprise. "I grew up in a restaurant. All I've ever wanted to do was cook."

"What about it do you like?"

"Everything. I love the smell of the food and the ovens. I love the sounds of the kitchen. Mostly, I love the rush." Tilly gestured with her hands, leaning forward into her excitement.

Dan raised his eyebrow at her as he chewed to encourage her to continue.

"A date took me to one of Chicago's fancier restaurants before my junior prom. Until that night, all I wanted to do was run Healthy Food, my mom's restaurant. Healthy Food was comfortable and it was—is—home. The food is always the same, the same retired old Poles eat there at five every day, and that's how the neighborhood wants it."

Tilly's mouth lifted up in a smile and her voice had the confidence of someone who knew exactly where she came from and where she was going. Currently floundering around in his own uncertainty, Dan was jealous. He wanted to share her faith.

"The restaurant was elegant, with white tablecloths and waiters who spoke reverently of each dish and of the chef, who must have been something close to God. The next day, I went to the library and figured out what I needed to do to become a chef at one of those restaurants. My grandmother helped me fill out the culinary school applications, against my mother's objections. Babunia insisted I reach for the stars and bought me my first knife set when I got the acceptance letter. I was using those knives at the Taste."

She held out her palm, where a scar ran from the fleshy part of her thumb to her pinkie finger. "I got this scar learning *not* to shuck oysters with my paring knife and no kitchen towel."

Dan could hear the clomping of her clog against the floor as she twitched her foot. Tilly enjoyed cooking, but she also enjoyed talking about cooking. Listening to her, he learned that her food wasn't just a combination of ingredients and heat. She put her family, history and memories into each recipe. He wanted to know about every scar on her hand, and how long it had taken her to get the knife callus on her left hand.

"Every day in Babka's kitchen gives me a high. I've heard professional athletes talk about the stress of the game and the adrenaline it produces." Tilly's face began to flush and Dan wondered what kind of reaction she had to sex if she got this hot and bothered by cooking. "I enjoy cooking at home, but in a restaurant kitchen, it's my own kind of competition. I'm racing the customers' expectations and my expectations of myself. I never played sports or did debate or anything else involving competition. Before I discovered kitchens outside my mother's, I never considered myself a competitive person. But in a restaurant kitchen like Babka, I'm in my own World Series and the restaurant is my stadium."

Tilly sighed and collapsed against the metal chair hard enough it rocked back on its legs before settling. "Besides the impending financial doom if Babka fails, in a slow restaurant, there is no rush."

"Do you have a plan B if Babka doesn't make it?"

"We will make it."

"If you don't?"

"I will. I have to. Babka is my grandmother's legacy. I should check on my staff." Tilly stood and walked through the kitchen, checking the control knobs on the stoves and wiping down counters. Dan got the point. This conversation was over.

Tilly returned several minutes later. Dan was finished with all of his meal except his wine, and his excuse not to talk about the drain was gone.

"About my drain?" Tilly's face was still tense from his previous suggestion Babka might not make it.

He followed her lead and left the previous conversation alone. Instead, he reached into his pocket, pulling out a washer that looked as if it had been chewed up and spit out by some large cat. The washer had been a bitch to get off so he could fix the sink and, given what Dan had found in the pipes, he suspected he wasn't supposed to be able to do so at all. Someone had tried to engineer an expensive plumbing repair. They just hadn't known much about plumbing when they'd done it. "There were two things wrong with your sink. First, this washer was worn—on purpose, I'd imagine."

"What do you mean on purpose?" She bent over to peer at the washer, their earlier conversation momentarily forgotten.

"The sink's new?"

"Yes."

"No new sink should have a washer this worn. Even a washer from an old sink shouldn't look like this." Dan took a sip of his wine. Tilly's bartender had made a smart match between his garlicky sausage and the Tuscan red he was currently drinking. "Secondly, I found something clogging the drain."

"What is it?"

"You don't want to see and I don't want to show you. It wasn't natural."

"What was it?" she asked, frustration raising her voice an octave. "I work in a restaurant kitchen. Gross is not new to me."

"It looked like a toupee." He took another sip. The wine was excellent, bold and rich. It had been a perfect pairing for his dinner, but he was glad he had saved some to savor alone.

"A what? Impossible. No one in my kitchen is bald. How would a toupee get in the drain?"

"Well…" Her skepticism amused him. "It was stuffed in there pretty deeply. I had to snake your drain and was lucky to find it."

"How do you know it's a toupee and not, not…"

"Not some other large clump of hair that wouldn't belong in the drain of a restaurant sink anyway? Does it matter? Something was stuffed deep into the drain. It wasn't accidental. It was a toupee and it was filthy." He grimaced at the memory. "I threw it out."

"But everything works now." She looked back at the sink and rubbed her hands together nervously.

"Tilly, I think you have a bigger problem." She didn't seem to be getting the point he was trying to make. "All of this was done on purpose."

"Don't be silly." She turned her head to face him and absently waved away his objections. "Why would anyone do this on purpose? I'm sure it was all an accident."

"The washer looks like it was put in the garbage disposal and torn to shreds and someone stuffed the hair down into your pipes. It couldn't have gotten that far down on its own."

CHAPTER NINE

"TILLY, DID YOU HEAR ME? I think this was done on purpose."

She blinked quickly several times but his words wouldn't go away.

I think this was done on purpose.

She tried to focus on what Dan was saying, but the millions of tiny things that had gone wrong to get everyone out of sync tonight flashed through her mind. The prepped ingredients in the wrong place. Spices missing. The knife she couldn't find. A missing six-top's reservation that they were able to seat, but not before looking unprofessional.

Little things went wrong in a restaurant all the time. Between the sharp objects, foods and heat, a restaurant kitchen was a disaster neatly hidden away from the paying public. She had assumed all those things that went wrong, those little things driving her entire staff batty, were everyday restaurant errors.

So what if they hadn't had such mistakes before? Mistakes were bound to happen. It was just bad luck they happened all at once.

Dan's words changed her thoughts. What if the cat had been let in on purpose, by someone who knew Bunny brought her dog everywhere she went? That person then sabotaged her pot sink, hoping for an expensive plumbing repair, forcing Babka to close for the night. This meant an employee was responsible.

She shook her head and blinked again. No, such a

scheme was too absurd to believe. The toupee got there by accident and the washer was simply defective. Thinking anything else was paranoid nonsense.

"Tilly?" She looked up at Dan, concern heavy in his eyes. "Are you okay? You blanked out for a minute."

"No, I'm fine. It was just…I don't know." Her voice dropped, her shoulders drooped and all her normal vim drained out of her. "Thinking about how a toupee would get into the drain." She shook her head. "I just don't know."

How was she supposed to lead the restaurant into offering a top-notch dining experience night after night after night if someone on her staff was interfering?

"Hey—" Dan reached out and placed his hand on her arm "—you aren't in this alone. You have a great staff and supportive family." His reassuring smile lit up her tiny office and gave her a quick boost of energy. "Now, was dessert part of the deal?"

"Dessert?" Tilly jumped up from her chair, grateful for something to do and someone to feed. "Of course! I have *legumina wiśniowa* for you. It's baked cherry pudding served warm with cold sour cream."

Dan admired the view as Tilly opened the refrigerator for the sour cream and got the pudding out of the warmer. The clangs of each door she shut echoed through the kitchen, pinging off the metal counters. It was much too quiet for a restaurant kitchen. The pot washer finally had his sink full of water, but the dishwashing machine wasn't running. The only noise was the light chatter of the staff breaking the kitchen down for the night and doing early prep for tomorrow.

Babka's business would pick up. Dan was sure of it. Tilly had made him a fabulous meal and what she served to her customers was probably as good. The oversalting was a one-off mistake by one of the line cooks.

Those people who ignored his review would find Babka's food and service were excellent, and they would tell their friends. His one review wasn't powerful enough to kill her restaurant. It would make things difficult for her for a bit, but if she was as good as he thought she was, Babka would pull through.

Tilly put a shallow dish of pudding in front of him and gave him a spoon. "I can't sit down to chat. It's getting late and I need to help close. Please come find me before you leave. I want to thank you again for fixing my pot sink."

"It was my pleasure."

Dan finished the tangy-sweet pudding and took his dish to the dishwasher. He found Tilly in the walk-in fridge, holding a notebook and mumbling to herself. "I came to say goodbye."

She jumped and clasped the notebook to her chest. "Oh, you startled me. I was just planning specials for tomorrow."

"The sausage was excellent. I recommend putting it on your menu."

"I'm glad you liked it." Her smile reached all the way to her eyes, where it acquired warmth and sent tingles down his spine. "Thank you again for everything. I don't think dinner even came close to being a fair exchange."

He smiled. If she only knew the heat in her eyes was thank-you enough. He wanted to kiss her, to feel the heat of her soft lips against his in the cold storage. He leaned into her a little. She looked at him as if she would welcome a kiss, but as soon as she found out he was the reviewer from *CarpeChicago* she wouldn't look at him that way again. He might not get another chance to hold her. He could slip his arms around her, pull her close to him so her breasts pressed against him, and she wouldn't protest.

What kind of asshole will you be when she finds out who you are? Think she'll remember your kisses fondly or rinse her mouth out with baking soda and lemon? The thought was more effective than a cold shower.

Dan pulled back.

"Dinner was delicious. It's been a long time since I've had such food and it is certainly a change from what is currently trendy in restaurants."

She smiled at his compliment and a second urge to kiss her hit him like a blast of hot air through the refrigeration. No thoughts of Tilly's reaction when she found out his duplicity could cool his hunger for her. Standing with her in her fridge, surrounded by cheese and butter with her chest rising and falling under her chef's whites, she was something out of every food lover's dirty dream.

He'd already kissed her once without telling her who he was, so what was another kiss? Of course, the kiss at the Taste had been an impulse. He hadn't known who she was then, either. It wasn't even fair to call the second brief peck anything more than what he had called it then, a good-luck kiss.

If he kissed her now, he would have to acknowledge he was no longer acting on impulse. There would be no question that he had talked himself first out of, and then into, kissing a woman under false pretenses. She stood in the fridge with her wonderful, bright hair sticking out in tufts from under her bandanna. He had wanted to kiss her since she walked out into the dining room, the red stain on her white chef's jacket as vibrant as her hair and her personality, and her face wary but her eyes hopeful.

"You have goose bumps on your arms."

"Pardon?" He looked down. Little bumps covered his arms, but he didn't feel cold. Warmth came off Tilly, a light from the way she embraced life.

"We should get out of the fridge. I'm sure you want to go home, shower, go to bed and get some sleep."

Shower? Yes. Bed? Yes. Sleep? No, he didn't want to sleep. He wanted to take Tilly home with him, to bring color into his stark, white house. Instead, Tilly walked past him out of the fridge. The moment was broken.

She was packing take-out food containers into a paper bag when he found her again.

"Here." She thrust the bag at him.

"What is this?"

"Leftovers for your lunch tomorrow. There's even dessert."

He took the bulging brown bag. "Thank you. You didn't have to."

"You didn't have to fix my sink, and you did."

"It was my pleasure."

The brown paper crinkled as he tightened his grip. He'd never noticed what a chiding noise paper made when clutched in nervous desperation.

They faced each other awkwardly. Tilly shifted her weight from one foot to another while Dan wished he had kissed her in his town house. Or in the walk-in fridge, before his conscience reminded him that she didn't know he had written the review.

If he wanted to kiss her, if he wanted to see her again, he had to tell her who he was. She would be hurt, understandably, but he could make her see that they could get past all of this. He could make her see that the review was business, but their relationship could be pleasure. She was interested. He'd seen the heat in her eyes and he hadn't been mistaken about what it meant.

Pans clanked together and someone in the kitchen cursed. *There was no audience in the fridge. You should've kissed her there.*

Tilly was staring at his lips and Dan cursed his alter ego.

"I should walk you to the front door," she said. "I'll need to lock up behind you."

He followed her out of the kitchen, past Candace wiping down the bar with smooth, even strokes. In the dimness of the closing restaurant, the bartender's dark eyes disappeared into damning, empty holes. Which was ridiculous. When he blinked, she turned back into the polished bartender of earlier that night.

At Babka's front door the bag crinkled again, scolding him. He had to tell Tilly the truth. Even if their relationship went no further than this front door, he couldn't let her look at him so openly, pack him lunch for God's sake, without knowing what he'd done.

"Tilly—" he put his tool kit on the floor and rested his hand on her shoulder "—I have something I have to confess to you."

"Yes?" She cocked her head in response, her eyes wide and her expression unguarded. He needed to enjoy that unsuspecting look on her now, as he might never see it again.

"I'm Dan Meier, the food writer, as you may have guessed…. No, don't interrupt," he said when she opened her mouth. "I also write reviews for *CarpeChicago* under the name 'The Eater.'"

SHE SLAPPED HIM. Hard enough that her palm buzzed with pain and the vibration radiated down her arm to tingle in her elbow. Her whole body shook. Not from the slap, though every cell in her body itched to slap him again and again until the sound of his brain being battered against the inside of his skull reverberated through the restaurant. Betrayal shook her.

But she didn't give in. Babka was her restaurant and Dan—The Eater—was an important person in the food business. Personally, she could justify slapping him once.

Unfortunately for her business, she couldn't give him the same punch to the gut he'd given her.

"Thank you for fixing my pot sink." That was polite, professional, and she wasn't doubled up with pain. She could do this. "I would appreciate your not returning to Babka." She opened her mouth to speak again, to say something else as if he hadn't just crushed her with his foot and scraped the remains on the stoop, but nothing came out. Something solid was lodged in her throat, blocking all access to breath. Before it could escape through tears, she turned and walked back through the dining room.

"Candace." She swallowed and the lump moved enough to get out another sentence. "Please make sure the door locks behind Dan."

She didn't go back into the kitchen. Instead, she turned past the bar and headed to the closet with the cleaning supplies. Despite the cleaning service that came in every night, Tilly was going to scrub the bathrooms. The bleach would sting her eyes and burn her nostrils, but it might also cleanse her heart of any remaining soft feelings for Dan. The chemicals would give her something to blame when Karen bounded in behind her and wondered why her eyes were red. If her cat wouldn't go near her tonight because of the fumes, she could add Imbir to the list of male creatures who had betrayed her.

CHAPTER TEN

"HELLO, BETH," Dan said into his phone.

"Beth took my phone and won't answer my calls," the gravelly, disappointed voice replied.

"Oh. Hello, Dad." Caller ID was wonderful, until it was wrong. He'd only answered because he thought it was his sister.

"Have you heard from your sister?"

"Not recently." *Not since you offered me a job while Beth was offering you a child.* He didn't say that, though. Even if Beth would tell him some nonsense about not seeking Dad's approval or that the desperate attempt to get a child was for the good of the company, he wanted her side of the story before he heard his father's. He needed preparation—and ammunition—against his dad's sugarcoated lies and cloying tone as Dan Sr. explained how Beth was wrong.

If the story Dan had heard was true, Beth was in the wrong, but not for the reasons Dan Sr. thought she was. Beth needed to get out of Wisconsin and away from their father if she was going to have any life of her own. Dan would like his mom to move away, too, but that was like wishing for the end of all wars, hunger and disease. Possible, sure, but completely improbable.

"It's not like her to run off," his dad said.

Having trouble running the company by yourself? Dan didn't say that, either. He could pretend not to care, but he still hoped every interaction with his father would be different. Better. That age would hit the old man and he'd stop trying to manipulate his children into submission, stop thinking of them as reflections of his self-worth and start seeing them as people. Dan was hoping gray hair was enough to change a leopard's spots. "If she calls, I'll tell her you're looking for her."

"I don't understand you two. I give you everything and you constantly disappoint. Like you and your worthless job. Did you hear about that reporter who faked his story?"

Being blamed for a stranger's mistake was new. "That wasn't me."

His father either didn't hear him or didn't care. "Imagine the embarrassment his family must feel."

"Dad, that wasn't…"

But Dan Sr. was on his favorite subject, the burden of children to their parents. "I don't think I could face walking down the street if one of my children did that to me."

Dan didn't have enough fingers and toes to count how many times his father had expressed a shame-driven fear of walking down the street.

"And now your sister is probably off doing something even worse."

"Goodbye, Dad. I'll tell Beth you wanted to speak to her."

Dan put down his phone and contemplated his lunch. He wouldn't let a conversation with his father put him off his appetite. One white-and-red take-out box held a roast chicken thigh, seasoned with juniper berries, salt pork and garlic. The other box bulged with roast potatoes and perfectly cooked green beans that snapped when he bit into them. As Tilly had promised, there was also dessert. A piece of flaky butter pastry spread with raspberry jam and a thick poppy-seed filling had been wrapped in tinfoil. Even the little details had been given painstaking attention. All the food would be equally delicious eaten cold at a desk or warm at home. Tilly took time to think of the needs of those eating her food, not just what they ate but how and when they might eat it.

He smiled at the image of Tilly in her restaurant kitchen packing his food. He imagined her surveying the food in her kitchen, a contemplative look on her face as she selected each piece with care. The love she had for the culture of her food would be shining in her eyes, even though she wasn't preparing anything new.

Tilly was a marvelous cook because her food was part of her soul. She was a first-rate chef because she paid attention to every detail in the experience of eating.

Dan sighed at the problem she posed. If she were a bad cook, or a terrible manager, he could have ignored how much he liked her. Her sparkling eyes and expressive face would be another memory he could pack away. Mike would have to accept he had lost a bet and camp out at the Cubs game with a smile on his face.

If Tilly had lived down to his review, he wouldn't like her quite so much. The memory of her vividness wouldn't haunt his austere dining room and he wouldn't want her sitting beside him, telling him the unpronounceable Polish name of the chicken dish. He'd told her he was The Eater because he would've been a bastard if he hadn't. So why did he still feel like horse's ass?

Dan picked up the thigh and took a bite. The chicken was, as Julia Child would say, "chickeny." Tilly didn't overdo the spices. She wasn't trying to hide inferior ingredients with salt or butter. All the flavors came together to make Tilly's roast chicken taste perfect, with the juniper berries hinting at a medieval hunt, exotic and powerful. One bite, and his mind traveled across the ocean and through time until he stopped at a small homestead in Poland where a family waited for the next invading army to bring new spices that would be integrated into the cuisine. The best food took the eater on a journey, exploring the history and culture steeped in the dish. Tilly's chicken was *that* kind of chicken. The kind a Polish grandmother made, that sang out with her heritage.

"Shit." The weight of his mistake was a ton of chicken poop piled on his back.

He had two things in common with Tilly. Neither of them could fully separate food from life, and his review had screwed up both their lives. He couldn't separate himself from food any more than he could cut off his right arm. He was a food writer. He ate and wrote about his experiences. When he was writing about food, he was also writing about culture.

Tilly was a chef. She made her living from giving people pleasure with the meals she cooked. Her customers depended on her feeding them flavorful, delicious food. Food they wanted to come back for, that they didn't think they could make at home. He was a betting man and he'd bet the customers who'd stayed in Tilly's restaurant after the cat disaster had enjoyed her food.

Even worse, Dan had screwed up their lives. They'd had an undeniable connection, the kind of connection the characters had in the romantic comedies his sister pretended she didn't watch. He'd felt the interlinking of their strengths and known she was a woman worth pursuing. Then she'd slapped him and told him never to come back. Standing in the way of their relationship was his job. He'd written a negative review and she might not ever be able to get past it.

Are you sure it's not your pride that's in the way? a needling voice at the back of his head asked. Dan shook his head to dislodge the thought. Bad reviews were part of the business and he'd given Tilly a bad review. Either she was mature enough to look past it, or she wasn't. He couldn't control her reactions; he could only control his own.

His doorbell rang. Dan rose to answer it, the chicken thigh still in his hand. Mike stood at the door.

"Shit." Dan wanted to luxuriate in his lunch and problems alone. He didn't need Mike here to harass him.

"If you're going to swear at your food, you should at least look like you're not enjoying it." Mike pushed past Dan into his house.

What did he want? "Who says I'm enjoying it?"

"You're a food writer. You don't eat food you don't enjoy. Plus, most men don't get that look on their face unless a naked woman is involved." Mike pulled a chair up to the table and sat. "Where's lunch from?"

Dan considered lying. It would be much easier than to tell Mike the truth. The truth would mean harassment, teasing and another lecture or fifteen on journalistic ethics. Mike might even think he'd won the bet if Dan told him the truth. On the other hand, Mike would find out eventually. He always did. Getting caught later would extend the harassment, teasing and add lectures. In the interest of getting the pain over with, Dan was honest.

"Babka." He could be honest without elaborating.

"You didn't tell her." Mike leaned back in the chair. He was making himself comfortable, preparing for a long lecture.

Dan took another bite of his chicken. If he was going to get lectured by his friend about the meal, he should at least get to eat all of it.

Mike kept talking. "Babka isn't open for lunch and those are leftovers. If Tilly was nice enough to pack you lunch, she doesn't know who she packed lunch for."

"The food is a thank-you for fixing her sink."

"Ah, avoiding my question and stalling for time." Mike

nodded. Perceptive and an asshole. "Perhaps you hope I have somewhere I need to be and if you avoid my questions, I'll leave you alone." Mike smiled. "My friend, that is not the case. I'm settling in for the long haul."

Dan snorted. "Her sink was broken and I fixed it. She gave me a thank-you dinner and lunch. Hell, you even got Tilly's delicious food to eat at home, while sitting on your butt in front of a White Sox game. There is nothing more to the story."

"Bull. You're eating roast chicken. You never order chicken from a menu until at least the third meal. It's how you judge a chef's ability to produce something—what's the phrase you use?—'simply delicious.' You don't want to let your thoughts on their roast chicken ruin your opinion of the rest of their menu. Even if you hadn't written the stupid review yet, it's not time to order roast chicken."

Dan took another bite of his chicken and enjoyed its simple deliciousness. Mike could continue this conversation without his help.

"Man, that look on your face. You really are a bastard."

"What the hell? You come to my house, interrupt *my* lunch and call me a bastard?"

"You go to a restaurant, eat a little of one meal, write a scathing review, finagle a date with the chef, go to her restaurant, eat her food, don't tell her who you are *and* you expect not to be called a bastard. Are you temporarily crazy or do I need to call a doctor?"

"I told her who I was." He regretted the words before they were even out of his mouth. Distracted by the chicken.

"Now you're a bastard and a liar. No woman packs a man a lunch like that after hearing 'Hi, my name is Dan and I ruined your career.'"

"I didn't ruin her career." Whether or not he wanted to admit it, once the people of Chicago tasted Tilly's food, they would forget his review. He had made her career more difficult, but he hadn't killed Babka. He was a respected food writer, but even he couldn't compete with this roast chicken. "And she packed the lunch before I told her."

Mike was stunned into silence. His lips were compressed into a thin line, ready to pronounce judgment on Dan for being an asshole and not telling Tilly the truth, but Dan's admission stalled him.

Dan kept eating, not offering Mike a bite. Finally his friend humphed, leaned back in his chair and folded his arms. "You're right. You didn't ruin her career. You made a mistake with your review and haven't admitted it to yourself yet. Or to her. Or to your reading public. She'll probably come out of the review singed but otherwise unharmed. You may need to buy stock in bandage companies."

Dan's cheek throbbed at the memory of Tilly's slap. "I didn't make a mistake." He took a bite of potato and chewed. Where did she get her produce? Her potatoes were fresh enough he could taste the soil they were grown in. "The night was a disaster and should never have happened."

"Meiers don't make mistakes. Meiers make cheese," Mike said with barely controlled sarcasm.

Dan choked on his potatoes as Mike echoed the conversation Dan had just had with his father. "Don't be ridiculous."

"I've met your father. I know the unofficial family motto. Face up to the facts, Dan. You. Made. A. Mistake. You. Should. Correct. It."

"She's got blue hair. Doesn't that say something about her sanity?"

"You think her blue hair is hot. I think that says something about yours."

Dan stared at Mike. Mike stared back. It wasn't even a fair contest. Dan wanted Tilly, but he couldn't change the past and didn't know how to reconcile those two facts. He put down his fork. "I know." His sanity was questionable because he believed he could figure out how to see Tilly again and make their relationship happen—a bit like believing in aliens. The connection he felt with her was too powerful to be ignored, even if a restaurant critic pursuing a chef was beyond stupid.

"Why I am sitting here lecturing you? I have better things to do than play moral authority with a grown man."

"I don't know how to fix it."

"Write another review. Isn't that your job?"

"Another review would ruin my credibility as a critic." This wasn't about pride; this was about *credibility*. Dan could throw his pride to the wolves, but he lived off his credibility.

"Sucks to be you, then. You meet a cute woman who is also a fantastic cook and you screw it up before you even shake hands."

"Chef."

"Pardon?"

"She's a chef. Nigella Lawson is a cook. A very hot cook, but still a cook. Tilly is a chef. They are both hot, but besides making food she has to be chief of the kitchen. It's an entirely different level of responsibility, even if they both are delicious to look at and make delicious food."

"Fantastic chef, then. Still doesn't get you out of writing another review."

Dan may be interested in Tilly, but it would have to snow someplace really hot before he'd write another review. Mike may be playing moral authority, but Dan was a restaurant authority. He hadn't gotten to his position by writing reviews that started with, "Remember the other review I wrote? Well, don't, because it was a mistake." Dan had gotten where he was by having an opinion and sticking to it. He was paid for his opinion and he was going to keep it.

Tilly was cute. He liked her blue hair and wanted to see it again.

Without getting egg on his face.

"I'll fix it."

"We'll see another review of Babka on the blog?"

"I said I'd fix it."

"Why don't I believe you?"

"Dammit. Who are you? 'Cause you're not my mother, father or priest, and they are the only moral authorities I subscribe to."

"With your parents, it's no wonder you're whacked. I'll give your priest the benefit of the doubt." Mike leaned forward in his chair. "When I leave here, I'm going to have coffee with Brian Urlacher. You may have heard of him. He's a linebacker for the Bears and eats quarterbacks for breakfast and running backs for lunch. I'm going to sit in front of this two-hundred-fifty-pound beast of a man and ask him if he thinks he's getting too old for professional football. Then, I'm going to ask him about missed tackles and his mother. If I can do that for my job, you can write a new review for yours."

"Why are you here?"

"I have those tickets to a Cubs game I promised you, behind home plate."

"Were your fingers too busy writing letters of advice to the pope to send a text letting me know you were coming over?"

"Stop making love to the chicken and you'll notice your phone is blinking."

Dan looked at his phone with its telltale light blinking a message at him. Tilly's chicken should be banned as a narcotic for making him miss the text from Mike. Tilly and her food were messing with his mind.

"I don't want to share my tickets with an asshole," Mike said, breaking into his thoughts.

Right now Dan didn't care. He had plans for the next several nights and they didn't involve a Cubs game. He had sworn he could never seriously date a White Sox fan. For Tilly, he was willing to make an exception. They'd have to have a serious conversation about how they'd raise their kids, though. "Then leave me alone so I can enjoy my lunch in peace."

Mike tipped an empty take-out box over onto Dan's plate. "I hate to tell you, buddy, but your lunch is finished. So are your excuses. You need to sack up." Mike didn't even wait for a response. He left, the disgusted look on his face matching Dan's own opinion of his options.

Dan stared at the closed door to his house long after Mike left. The chicken was gone, as were the potatoes and green beans. Only his dessert remained, which wouldn't be enough to keep him occupied until he found a solution to his problems. He needed more food and more time.

More time. Was the solution so easy? He liked Tilly, wanted to get to know her better. Wanted to find out what she dreamed about at night and fantasized about during the day. He needed more information about her. Maybe she was a woman for the long term. If she was the woman he imagined, then he'd think about how he could get Babka some better press. Not a new review from him, but maybe a short mention in a newspaper or magazine; enough to push a few new customers her way.

If she wasn't, well, no need to stress them both out with his review. He could fade out of her life. They were adults and could separate business from their personal lives. The end of their relationship didn't have to be a nasty scene about the review and its unfairness, especially because it wasn't unfair. The review had been an accurate representation of his night.

Dan had only met Tilly on Monday. This was Friday. He'd gone to eat at Babka last Thursday. He'd known Tilly a grand total of five days and had only talked with her for two of them. A weekend of talking to a woman did not make a relationship. Thinking about a woman all day, every day for five days didn't make a relationship. When they had a relationship, maybe his choices would change.

Dan took a bite of his pastry. His problem wasn't solved, but it was pushed far enough into the future that he could enjoy his dessert. The poppy seeds still retained a little crunch against the buttery, tender pastry and the sweet, tart raspberry jam. If he hadn't been busy chewing, Dan might have cursed again.

CHAPTER ELEVEN

STEVE WAS WORMING his way through the line cooks and kitchen equipment to Tilly, though he should have been busy running tables. It was Saturday night and Babka had been, pleasantly enough, half-full most of the night. Her restaurant should have been completely booked on a Saturday night, but Tilly would take half-full to the more recent alternative of mostly empty. For once, Babka was busy enough to require her presence on the line. There weren't quite enough customers to keep them jumping, but she didn't need a rush right now. So long as she didn't have time to think about blond hair hanging over blue eyes and the hint of a smile, she was content. Not happy. She wouldn't be happy until she'd read a new review of Babka and customers started pouring in, but distracted enough not to...

Nope. There she was, thinking about him again. She willed another ticket to print out, but service was almost over and the kitchen was starting to close down. What she got instead was Steve's spindly arms twitching next to her.

"That guy is here," he said, his voice barely loud enough to be heard over the commotion of the kitchen.

"What guy?" she asked, distracted by the plate PM Carlos put in front of her, roast chicken for the last four-top. "Where's the trout?" she called out to Enrique.

"*Uno* minute." Enrique didn't even turn around to look at her.

"You said that a minute ago and I still don't have it."

Enrique ignored her. It was a game all the line cooks played. She'd yell at them to get her the food and they'd promise her the moon, while steadily continuing to cook the food. Her job was to yell at them to be faster. Their job was to make sure every dish that left their station was perfectly cooked and perfectly seasoned. If they gave in and handed her undercooked fish, she'd fire them.

"Tilly, the guy outside?" Steve's hands shook.

"Are you using again?"

He clasped his hands together and held them behind his back. "No. Just too much coffee." His weight shifted from one foot to another. "That guy who fixed the sink. He's sitting at the bar."

Dan. Anyone who said you got what you asked for was a liar. She'd asked for another ticket, another customer. What she'd gotten instead was a jerk. Well, he was in the dining room and she was in the kitchen. She didn't have to go out there and he wasn't supposed to come in here, she thought, purposefully forgetting that he'd undressed her with his eyes in her walk-in, so it wasn't as if he hadn't been in the kitchen before. She'd allowed that breach when she'd liked him. She didn't like him anymore.

"Tell him to leave."

"I came back for my toolbox."

She looked up and wished she hadn't. Why did his eyes have to be so bright and his shoulders so broad? He deserved a hunchback and the flat, emotionless eyes of a psychopath. "It's in my office. You know where it is, so you can get it and then you can leave."

"Can we talk?"

"No." Enrique, bless him, decided at that moment the trout was ready and put it in front of her. "As you can see, I'm busy."

"Tilly…" Her sous chef scooted over from his station. "This is our last table of the night. I can finish up."

"Fine." She ripped her towel off her shoulder and threw it on the counter. If Dan wanted some painful, useless back-and-forth about his review, she'd give it to him.

DAN WASN'T SURPRISED when Tilly didn't greet him with open arms, but he'd hoped her tendency toward violence had dissipated in the past forty-eight hours. If the force with which she threw her towel and slammed her office door was any indication, he should make sure she didn't have a butane torch nearby. She stood by her office door, hands on her hips and face puckered with anger.

"Well," she said. "Your toolbox is on the floor by your foot. Say what you have to say, take the damn thing and go."

He swallowed back doubt. If he wanted to spend any time with her, he'd have to push her past the review. "I think we should get to know each other better."

"I think you're crazy."

She was the second person to accuse him of madness in thirty-six hours. Hell, he deserved it. There was a clear line in the sand between reviewer and chef and he wanted to cross it. More than cross it, he wanted to leap across the line and sweep the steaming woman standing in front of him off her feet. Even though she probably had a fillet knife tucked in her clothes to gut him with.

"Look, I'm not looking for you to give me the keys to your kitchen, just don't try to kick me out when I come here for dinner."

"I won't *try* to kick you out. I went to high school with half the Polish cops in Chicago. I'll let them do it for me."

Her words and the nasal *a* in Chicago—years of living in New York couldn't entirely erase her accent—were a fine reminder that she was more than just an owner of a small restaurant in Bucktown. He may have lived here more recently, but her roots were deeper. The popularity of *CarpeChicago* couldn't overcome the established Milek family. So far she'd only threatened him with cops, but her brother was also the city's inspector general. It wouldn't surprise him if she had an alderman ex-boyfriend.

"This is more than just about the bad review."

"Of course it's about more than just the review," she yelled, throwing her arms in the air. Then she looked over her shoulder at the door as if waiting for one of her employees to come in and see what was wrong. "You're a restaurant reviewer—it's your *job* to write reviews and sometimes you have to write bad ones. Maybe you're even one of those twisted bastards who gets enjoyment from skewering chefs. I don't know and I don't care."

Her breasts lifted the buttons on her chef's jacket as she took a deep breath and her hands returned to their enraged position on her hips. "What really pisses me off is that you panned my restaurant and then *cozied up—*" she said the words as if they were rotten food at the bottom of her Dumpster "—to me. Did you get some sick thrill knowing you were kissing the woman whose career you tried to destroy?"

He exhaled his frustration. She kept trying to make the review personal.

"I didn't know who you were when I kissed you." She raised an eyebrow at him and he corrected himself. "Kissed you the first time. Then I didn't tell you who I was before your demo because I liked you and wanted you to succeed. I didn't want to pressure you."

"I'm supposed to believe you don't want to pressure me now?"

"I'm not asking for special treatment, just to be another

paying customer. I'll eat your food, drink your alcohol and pay my bill."

She was weakening. Her arms had relaxed at her sides and her face was no longer at a rolling boil. A gentle simmer wasn't much of an improvement, but he would take what he could get. If he came here for dinner every night…

How could he have been so blind as to miss the giant carrot he could dangle in front of her? He didn't have to promise anything, just hint enough to persuade her not to bar the door to him. They'd get to know each other and either they were as compatible as he was hoping and she'd forget about the review, or they'd part and his small deception wouldn't matter.

"I can't revise my review if I can't eat here."

Mike would be appalled. His sister would be appalled. His mother would be disappointed in him, but desperation bred shady behavior. He couldn't leave the brilliance of her presence without knowing he'd tried everything.

Her mouth flapped open and shut like a caught fish. When she finally got control over her lips, she crossed her hands over her chest and regarded him. "You've already eaten my food."

"I've only eaten here twice, and one of those experiences was terrible."

"It wasn't—"

"I'll grant you the dog-and-cat fight wasn't your fault. But my food was inedible. One delicious dinner eaten in your office isn't enough to make up for my mother's ruined birthday." And the aftereffects of the ruined dinner. His dad had learned about the review and thought it was hilarious. His mom was trying, in her timid way, to get his father to stop referring to a night she'd found painful. In typical Meier family dynamics, his mother's unease only encouraged his father to be more offensive. Dan wished he'd never written the damn thing. Life would be so much easier if he'd just considered his dinner ruined and gone on with his life.

Though he never would've gone to the Taste and met Tilly.

"I can't explain how your food got oversalted." Hurt-Tilly wasn't talking to him any longer. His argument appealed to businesswoman-Tilly and she needed the chance of a better review. She also needed to know what had gone wrong that night. But there was still no warmth in her eyes when she looked at him. "How do I know I can trust you?"

"Just don't kick me out when I come here to eat."

CHAPTER TWELVE

DAN HEARD TILLY MURMUR, "Special treatment my ass," as she walked to the bar. Her face was flush from the heat of the kitchen, but her flamboyant hair was all tucked under her white bandanna. Too bad, he'd been looking forward to seeing that hair for two days.

"Not too salty for you?" she asked, a hand on her hip and eyebrow raised. She was looking directly at him and he couldn't miss her slight sarcasm. His dish wasn't empty yet, but would be after he dragged a piece of bread through last bits of mushroom, potato and sour cream in a white wine sauce.

"No. It's rich and earthy and perfectly seasoned. Is it really named after Horatio Nelson?" The menu had called the dish *zrazy grzybowe po nelsońsku* and made that ridiculous claim.

"Yes. People tend to name things after heroes who right wrongs and fight the good fight." She paused, and he hoped she was done.

She wasn't. "Are you going to include that tidbit in your new review?"

"The new review is only a maybe." He wished she hadn't asked about it, though he kept that thought to himself. Next time he ate dinner here, he didn't want his food poisoned. He liked mushrooms and the line between a wild-mushroom dinner and death was a good eye and a gracious host. Tilly had the first; he wanted to make sure she remained the other.

"How can you say that after eating food you just declared perfectly seasoned?"

The clinking of his fork on his plate covered up his sigh. He'd come here to see her and to hear more interesting morsels about Polish cooking, not to be scolded about a review. If he wanted scolding, he'd go find Mike. "I'm a critic. I write reviews. They're sometimes negative. It's not part of my job to write retractions, especially when I don't have a reason to."

Her face turned a new shade of red, no longer attributable to the heat from the kitchen. She didn't look homicidal, though, and he wasn't going to take back what he said.

"Was the food of mine you ate last week good?" Her hand was still on her hip, but her eyebrow had fallen. She somehow managed to convey nonexistent angry gestures with the power of her stare. He looked around the mostly empty dining room. She must be controlling her reaction for the benefit of her staff. Too bad. He liked the way she talked with her hands.

"Yes. Did that chicken you packed me have juniper?"

"Your bio on *CarpeChicago* says you eat at every restaurant you review three times. When you wrote the first review, you'd only eaten at Babka once. Now you've eaten at Babka *three times,* plus having leftovers at home. It's not time for a new review. It's time for a review that meets your own standards."

"If you're looking that closely at The Eater's record, you'll also notice I've never written a second review."

"I read all your old reviews. I don't think another restaurant has deserved one."

Dan took a sip of his beer and wondered if she realized the double standard she was applying to his review of

Babka. "If I started giving out new reviews, I'd have chefs and restaurant owners hounding me day and night. That's not a precedent I'm willing to set."

"But if you had just come back here to eat another time…"

"My first experience here was terrible and you expected me to come back?"

"You're back now."

"To see you." A good dinner was just a bonus. He'd have come see her if she'd been serving cow pies for dessert.

His baldly honest statement disarmed her long enough for both her arms to drop to her sides. She wasn't the only one surprised by what he'd said. Dan knew why he'd come back to Babka; he just hadn't expected to tell her.

She wasn't defenseless long. "You come here to see me, you eat *my* food in *my* restaurant, and you still won't write *me* a new review."

"The Eater, the review, all of that is business. My interest in you is personal. One shouldn't affect the other or my professional reputation, the authenticity of The Eater, dies."

"Maybe you can separate business and pleasure, but Babka is my restaurant and I can't." She gave him one last glare before striding back to the kitchen in righteous anger. Dan let her have the last word. He'd be back at Babka tomorrow. There was something about Tilly he couldn't stay away from.

TILLY HAD THOUGHT THEIR conversation on Tuesday was final. After all, what more could he have to say to her? But on Wednesday night Candace slipped into the kitchen to inform her that the quail with mushrooms she'd just called out was for Dan. Candace had said it under her breath, but movement had stopped in the kitchen for a brief second

as everyone heard. Tilly glared and her staff went back to
their business of cooking.

Ignoring him would serve him right. If he was at Babka
to see her and not to eat the food, she could ensure he didn't
get what he wanted. She could stay in the kitchen, swiping
stray breadcrumbs off plates and reminding Enrique that
he wasn't taking a walk in the park. But she wanted Dan
to write a new review, his dumb excuses notwithstanding,
and he was unlikely to do so if she snubbed him. Separating business from pleasure, she scoffed. What a crock.

If she wasn't going to ignore Dan, she was at least going
to ignore the gooey feeling in her stomach at the thought
of his smile. For a judgmental ass, he had a winning smile.
She could look at his smile and pretend he wasn't a jerk for
enjoying her food and not writing a new review. When the
already slow kitchen slowed down for the night, she asked
her sous chef to expedite—call out the orders and finish
the food at the pass before it went out to the dining room.

She didn't have a chance to question Dan about the review because the first words out of his mouth were, "This
is delicious. Where did you get the quail?"

Like a fool, she answered, telling him all about the local
poultry farm and her mushroom grower. Then, because he
was interested, she told him about her struggles to re-create
medieval Polish dishes that called for extinct or threatened
wild game. Imbir would listen to her as long as she kept
petting him, but Dan understood when she explained that
while bison meat was probably an acceptable substitute for
żubr, a European bison currently threatened with extinc-
tion, she was certain no beef approximated the flavor of
tur, an extinct wild cow.

Candace stopped her before she could launch into the
difficulty of finding hare, when even the finest U.S. suppliers confused hare and rabbit. Despite leaning forward and

watching her intently, Dan couldn't possibly be interested in sources of game meat. She left, a little embarrassed with herself for pouring her troubles out to Dan and monopolizing the conversation. Ticked off, too, because she'd not mentioned a new review once.

In the kitchen she learned a customer had complained about a watery salad. The proof was undeniable. Boston lettuce and cucumber were drowning in water on the plate. The vibrant red French breakfast radish looked like a flotation device for other vegetables. With so much water, the sour cream in the dressing couldn't cling to the lettuce and rested like an oil slick in the ocean. Even the normally peppy dill drooped on the plate. She had been the last person to touch the salad and she knew it had been as fresh as a spring day when leaving the pass. Dan left her thoughts and was replaced by the uncomfortable possibility that an employee was sabotaging her restaurant.

Dan came back again on Thursday night. And Friday. Each time she tried not to let herself talk too long. He asked about her food and the farms she used, and her reluctance to talk lasted only until he smiled. Then she would ease into conversation with a man who understood that being a chef wasn't glamorous, but involved long hours, butchering sides of beef and feeling like a mom to her employees because she had to check to make sure they all washed their hands. At least on Friday she remembered to ask him about the review again. She might be charmed, but she wasn't charmed stupid. Or, she wondered, was there a middle ground between the two where she was stupid enough to look forward to his visits, even without a new review in the works?

In her office the next morning Tilly updated the website menu for that day. The mouse hovered over the address bar and the chance to read The Eater posts again. The knowledge was like a durian fruit, luscious and frightening at the same time. Certain doom lurked in losing herself online.

She had a restaurant to run. Cyberstalking the critic who ruined her career was not cool. It was admitting The Eater had defeated her and she wasn't defeated yet. It was admitting Dan meant more to her than just a customer and the potential for a better review.

Her ringing cell phone decided for her.

"Tila, you haven't called in a couple days. Should I be worried about you?"

"Good morning, Mom. How are you? I'm fine. I was working."

"I'm sure you were. Are you coming home on Sunday?"

"Hadn't planned on it. I have some work I have to do for Babka."

"You should go to mass. How long has it been since you went to mass?"

"Oh, Mother, I don't know, a couple of months." A year? More? And now she had that petty desire to cyberstalk to feel guilty about. Just what every Catholic needed, more guilt.

She looked back at the computer and the empty address bar. If she was going to feel guilty about the thought, she should at least have the enjoyment of the action.

"Father Szymkiewicz misses you."

Or not. She turned away from the laptop. No cyberstalking while talking on the phone with your mother about the priest missing your presence at mass. If that wasn't a sign from God, may lightning strike her dead.

"Yes. I'm sure he does, but I need to get Babka off the ground, then I will go to mass with you and the rest of the neighborhood."

"Monday, then. You don't work on Monday, either. I'm

taking the night off from Healthy Food and cooking dinner. Karl and Renia are coming. I expect you to come, too."

"I'll be there, Mom. Just let me get some work done on Sunday."

"Good. I'll call Renia and Karl."

"Wait, I thought you said they were coming already." But she was talking to an empty line.

CHAPTER THIRTEEN

BEFORE GOING TO her mother's for dinner, Tilly spent the day in Western Illinois visiting one of the farms that supplied Babka with produce. The sun was shining on a neat field of green with a few wispy clouds in the sky. After a discussion about the upcoming crops, she and the farmer sat on a gravel patio near his fields and drank iced tea. As on her previous visits, he hinted she should stay the night and, like her previous visits, she casually turned him down.

Unlike her previous visits, she didn't look at the young farmer with his broad workingman's back and wonder, "What if I stayed?" Instead, she thought of Dan's easy confidence and talked about going to her mom's for dinner. Dan had crashed her dream and was now ruining her sex life. What the hell did he know about separating business and personal?

Karl picked her up and drove her to their mother's in his BMW. Tilly was, as always, a little in awe of her much older brother and spent most of the ride in silence. He was so…put together, successful—like Renia, but with more presence. When their father, grandfather and brother had died, a teenaged Karl had pulled the family together and taken care of everything while her mother and grandmother grieved. All while maintaining perfect grades and getting into Notre Dame with a scholarship for children of Polish descent. He followed college with a law degree and had practiced corporate law until going to work for the state inspector general's office, hunting down and prosecuting business owners who thought they could make a profit through waste, bribery and corruption. He had recently been appointed inspector general for the City of Chicago. Mom wanted him to run for a city office—alderman was acceptable, but she would prefer mayor. Karl had no interest in the dog-and-pony show. "Too dirty" was his response whenever she mentioned it.

The one complaint her mother had about him, other than his lack of interest in eventually running for president, was Karl's divorce. Instead of pursuing a new wife, he dated beautiful women and got his picture in the paper. Their mother could only complain briefly—she loved to see her little boy in the paper. Though she still told anyone who would listen that her son was going to be president one day.

All in all, it meant Tilly felt like overcooked cabbage around her brother. She didn't think she was a washout of a person, but her brother was enough of a success to get compared to the Kennedys in the papers. Only a Kennedy could sit in a car with the man and not feel overwhelmed.

"No hot date tonight?" Overwhelmed or not, he was still her brother, which meant she could give him a ribbing.

He didn't even glance over at her. His handsome face stared straight ahead, looking at the road. "I can't turn down Mom."

"When did she call you?"

"About tonight? She called me Friday."

Tilly snorted. "I'll bet she told you I had already agreed."

"Hadn't you?"

"Yes, but she also told me *you* had already agreed."

"She knew I would. I always accept her invitations to dinner."

"What is it like to be the favorite child?"

The only movement in her brother's chiseled face was a slight upturn of his lip as he said, "Pretty damn good."

Tilly huffed and turned to stare back out the window.

The instant she walked into her mom's house, she knew something was up. Dinner was in the dining room, a special-occasion-only room, and her mom had gotten out the lace runner. She'd even decorated with candles and flowers. The wood gleamed from a fresh waxing. If Tilly was lucky, Karl was announcing a senatorial campaign when he finished his term with the city. Maybe Oprah was getting married and Renia was the photographer.

The smell of stuffed cabbage wafted into the dining room ahead of her mother. She put the dish on the table, signaled to Karl to pour some wine, and they all served themselves.

"I hear we have some news."

Tilly looked at Karl, then at Renia. Then at her mother, who was looking straight at her.

"What? I don't have any news."

"I understand you are being courted."

Tilly looked back at Renia, glaring hard enough to set her sister's hair on fire. The tightly wound bun didn't ignite, and Renia's innocently raised hands meant her mom had gotten the information from somewhere else. "First, I don't think people get 'courted' anymore. Second, even if they do, no one is courting me. Third, if someone were courting me, I'm a grown woman who should be able to have a boyfriend without her mother planning a celebration dinner."

Her mother completely ignored Tilly's outburst and focused on the information she was desperate to hear—that one of her children might get married and provide her with grandchildren. "Chuck and Sharon Biadała were at Babka for dinner on Thursday, and he said a man was sitting at the bar talking with you and it was more than just a casual conversation. *Courting* was his word."

How had she missed seeing Mr. Biadała, her American History teacher in high school? And Mrs. Biadała had worked at Healthy Food as a waitress for years. The woman had had monthly arguments with Tilly's mother about diets. If the diet was on Oprah, Mrs. Biadała tried it, making working at a Polish buffet difficult.

Tilly should've stood firm when she banished Dan from the restaurant. He was messing with her concentration.

"That was Dan Meier, The Eater. Do you want me to be courted by the man who said such terrible things about Babka?" That ought to shut her mother up.

"What else does Dan do for a living? I can't imagine writing for a blog makes him any money." Her mother must despair about getting grandchildren if her response was to ask about Dan's income. Of course, she had resorted to a celebration dinner at just the suggestion that a man was "courting" one of her children. What would she do if one of them actually had a date? One of them besides Karl, who only ever had dates. Or Renia, who never seemed to like the men she dated. God, no wonder her mom was desperate.

Stop thinking uncharitable thoughts. This is your mother and she cares about you.

"He's a freelance writer."

"Does he make a good living?"

Tilly thought about the town house in a fashionable part of Chicago and the Subaru. "He seems to do fine."

"It's not a steady career."

And owning a restaurant is?

"Maybe we can find some of his articles," her mother continued.

"You've read some of his articles already. I've ripped them out of food magazines for you. I mailed you one on

Eastern European dumplings three years ago. You were mad because the only Polish dumpling he talked about was the pierogi."

Her mother humphed. "Everyone knows about the pierogi. I just thought he should introduce the world to some of the lesser-known dumplings, *kluski kladzione* or *kluski ptysiowe*. At least a sweet pierogi instead of the standard cabbage."

"Why are you so concerned? He gave Babka a terrible review and I have no interest in him."

Renia raised an eyebrow from across the table, but she didn't say anything. She didn't have to. Tilly could hear her sister's thoughts, *Tsk, tsk, Tilly. Lying to your mother.*

"The Biadałas said the man wasn't the only one doing some courting. Sharon said you looked pretty interested."

She should've opened Babka in another city with a large Polish population—Pittsburgh or Cleveland—not in Chicago, where people from the neighborhood would spy on her for her mother. There were a lot of Poles in Western Massachusetts and she could escape spies by hiding in the woods. "I've expanded my business plan. I'm going to trade sex for a better review."

"Tila Marta Milek, I can't believe you would say that to your mother!"

Renia was clearly trying not to laugh. Karl's expression didn't change at all, but he coughed after taking a sip of his wine and his hazel eyes danced.

"Mother, we're having a family dinner in the dining room because Mr. Biadała said a man was courting me. How do you expect me to respond?"

"You're my baby girl and I worry about you."

Tilly smiled through her frustration. Once the baby, always the baby.

"Dan Meier?" her brother asked.

Tilly turned to face Karl, who was looking at her with curiosity. "Yes. Do you know him?"

"Karl knows everyone," her mom said with pride. She always said everything with pride when she talked about Karl. "You should have him look into your Dan's background."

"He's not *my* Dan!" What a horrible thought, even if she was wondering if he'd be back at Babka on Tuesday. "Karl wouldn't do such a thing." She looked back at her brother. "Would you?"

Karl raised his eyebrow at her and for the first time it occurred to Tilly how much influence her brother might have in the city. *My brother, political machine master.* Except the point of his job was to be above all the political fray and corruption. Tilly shook those thoughts out of her mind. She liked her brother more when he was her brother than when he was big man on campus.

"You're my sister."

"Thank you, Karl, but I can handle my own problems." What must her family think of her if they didn't trust her ability to handle her own business or her own love life? And her mother, thinking she'd have to settle for a relationship with a man who defended stomping on her dreams by lecturing her about business versus personal. Did they think Babka would fail and she'd need a man to support her?

Silly Tilly. Always messing everything up but dinner.

Of course, it was easy enough for them to judge. Renia was a sought-after photographer. And Karl. Well, right now Tilly didn't want to think about Karl. He had looked scary for a minute.

While she wasn't feeding the famous yet and she couldn't sound like the Godfather, she was no longer the helpless baby of the family. She had opened a restaurant in a big city. Even if Babka failed, opening it was already an accomplishment. She was the first one of her Culinary friends to reach her goal—which was why her hair was currently a vibrant shade of blue.

"Tilly, I don't think Mom wants you to date The Eater." Renia tried to sound soothing, but Tilly's ire was already up. Renia sounded patronizing. "She just cares about you and wanted to know more about him."

In front of the family? Most families were fabulous some of the time. Her family was fabulous most of the time.

This was one of those *other* times. She lobbed a new topic of conversation into the air and hoped for the best. "I hear the Twenty-third Ward seat is going to be open again." After being filled by the same person for over ten years, Archer Heights' alderman's seat was anyone's game.

Karl changed the subject before their mom could suggest he move back to the neighborhood and run for office. "How is Babka? I haven't been there since before the review."

"It's slow. Our one regular customer has been Dan." She didn't want to think about what it meant that her regular customer was also her most famous critic. "But no night has been truly empty." She sighed. "Just slow."

"Has Dan been in every night?" her mother asked, hope in her voice.

"Mo-o-om." The whine escaped before Tilly could stop it. "Why do you keep harping on Dan? I thought you'd be leading the campaign to lynch him."

"The way Sharon described the look on your face—oh, well…I want my children to be happy and I can forgive him if you can."

"We are happy." Tilly looked around the table. Scary Karl had been divorced once already and Perfect Renia never dated a man she couldn't push around. She ignored the second point about forgiveness. Dan had to acknowledge he'd done something wrong before forgiveness was even an option. "It's different now than it was when you and Dad married. I have a career to get established and Dan got in the way of that."

Her mother looked up to the ceiling and sighed. "It's only your generation that thinks there is a conflict between work and love." When she looked across the table there were tears in the corners of her eyes. "I managed to build a small restaurant into what it is now and I couldn't have done it without the love and support of your father. This, *this* is what your generation has missed."

CHAPTER FOURTEEN

"YOU CAN'T REEVALUATE Babka on beer alone," Tilly said to Dan when she came out of the kitchen the following Tuesday. She wasn't going to let him forget he was only here because she needed to prove him wrong about the review. Maybe she needed to make sure *she* didn't forget that detail.

Candace coasted to the far corner of the bar without making a sound, leaving Tilly and Dan as alone as possible in an open restaurant.

"I ate dinner at another restaurant, but I still wanted to come here and see you."

"Are you going to slam that restaurant, then go back and charm the chef with your smile?"

She regretted the emotion in her words as soon as she said them. He knew what her slip revealed. His smile wasn't the widest and most charming she'd seen, but the light in his eyes made it more honest. "I have no interest in charming him. Besides, I wanted to be here. I wanted to see you."

Stupid, she knew, but she couldn't even work up enough indignation to be pissed. His smile enlivened his face, reminding her of the man who'd made her laugh and bought her a hot dog. How could that man be The Eater?

He patted the barstool next to him, but she ignored the invitation. It wasn't just that she was at work and couldn't chat, but that she wanted to. She wanted to return to the moment before she knew who he was, when he was standing at the bottom of his stairs holding a toolbox and she was innocently thinking dirty thoughts about him. She still fantasized about him, but she could no longer pretend to be innocent. Dan was more dangerous than she could ever have imagined. She thought she'd been prepared to always put Babka first—to always put Babunia's dream first.

She was a fool. He smiled at her, his lips full against his white teeth, and she wavered in her resolve. How could she look at the man who'd written a bad review of Babka and want to sit next to him? Not just a critical review, but an unfair one based on a single freakish night that had made her a laughingstock. And he didn't seem to understand what he'd done to her—at least not enough to fix it. She couldn't even trust that he was here to reevaluate Babka, as he'd claimed earlier. He was both the serpent and the apple.

And a barstool had never looked so tempting.

"I need to get back to work."

"Okay." He took his hand off the barstool and she willed her feet not to walk around the counter and sit. "Tell me, how do you research your beers?"

Fool that she was, she told herself his question was business related and she relaxed enough to answer it.

When Karen bounced into the kitchen on Wednesday to inform her they'd served dessert to the last table and Dan was waiting for her at the bar, her traitorous heart didn't give the smallest blip of irritation at his gall. She finished the pressing tasks, left for later what could be left for later and headed out to the bar. His smile, his easy understanding of her business, even the curl of his hair over his ears, lifted her spirits. Her feet didn't even hurt.

She eyed the barstool again, just as she had the night before, but didn't come around the counter to sit. She hadn't completely forgotten about the review, soothed toes or not. The delicious gleam in his eyes was too enticing and she didn't trust her response. Babka still needed her and she had no time for a handsome man who disparaged her life's work, but couldn't take his eyes off her lips when she talked.

Renia snorted when Tilly told her this over the phone after closing. "Tilly," she said. "No man goes to a restaurant every night for a beer. Especially a restaurant like Babka. God made dive bars for cheap beer. Candace is serving him the most expensive glass of beer in Chicago and he's just sitting there enjoying it? The man wants something. You."

"Why am I even interested in a man who nearly ruined my career?"

"Women make stupid decisions about men when they're under stress."

Her sister's answer was too easy. Babka hadn't fully recovered from the damage of Dan's review, but her restaurant was out of intensive care and limping along. Besides, chefs were thrill seekers disguised as respectable professionals. Just because she wasn't hopped up on pep pills didn't mean she didn't crave the adrenaline rush of stress. "I've never made bad decisions about men while under stress before."

"Ask him out. You have Sundays and Mondays off."

Tilly rolled her eyes, but her reaction was lost over the phone. She had Sundays and Mondays off, and she spent them at work.

Renia continued. "See him outside of Babka and maybe location will change your opinion."

"Good girls don't ask men out. They let the men do the asking." Their mother had raised them both to be good girls, although Tilly was the only one who'd listened. Or, to be honest, Tilly hadn't actually listened. She just hadn't been interested enough in boys to care until culinary school, when her mom wasn't around to spout off rules of behavior.

"I love Mom, but that's crazy. Women ask men out all the time and the world does not stop turning." Her sister snorted. "Not to mention that you didn't say, 'No, I don't want to go out on a date with him.'"

"I don't have time. And I don't trust him." *I don't trust myself when I'm around him.*

"If you're so suspicious, why do you want him to ask you out?"

Because he's funny. And charming. And handsome. And when I forget he's The Eater and think of him as Dan, I feel as if I can conquer the world. She said none of these things. "I just want to know why he's coming in every night."

"Have you asked him?"

"At first, he said he'd reevaluate Babka, but then he said it was a maybe. So now I have no idea."

"What do you talk about?"

My dreams. "Nothing. I don't have time to talk." She was either a big fat liar or shirking work since she talked to him every night. His nightly visits had turned into the highlight of her workday.

"Tilly." Renia's exasperation came through loud and clear, even over the bad cell connection. "You're pathetic. Admitting you want a man won't kill you."

"I need sleep. I have a business to run."

"Whatever. Good night."

"Night."

It was probably better she hadn't told Renia she'd started sending Dan home with packed leftovers every night. Renia had funny ideas about Milek women and their need to feed men. She might get the wrong impression.

LATE SATURDAY MORNING, Tilly sat at her desk, chewing on the end of her pencil. The numbers didn't work. At the rate she was making money and the rate she was spending money, she would be broke and Babka would be done in six months to a year. Limping along wouldn't get her far enough to cross the finish line and into the black. In the two months Babka had been open—the before-review months—Tilly had pegged fifty people as potential regulars. She needed three hundred regulars. Three hundred people coming in at least once a month would keep Babka afloat through the slow months after the holidays. Fifty was a start. She wasn't complaining about fifty.

Only a few of those potential regulars had come in since the review. They had expressed their sympathy, shaken their head at The Eater's mistake and shared in pained laughter about the dog-and-cat incident. But no matter how loyal those few people were, they couldn't eat enough to nudge Babka into the black. Especially if her meat delivery got messed up again and she had to make dinner menus with organ meat and whatever cuts she had in her freezer.

Bunny, the owner of the infamous terrier, had not been back.

Six months. A year.

If I'm lucky.

The phone buzzed and Tilly grabbed it before the second ring. Until AM Carlos came in, it was just her and the pastry chef in the building.

"Babka. Can I help you?"

"Tilly? Is that you?"

"Renia?"

"Oh, Tilly, I'm glad you answered. Are you busy?"

Tilly laughed uncomfortably. There were no reservations to confirm. Her menus were done and the bookkeeping nearly finished. She'd trade her beloved knife set for a little busyness right now. "No. I'm not busy. The day has barely started for us."

"I need a favor. A big favor."

"Okay."

"The wedding I'm photographing next weekend is a mess. It's a big wedding, with ten bridesmaids and grooms-men, plus an enormous family. You have no idea how many pictures are on their required list…"

Renia never ran her mouth. Whatever was troubling her was a *big deal*. "Renia, what does this have to do with a favor?"

"I just got a crying call from the bride, who seems to think I know everyone in the business. The restaurant they had booked for the rehearsal dinner got shut down, some-thing about massive tax fraud and a money laundering scheme. The owner has apparently fled the country."

"Mother Mary! I thought I had problems. At least I'm not on the lam."

"Yes, well, I told the bride my sister owns a very nice restaurant and I'd see if you were free."

She wanted to be mad at Renia for assuming she would have the time and space, but instead she was thankful her sister had thought of her. Money from that dinner would be a welcome change, and she might get new customers out of the evening.

"When?"

"Next Friday. I know it's a big restaurant night, but…" At least Renia was kind enough not to point out the ob-vious.

"I've had few customers since the review. Don't worry. Let me check to make sure we don't have any reserva-tions—" Babunia had said always said to believe in pos-sibility "—and I'll be back."

She put her sister on hold and looked at next Friday's reservations. Nothing. Tilly blocked out the whole night. This dinner was a chance and Tilly intended to grab it, wrestle it to the ground and feed it Polish.

Some of the guests had to live in Chicago and they would want to come to Babka again. She had been raised a good Catholic, but if she had to swing a live chicken over her head at midnight with the witches from *Macbeth* to make the evening a success, she would. A shudder ran up her spine and she looked around for the ghost of a Catholic school nun scowling at her for such a sacrilegious thought. No nuns. Maybe they were finding her a chicken to swing.

"Renia, I can do it."

"Oh, Tills!" If it wasn't her perfect, emotionally-controlled-at-all-times sister on the phone, Tilly would think she was gushing. Renia never gushed. "Thank you so much. I'll give you the bride's information and you can work out the details with her. I know she'll be grateful."

"Yeah, maybe. Maybe she read the review."

"Hush. That review was bull and we both know it." The phone line went silent for a minute. "He still been coming back every night for a drink?"

He didn't need a name. "Maybe."

"I'll take that as a yes. Have you learned anything about him? His family? Where did he go to college?"

"He probably has family. Everyone has family. Mine won't get off the phone right now."

Renia, the perfect sister, ignored her. "Call me as soon as you know more."

"I will, I promise."

"I'm going to call you tonight anyway, just to check in."

Tilly rolled her eyes at the phone. "Thanks, Mom. Can I just get the bride's phone number?"

Grabbing a pen, she took down information, then told her sister goodbye. She'd never had to deal with brides—Renia was the one with the skill to calm even the worst Bridezilla—but she wasn't going to second-guess this opportunity.

Calm deep breath. Calm deep breath. She didn't want the bride's jitters to get to her. She wanted to be calming, like her sister. She could take care of this, no problem. It was better than a cat, toy dog or a toupee. A wedding rehearsal was positive news.

She dialed the numbers. "Hello!" A woman's voice screamed through the phone, on edge, the way Tilly imagined a bride within a week of her wedding would be. Tilly moved the phone a little farther from her ear.

"Hello. My name is Tilly Milek." *Think calm.* "I'm Renia Milek's sister. She called me about your rehearsal dinner."

"Oh, thank you for calling." The scream lowered to a shrill shout, but at least she could hold the phone against her ear. "Can you help us?"

"Yes. I've had to rearrange a few things…" God forgive the lie, but she didn't want the bride to think no one else wanted to come to her restaurant. "…and we can give you the whole night."

"What about the price? I mean, we already paid another restaurant a down payment that he's taken to some godforsaken place. My fiancé's family is having a fit about the extra cost. Like it's not the most important day in our lives."

"Yes, my sister told me what happened. I'm sorry to hear about the other restaurant. Let's discuss what type of food you want and how you want the bar to operate before we talk about price. What was the other restaurant going to serve?"

"Some chicken dish and something vegetarian. My fiancé's sister and some of my cousins are vegetarians."

"Okay. We can easily accommodate chicken and vegetarian. What kind of appetizers were you thinking of?"

The negotiation continued until Tilly had worked out a menu and price. For the first time since opening, Babka would make a Friday goal, plus some. The money would put off the inevitable for a couple more weeks at least.

Tilly looked out the small window from the kitchen into the dining room and tried to judge the crowd. There were empty tables, but it was a Thursday night and few restaurants were packed on a Thursday. Babka didn't look barren, which was enough for today.

"Tilly." Steve spoke from behind her. "You need to get away from the window."

Tilly turned to face him. "I'm seeing how our business is doing. Part of my job as owner."

"You keep telling yourself that." He moved the tray to rest on one arm and took Tilly's hand. His hands weren't shaking tonight, which was a good sign. Maybe his shakes *were* just too much coffee. "I'll make you a deal. If Dan comes tonight, I'll come straight back and let you know— if Karen doesn't beat me to it. We're busy tonight."

Am I that transparent?

He was right—she was both happy and loath to admit it to herself. Happy because, well, it was business and she'd been praying for more business since she opened and especially since the review. Loath because she was needed in the kitchen as expediter and working cold apps, not staring out the window, looking for a man she didn't trust anyway.

Her problems were no longer only the lack of customers, clogged sinks and messed-up prep. She now had employees complaining about their wages. Someone had found, and left lying around, information about how much the servers were making compared to the kitchen staff. Normally this would anger the kitchen staff, who didn't make tips. In a slow restaurant, this angered the waitstaff, who didn't make a decent hourly wage and needed tips.

Each staff member she'd questioned about wrong orders and soggy salads had claimed innocence. Talking about

Babka's problems during family dinner hadn't helped, either. Everyone had denied involvement, then proceeded to offer up suspects until it was as though the entire staff were playing a game of Clue. It was Candace behind the bar with the seltzer hose. Karen at the hostess station with the stray cat. AM Carlos at the sandwich units with the butter.

Every small slight in her normally easygoing staff took on nefarious undertones as they suspected each other of trying to ruin the restaurant and put them all out of jobs. Tilly had finally had to tell everyone to call or email her—they could call her at home—if they had ideas about the saboteur and she would keep everything confidential. Then, at the worried faces of her employees as they tried to guess who secretly didn't like them enough to frame them for ruining a restaurant, Tilly had assured everyone that this wasn't a witch hunt and she wouldn't fire anyone on a rumor.

Since that botched family meal, every staff member had been on their best behavior, as if one slip would peg them as the saboteur. As grateful as she was for their hard work, she liked them better when they were people and not robots.

The printer spit out tickets and Tilly called out the orders, careful to keep her voice steady. If she allowed her fears and frustrations to show in the kitchen, Babka would swallow her whole. She had to be calm and in charge at every moment while at work. She could express her fears later, to Imbir as he kneaded her thighs. Even if he didn't listen, he purred and closed his eyes, so she could pretend he did.

Or to Dan, to whom she found herself turning, forgetting that he was The Eater. Some nights she would remember halfway through their conversation, but by then she was searching for support and he provided it. He listened, understood and reassured without being patronizing. If he really understood what Babka meant to her, he would be a man she could fall in love with. That was a mighty big if.

The sous chef kicked her foot and Tilly looked up to see tickets hanging off the printer, waiting to be called. She closed her eyes for a split second to get her head back in the game, then hollered out the next orders. *If* he gained her trust, if they could make this work, she had to learn how to be at Babka and not think about Dan.

If she got distracted, Dan would have to go.

"Tilly?" She looked up from the food she was plating. Steve had slipped into the kitchen, a wide grin on his face. "Karen just seated Dan at his usual seat at the bar."

"Thanks, Steve. I'll be out in a minute."

He nodded and walked back into the dining room. Tilly finished her task, rinsed her hands, gave some instructions to her sous chef and followed Steve out. She could take a short break. Babka was busier than it had been, but her staff could handle the extra rush for ten minutes, especially in their new perfect-employee mode. If it wasn't so stressful to run a failing restaurant, she'd be bored.

Dan smiled his glorious smile at her as she walked toward him, but movement at the front door distracted her. Two men in suits carrying bags leaned in to talk to Karen before moving in her direction. They were both pretty average looking, average height, average build—nothing compared to Dan—but the way they walked with such purpose commanded all her attention.

"Ms. Milek?" The one on the right spoke. He had a bulbous nose and a single hair stuck out of one nostril, making his nose look even bigger on his face.

"Yes. What can I help you with?"

"Perhaps you would be more comfortable talking with us in the back," the one on the left said. He was softer looking with bright red cheeks and kind eyes. "We're from the health inspector's office."

His words made no sense. What were they doing here during dinner service? "I've just recently had my health inspection and passed easily." Her heart sped up. It wasn't pushing out of her chest yet, more like a car revving at a red light, waiting.

"Miss, I'm trying to be nice and not talk in front of your customers."

"Yes, yes. Of course." She nodded quickly, several times, not sure what else to do. "Please, follow me into the kitchen." She looked back at Dan and gestured that she'd be there as soon as she could.

Once in her office, safe behind her desk, Tilly faced the two men. "What can I help you with? As I said in the dining room, I had my last inspection recently and passed, no conditions. You can see the report behind the bar."

Bulbous nose didn't beat around the bush. "We've had a complaint about rats in your restaurant."

"Rats! I haven't seen any evidence of rats and I'm here more than anyone else."

"We've had complaints and we're here to inspect."

Did they have to come during dinner service? On a night she had customers? Couldn't they come back tomorrow, before they opened?

Smile and answer their questions, Tilly. You don't have rats. They'll see the truth and be gone soon enough.

"Of course. Can I see your IDs? Then you're welcome to inspect my restaurant. I have nothing to hide."

They showed her their IDs, got black lights out of their bags and proceeded around the kitchen. Tilly could only watch and hope.

"What are the Men in Brown here for?"

Tilly turned back to find Dan leaning against the hand sink. "Shouldn't you be in the dining room ordering?"

"I thought I'd come back and offer you some moral support."

Her heart grew nearly twice its size in her chest, although it was still pounding as if it were trying to flatten a veal cutlet. "Thank you. That's sweet."

"What are they here for?"

She didn't want to tell anyone what the men were doing, especially The Eater. But he was also Dan, so she said, "Oh, they're health inspectors."

"The place looks spotless. What could you be worried about?"

"Well," she stalled again. "They've had complaints."

"What kind of..." Dan didn't get a chance to finish his sentence.

"Eeewww!" The scream came from the refrigerator area and a white rat raced under the counter. It tried to hide behind PM Carlos's legs, but one solid kick sent the rodent racing through the kitchen again, dodging Enrique and the dishwasher, squealing all the while. Tilly grabbed an empty milk crate and threw it over the rat, barely catching the nasty thing.

I'm getting too good at catching loose animals in my restaurant.

Dan wove his way through the employees and appliances, putting his foot on the crate to hold it down as Tilly leaned against a rack of dishes for support, making the plates rattle. She hated rats and they were in her restaurant. It was true. What the health inspectors said was true.

She took a deep breath and forced herself upright. She had to deal with this problem.

The health inspectors gathered around Dan and all of the kitchen employees looked up from their tasks. She

looked at them and they all went back to working. Or, working as well as they could with three extra people in the kitchen. And a rat trapped in a milk crate. She couldn't forget the rat.

Everything crammed into an already tight space. *Thank you, Mary, Mother of God, that I don't have an open kitchen, just this silly window.*

The younger inspector's eyes were no longer kind. Instead, they were hard as he reached into his bag to pull out his notebook.

"Wait—" Dan held up his hand to stop them. "Before you do anything that might threaten Tilly's restaurant, I want a look at this rat."

"Who are you?" the Nose asked.

"I'm the guy keeping the rat caged. You can still write your citation, close the restaurant and whatever else you need to do about the rodent later, just let me look at it first. Tilly, can you hold the crate down while I look at the thing?"

She shuddered. The thought of getting close to the disgusting, beady-eyed rodent nearly made her retch, but she held her ground. *This is my problem. This is my problem. This is my problem.* She took a deep breath and put one foot on the crate. The rat looked up at her through the holes and she could have sworn it smiled at her.

Dan crouched down on the floor and peered into the crate at the dirty sewer monster. Tilly swallowed hard, the bile rising in her throat. When he stood back up, Dan was smiling at her.

"I think it's a plant."

Her jaw dropped, but she couldn't take her eyes off of the little fiend. What if it escaped and ran into the dining room?

"Sir, perhaps you are a little soft in the head. It's ob-

viously a rat." The Nose smirked, looking quite satisfied with his poor joke.

"That is no sewer rat."

"Excuse me?" Tilly forced her attention away from the rat, which could chew its way through the hard plastic in seconds to rush up at… She swallowed and looked at Dan, who was speaking nonsense.

"Tilly, look at the rat."

"I've been looking." The thing had curled its hairless tail around itself, as if it was harmless. The lying little rat.

She slapped her hand over her mouth before a hysterical giggle could escape. *I'm losing my mind.*

"Look again."

She looked. "It's still a rat," she said through her fingers as her hand continued to hold hysteria in. Just what she needed, more publicity. Maybe she should start collecting the animals in her restaurant and open a petting zoo.

Dan made a noise somewhere between a laugh and a sigh. "When was the last time you saw a white sewer rat? Moreover, when was the last time you saw a sewer rat without marks on it anywhere? Not missing an ear or no scars? This is the cleanest, healthiest, *fattest* rat I've ever seen."

"I try not to look at rats." The thing sat up on its hind legs—*now it was close to her foot!*—and her stomach heaved. *Can I barf and be hysterical at the same time?*

Why couldn't Dan take over the job of holding down the crate?

But if he was right, he was saving her restaurant. Whining about being close to the rat seemed a touch ungrateful and having a fit would ruin his rescue altogether.

"I've lived in a lot of cities and seen a lot of rats. This is a pet and I'll prove it. Tilly, step back."

"But…I'm all that's keeping the rat caged." Heaven was a place where she wasn't holding a rat in a milk crate with her foot, but she couldn't have it racing around her kitchen, either.

"I don't think it will run away." He reached down and pulled Tilly's foot up off the crate then lifted the edge close to his arm.

The rat raced out and up Dan's arm, perching itself on his shoulder. Tilly coughed back more bile as the hairless tail twitched back and forth on his arm.

"A sewer rat would never be so friendly. Since Tilly would rather kiss a snake, I'm going to guess it's not hers."

"Bill—" The younger inspector turned to the Nose and hope entered Tilly's body for the first time since the men had entered her restaurant. "The man's got a point. You and I have seen a lot of rats in restaurants around the city. Never has one been white—or friendly."

"What do you propose we do? This is a critical violation. We've not just seen evidence of rodents, but we've seen the actual animal. We should give her a citation and close the business until the problem is taken care of." The Nose looked at the rat sitting happily on Dan's shoulder and shrugged. "I'm not sure we have any choice."

The Nose talked tough, but he was wavering. She had the advantage and she took it. "I have some ideas. If the rat," she said through a shudder, "is a pet, he hasn't been in here long. Someone would have seen it, since it seems friendly." *Gross!* "We'll put the rat somewhere else and you men can take your black lights around the kitchen to search for urine. The health code says I must correct the problem immediately. If the only urine you find is where we've seen the rat tonight and we clean up with you watching, then I don't get a citation. Come back as often as you feel you need to in the next month and we'll call ourselves even.

"If you find evidence of rats all over the kitchen, you can…" She took a breath and used the air to finish the sentence. "You can shut down my restaurant and I'll hire an exterminator. Sound fair?"

"Bill, what do you think?"

"I don't want to write a citation if this is some neighbor's rat that got out. Miss, how do you know this rat hasn't been holed up for weeks and you've only now seen him? That's a big risk you're taking."

"If we had a rat, I would have seen evidence before tonight. This restaurant is my baby. I refuse to believe I wouldn't have known."

"All right." Bill raised his eyebrows at her, but nodded. "You have a deal. What are you going to do about the rat?"

Every muscle in Tilly's body weakened with relief and only the sheer force of determination held her up.

She had no idea what to do about the rat, other than get it the hell out of her restaurant.

Dan chimed in. "I'll take it out of here. I can get a cage and I'll take it home. I have bread and some other stuff to feed it until I can make it to a pet store."

Tilly turned to the inspectors. "Dan can go out the back and we can start tracking how the rat got in Babka. Sirs," she said as she held her hands out, palms up in supplication, "I am at your mercy."

DAN FOUND TILLY in her office later that night, the restaurant mostly cleaned and closed down, seated at her desk holding her head in her hands.

"Will the rat story be in the next column of The Eater?" she asked her desk.

"What?" Did she think so little of him? "I wouldn't do that to you. This, this was a fluke. The city of Chicago doesn't need to know about a fluke."

"Did you think the cat and dog were normal?" Her fingertips pulled the corners of her eyes down as she lifted her head to look at him.

His inner rationalizer kicked in. "There was the over-salted food, too. I might have ignored the cat and dog or spun things differently if it hadn't been for the food."

"Have you had oversalted food from my kitchen since?"

"Tilly, you know I can't just…"

"Actually, I don't know anything."

He didn't want to have this conversation with her now—or ever. He wanted to hold her in his arms and give her a shoulder to cry on. He wanted her to let him comfort her. "Did they find anything?"

"No." She let him change the subject, which was close enough for now. "The rat had been put behind the Hobart mixer with a bag of cereal. The only trace of any rodent was from the cereal to where we caught him."

"Cereal?"

"Cheerios." Her voice was small, but relieved. "I thought that was weird, too. As I showed the men, we have no cereal anywhere else in the restaurant, so it didn't violate our agreement. I think by the time I was leading them through all our pantry items so they could see I didn't own any cereal they were sick of me."

"No citation?"

"No citation. I felt dirty bargaining with them, but I didn't want my restaurant shut down. We've never had any problems before."

She closed her eyes and rested her head on the back of her office chair. Dan let her have her moment to collect herself.

When she lifted her head and opened her eyes, the spark was back. "I'm still not convinced that what I did was legal, but it's done and Babka stays open. Karl would kill me if he knew I bargained with a health inspector."

Ah, yes, Karl, the overly rule-bound, inspector general brother. Rich, who was more in tune with Chicago politics than Dan ever cared to be, predicted Karl would be the scariest inspector general Chicago corruption would ever have to suffer under. Corrupt city contractors must be quaking in their Salvatore Ferragamos if Karl was the type of man to get after his baby sister for bargaining with health inspectors.

"You don't tell him and I won't tell him." Dan walked behind her, put his hand on her shoulder and squeezed. "The health inspectors sure won't."

She leaned her head against his hand. God, he wanted more from this woman than a beer at her bar and stretches of conversation interrupted by her moments of doubt. He contented himself with inane chatter to take her mind off her Catholic guilt. "Paulie's been taken care of and is happily stationed at my home."

"Paulie?"

"The rat from the first Godfather movie. It seemed appropriate." He could feel the ghost of a smile against his hand. But, like a specter, it was fleeting.

"A cat, dog, toupee and now a rat. What next?"

Helpless, Dan squeezed her shoulders. The only thing he had to offer her right now was his presence. "Do you want me to stay?"

"Do you mind?"

Mind spending more time with Tilly? "No. Of course I didn't mind. I'd be happy to." He looked at her drawn face and knew she needed action. Something to do with her hands to take her mind off her problems. "I suppose I get dinner again."

"Of course." Tilly slowly closed her eyes. When she opened them again, her entire person was brighter with the prospect of something to *do*. "Don't worry. The whole kitchen floor has been sanitized and all the counters inspected. It's clean."

She took his hand, led him through the small door into her kitchen. Babka ruled her life.

Selfish bastard that he was, Dan wanted all of her attention to be on him. Not on the dinner she had saved for him, not on the restaurant she was barely keeping alive, but on him. Her eyes seeing only him. Her lips touching his. Her hands on his body.

He was moving before he even finished the thought. The kiss he gave her was different from the impulsive kiss at the Taste. This kiss was purposeful. He was going to kiss Babka out of her mind so she could focus on him. He'd give her back to the restaurant later. For now, Tilly was his.

She tastes like butter. He licked her lips and her mouth opened with a soft moan. She stood, pushing her body into his and wrapping her arms around his neck, her fingers pulling gently at the hair at his nape.

He wanted more. He grabbed handfuls of her chef's jacket in his fists, resisting the urge to lay her down on the desk and plunge himself deep into her. *I am not a caveman.* His conscience quickly informed him she still hadn't forgiven him for the review.

"Tilly," he said hoarsely, any objections halted when she pulled up his shirt and put her hands to his bare skin.

Dan was suddenly thankful for her lack of a manicure. Her hands were dry and calloused. Rough edges of her fingers tickled lines of pleasure over his stomach.

His entire body tensed with pleasure at the thought of what those hands could do on other parts of his body. What she could do with his body. Tilly didn't act unless it was with her whole heart, mind and body. He had imagined what such type of single-mindedness would be like when applied to sex, and he wanted to find out.

His hands found a thin tank top before he reached his goal. The skin under her top was silky smooth, just like he'd dreamed, and he didn't stop to think how his hands got there. He didn't care. Perfect. She was perfect.

He moved his hand over her bra to her full breast and rubbed her nipple with his thumb. She sighed. Her nipple was already hard.

He turned his attention to her neck, kissing under her chin and smelling the wonderful scent of Tilly. She smelled like every delicious meal he'd ever eaten, the scents of the kitchen having been absorbed into her skin. She smelled good enough to eat—real and ready for him.

"Tilly, I'm done…"

The door from the dining room to the kitchen was still squeaking on its hinges when the footsteps came to a quick halt. Tilly pulled back from him. His body missed her immediately.

"Candace, I'm…" Tilly was beet-red. "I'm sorry."

"Nothing to be sorry about. I'll wait at the bar. I'm ready to go whenever you are." The footsteps receded through the squeaking door.

"I, uh, have to, have to go," Tilly stammered.

"Not yet." Dan pulled his hands out from under Tilly's jacket. After he smoothed the fabric, he wrapped his hands around her waist and pulled her tight against him, just to wrap his arms around her, to be enveloped in her warmth and delicious smells. She smelled like home, like all he would ever want home to be. "Let me hold you for a minute. Candace can wait."

He needed to keep her here, with him.

They relaxed against each other, each one holding the other up.

CHAPTER FIFTEEN

"HAVE YOU WRITTEN YOUR new review yet?" Mike sat, his arms folded against his chest, outside the racquetball court with Dan while they waited for their reservation.

"No, dammit. And I'm not going to."

"Think Rich will let me run an essay contest on the blog? The details of the contest are still under works, but something like 'I did something douche-y. Best excuse for not copping to it like a man wins a case of Summer's Eve.'"

"Do you even care *why* I won't write a new review?"

"No," Mike said matter-of-factly. "You'll keep coming up with excuses until she gives up and calls the cops on your ass. She might forgive you if fix it and cover your douchiness in lavender and roses. Right now, you just smell like shit."

"I can make her understand."

"Are you willing to bet on it?"

Dan's gut clenched. Betting on Tilly now felt wrong. What kind of asshole bet on the woman he…the woman he what? *Loved?* Could he love a woman after knowing her two weeks?

He liked her. A lot. He looked forward to every moment he spent with her, even when she only came out of the kitchen for a couple of minutes. He loved the way she looked, not just the deep brown of her eyes and lushness of her lips, but the way exuberance and life sang in her every movement. When life pushed her down and got her dirty,

Tilly stood up—never bothering to dust herself off—and kept going.

He admired her.

More than wanting to touch her and share her bed every night, Dan wanted to stand beside her as she succeeded and as she failed. He wanted to be the man she kept up late into the night talking excitedly about her ideas for her restaurant and hopes for the future. He wanted to be the person who held her in his arms when life threw her lemons. He wanted to help her figure out how to make the perfect lemonade.

If that wasn't love, he didn't know what was.

"Are you willing to put your money where your mouth is?" Mike interrupted his thoughts.

"What are we even betting on?"

"Just an amendment to our original bet. That review is screwing you over and you're going to root for the White Sox at the next Crosstown Classic. After you write your new review, I think you'll be a Sox fan for at least a year and I don't mean telling me you watched a game on TV. That Cubs hat will be replaced by a Sox one and I think a White Sox license-plate holder would be a good addition to the Subaru. Plus going to games."

Had Mike fallen on his head recently? "The first bet I can understand, because Rich arbitrates, but I decide if I write a new review and I bet I'm not going to. It would be going against my self-interest." Even if Tilly was a White Sox fan and Dan would love to see her blue hair sticking out from under a black Sox cap.

Mike shrugged. "Your self-interest is to write a new review. Of course, if you're not sure about the review…"

"Fine." He was being goaded into this, but Mike was the one who was going to lose. So why did Dan feel like the bad guy?

"It's not fair to get insider information, Mike." Shane arrived, whacking his racquet against his hand.

Dan stared at the racquet, willing with his body and soul for the thing to fly out of Shane's fingers and hit him in the face. But Dan had no superhero powers today. The racquet kept swinging and Shane's face remained unsmacked. Then the meaning of the words struck Dan's brain and he looked closely at Mike. His honest, upstanding friend Mike.

"What insider information?"

"Mike didn't tell you? There's a pool going, about when you'll write a new review. Pot's up to a thousand bucks."

Shane stretched out comfortably on the bench next to Mike. Almost close enough for Dan to hit.

Feeling violent today, Danny?

The person he should be hitting was himself. Shane was an annoying little gnat of a man but, like a gnat, he was essentially tiny and harmless. The betting pool was tasteless, but not personal. Of his friends, only Mike had met Tilly. Of course, Dan had nearly had sex with Tilly on her desk and he was still betting on their relationship.

Dan unclenched the fist he hadn't realized was in his lap. He couldn't hit Shane, wrestle him to the ground and keep him in a choke hold until the gnat pounded the floor for mercy. Dan was the bad guy right now. Shane was just the stooge.

Dan looked at Mike. His friend. "Are you in on this pool, too?" How many bets did Mike have running on him right now?

Mike held up his hands. "Wasn't my idea. I warned Shane you might display some of the moves that made you a college wrestling champion when you found out, but he insisted."

"I think Mike has forfeited his chance at the pot, coming

to you for insider information. That's cheating. He's trying to get you to write a new review so he can have the money."

Mike turned to the buzzing whine of Shane's voice, his face red with anger. "Shane, Dan won't punch you because the person he's really mad at is himself. I have no such qualms and you called me a cheater."

Shane looked at the sports agent and shrugged. "Give me an equal shot at convincing Dan to skew the bet my way." He turned back to Dan. "I'll even split the pot with you. Seventy-thirty."

"Right now, I'd pay three hundred dollars to watch Mike punch you in the face." Just because Mike was right and Dan was mad at himself didn't mean he wasn't also mad at Shane for starting the pool. Violence wouldn't solve his problems, but it might make him feel better for a little while.

And it would shut Shane up.

"Fine. Sixty-forty."

Mike turned to Dan. "The little shithead has no shame and no fear."

Shane chuckled. "You guys talk big, but neither of you are real bullies. I believe Dan would wrestle me to the ground and make me say uncle, but that wouldn't cause lasting damage. And neither of you would punch me. Or not yet anyway. I know the line I can't cross and I haven't even come close to it yet. So, Dan, sixty-forty?"

"You're not invited to play racquetball anymore." Dan would find some random guy on the street to make up their regular foursome.

"I'll take that as no. When does Mike want you to write the new review?"

He'd expected to argue with Tilly about the review, but his friends should know he couldn't write a new one. "I'm going to pretend you aren't here," Dan said. He and Mike could play racquetball one-on-one.

"I just want to know if he's cheating," Shane whined.

"I wouldn't tell you. In fact," Dan added, "I might even lie to you so you thought he wasn't. Shut up about the bet in the next thirty seconds, or I'll make sure Mike wins the pool."

Shane might not believe Dan or Mike would commit violence, but the threat of losing a thousand dollars had some power. He took one last look at Mike, eyebrows raised, and shrugged. "Fine." He gestured with his racquet to the court. "Where's Rich so we can play?"

Dan turned to his friend, his rat fink, double-crossing asshole friend. "I wish we were bully enough to punch him."

"Think of it as motivation. Shane bet Tilly would dump you before you got around to writing a new review."

Looking out at the dining room between rushes, Tilly contemplated the number of tables she needed filled and the number of tables actually filled. The difference between those two was getting smaller, but she didn't want to get her hopes up. If the party that had ordered almost everything on the menu was any indication, she'd had a visit by another restaurant reviewer. No cats had busted in the door, so she hoped for at least one good review.

The staff was all working in sync. No missed reservations. No prep in the wrong place for the line cooks. Steve had called in sick, which meant the waitstaff had to run their own tables, but that didn't seem to be slowing anyone down. All in all, Tilly couldn't complain about the night.

She just wished Babka had more customers.

As usual, Tilly riffed the dishes she was finishing in her head, and, although she knew she shouldn't let him, Dan influenced her alterations. She had gotten a sense of what food he liked: simple, classically prepared food with a kick of something unusual and, in Babka, distinctly Polish. Everything about Dan was classic and clean.

She should stop packing him a lunch. Feeding someone so personally implied a relationship and they didn't have one. She wasn't confident she could rely on him, no matter how much she looked forward to his visits. He still couldn't see that his review had nearly ruined Babka's reputation, or that he should make amends for it.

And apparently she was a glutton for punishment, because she still hoped he would come to Babka tonight and make her laugh.

Tilly shook her head. This train of thought was useless. They didn't have a relationship. They weren't going to have a relationship, because even if he asked her out on a date, she would say no. All this, the lunch-packing and relationship-contemplating, had become a habit; the tasks had worked themselves into her daily routine.

Continuing with her new routine, Karen skipped into the kitchen to tell her Dan was at the bar, waiting for whenever Tilly was free. As she had for the past two weeks, Tilly thought about saying she was busy, wondered who she was kidding and walked through the swinging doors to the restaurant.

Dan smiled at her and she wanted to toss Babka to the culinary wolves and go out on a proper Saturday-night date with him. Dancing or to the movies—whatever it was normal people did on Saturday nights. He looked at her as if she were all the courses in a seven-course meal. She wanted him to look at her like that when it wasn't late at night, in her restaurant, with all her staff watching.

But she had a restaurant to save.

"How were last night's pierogi?" she asked as she placed a bag packed with food on the bar.

"Perfect, of course." Dan didn't once glance at the bag of food. He looked at her.

As usual, Tilly thought about going around the bar to sit next to him and decided against it. She would talk longer with him if she sat at the barstool. Anyway, they had established a routine and she intended to stick to it. The routine involved her on one side of the bar and him on the other.

Then Dan broke the routine. "I'm taking you out for breakfast tomorrow morning."

CHAPTER SIXTEEN

WITH THOSE EIGHT WORDS, Dan proved himself as much of an ass as Mike accused him of being every day as he ate Tilly's carefully packed lunches. Every day he enjoyed a delicious lunch and every day Mike sent him a text asking if he was going to write a new review.

The answer, of course, was *no*. He liked Tilly. He liked the way her blue hair escaped her bandanna, no matter how often she tried to tuck it back. He liked what the strength in her forearms when she rolled back the sleeves of her jacket meant about her dedication to her restaurant. And he liked the way the roundness of her hips cradled in his hands just so, and how that roundness spoke to her passion for food.

That was his personal life. The review was professional. His feelings for Tilly couldn't influence his obligation to write honest reviews. Her business was so personal to her she didn't understand how he could separate them. He wanted her to try, though, enough to surprise himself by asking her out on a date. After spending nearly two weeks perched on this barstool like a roosting chicken, he wanted to see Tilly when she wasn't distracted by Babka.

No denying he was a chicken. Or an ass. A blind and deaf jury could convict him of being an ass. His presence here was evidence enough. He should never have come back to Babka, his bet with Mike be damned. But when he had eaten a tasty dinner at one of the many Chicago eating establishments, he had wished he was eating Tilly's food, with Tilly there. Remembering how she didn't simply talk with her hands, but rather with her entire body, her eyes and her smile. How the color on her face matched the occasional stain on her jacket. Then he would wonder whether all her underwear had red polka dots or if she had any with green stripes. Maybe a heart or two. Lace. Lace would be good.

He wanted to take risks around her.

Almost without thinking, he would be at Babka, just as he was tonight, drinking his beer and listening to her talk about her restaurant and her troubles. And fool that he was, he felt like mistakes—the cat, the oversalted food, his relationship with his family—didn't matter and there were only happy accidents. He would stare at her and think crazy thoughts. About painting his bedroom walls the color of her hair and taking her to meet his parents. But no matter how much she laughed, she always held a part of herself back because he was The Eater.

He would think about what it would take for her to enjoy his company without reservations and think about the reputation he'd spent years trying to build. He'd think about how he defended his existence whenever he spoke to his father and how little his existence would mean without reviewing for *CarpeChicago*. He'd wonder how far his reputation had to fall before Dan Sr. saw the death throes of Dan's career as an opportunity to pull him back to Meier Dairy. How bad would things have to get before Dan gave in?

Writing a new review wouldn't kill his career, but if he opened those doors once, even for good reasons, could he shut them again?

He would finish his beer and head the couple of blocks northwest to his home. He would pretend he was happy about his white walls and he didn't care what his father would say about Tilly's blue hair. He would pretend he wasn't a complete asshole because he was The Eater from

CarpeChicago and she was the chef of a restaurant he'd panned.

Tonight was different. He couldn't pretend any longer. Tonight he proved himself a complete asshole. But he couldn't stop himself. Tonight was Saturday. Babka would be closed Sunday and Monday. He couldn't go another two days without seeing her smile, hearing her laugh, catching the sparkling life in her eyes.

He wanted to kiss her somewhere other than her restaurant, somewhere there would be no interruptions and they could taste each other until their hunger abated, though he doubted their cravings would ever fully go away.

"This memory of you and a hot dog pops into my head every time I pass a Vienna Beef sign." He smiled. "Do you know how many Vienna Beef signs there are in Chicago? I get hot and bothered just walking around. If I'm going to have dirty thoughts about you and food, I'd like to add cinnamon rolls. Ann Sather's makes the best. I'll pick you up at noon for brunch."

"I haven't said yes yet," she replied. "I might have to work tomorrow."

"Babka is closed on Sundays and Mondays. You can spare time for brunch, especially since I want to watch you lick frosting off your lips." He'd asked her out. Committed himself to being an asshole. If he was going to make an enormous mistake—the best kind of mistake—he was going to do it right. They would have the whole day. He would have time to plead his case.

"I don't trust you."

"You look at me and see the review. Give me a chance to show you I'm more than The Eater."

She bit her lip and his breath stalled. It hadn't occurred to him she might say no.

"Okay. Noon?"

He breathed again. "Let's make it a whole day. The Chicago Symphony is playing an afternoon show at Ravinia. I'll pack us a picnic lunch."

"I should do *some* work tomorrow," she said, without any conviction in her voice.

"I won't keep you out late. You can work tomorrow night. And Monday."

TILLY LOOKED AT HER WATCH. Eleven fifty-two. He wasn't late, not yet, but she was beginning to worry. She was headed out on a date for the first time in years. Of course she was worried. She wasn't working on Babka. Babka should concern her every moment and instead she was going on a date. With The Eater. *His review nearly pushed Babka off a cliff.*

When she forgot he was The Eater and let herself remember he was Dan from the Taste who listened to her problems and made her laugh, she wanted to spend all her time with him. She went to her window and looked out over the trees. But he wasn't just Dan and she shouldn't be doing this. She drooled at the sight of his legs and he had a nice smile, but neither quality was enough of a reason to go out on a date with the man who had nearly crushed her dream.

Renia might say the purpose of dating was to learn if you could trust someone, but her sister had never dated a man she trusted, so what did she know? Tilly liked Dan, and that scared her. He could claim a separation of business and pleasure all he wanted, but he wasn't still trying to make a go of his dreams. She should be back in her kitchen at Babka, where she had control over her environment and problems could be fixed with extra salt or lemon juice.

Except for the tiny little problem of not having enough customers to keep Babka in the black.

Movement caught her eye and she looked down from

her window to see Dan stepping out of his Subaru across the street. He had a nice form. Khaki shorts revealed muscled calves and broad shoulders stretched out a light-green check button-down. Dan wasn't tall, exactly, but lean and strong without being overly thin. Complete with aviator sunglasses and sandy-blond hair, Dan looked as if he was stepping out of his car into an Eddie Bauer ad.

He looked up at her building, caught her staring down at him from her window and grinned. He held up a finger as if asking her to wait, then opened the passenger door. When his head popped back into view, he held up a small potted plant.

He would be perfect for her, if only...

The buzzer rang and Tilly pressed the button to let him in.

"You look good enough to eat," he said when he handed her the plant.

Potted mint. She sniffed it and took a piece off to taste. Chocolate mint, not rare, but he would've had to search it out. It was a thoughtful gift for a cook.

"I'll put it on the window with my other herbs. Does it need to be watered?"

"Probably. As I said at my house, I don't have much of a green thumb."

"Okay. Please make yourself at home." She gestured around the single room packed with a small dining room table/desk, two armchairs and a bed with her fat orange cat curled up on the pillow. Imbir didn't even lift his head in greeting, lazy beast. "I'll go get this some water."

DAN WATCHED HER walk into her small kitchen, separated from the living space by a bar. She wore a lemon-yellow dress with low V front and purple sandals, the bright colors made brighter by the same fresh scent of lemon he remembered from the Taste. It wafted like a ghost in her apartment. Not cloying, but clean and refreshing.

As she walked, Tilly's skirt swayed over her round butt and full hips while the shoulder straps highlighted her strong, sleek arms. At the Taste, he had wondered if her firm arms were a sign that she was a potter and he was partially right. Tilly worked magic and art with her hands, but the power in her biceps and forearms came from rolling out and kneading dough, particularly the tough pierogi dough.

He smiled to himself. Tilly was no waif. She was average height with plenty of curves that invited his hands to explore. He could watch the swing of her hips and bounce of her skirts all day.

Rather than sit down, he walked to the deep windowsill behind her two armchairs. Nestled among the pots of herbs were framed photographs. These weren't snapped pictures, but beautiful portraits of family and friends. They had to have been taken by a professional. In one photo, a woman who looked enough like Tilly to be her mother sat on a towel on the beach, reading. The woman was one second away from looking up and scowling at the photographer, but the photo captured the happy lack-of-awareness moment before the shutter snapped. The largest one, in a prominent position, was an older woman standing by a 1970s avocado-green stove, laughing and admonishing the photographer with a wooden spoon. She wore a white half apron and old-fashioned clunky shoes.

"My grandmother. Wasn't she beautiful?"

Tilly was back in the room, a small brown purse over her shoulder.

"Very. You have her eyes." He gestured to the other photographs on the sill. "The pictures are fabulous. Did you take them?"

"No. Renia, my sister, took them. She was at the Taste

for my demonstration. She's not in any of the pictures, because she won't give up her camera." Tilly laughed. "And the pictures I take of her don't belong among these portraits. The photograph to the right is my brother at his college graduation."

He looked closer at the photographs. "Your sister was the woman sitting behind me taking pictures. She's a fabulous photographer."

"Yes, she does weddings and portraits." Love and pride were evident in her voice and the softness of her eyes. "Are you ready to go?"

Dan grinned as she shifted her weight from foot to foot. "Antsy to get the day over with?"

Tilly looked him directly in the eyes, her unease clear. "Nervous, but you promised cinnamon rolls and I promised I'd give you a chance."

"Then let's neither of us go back on our promises." He captured her warm hand in his. "We're going to get the best cinnamon rolls this country has to offer."

"This country?" Her playful disbelief lifted one eyebrow and he relaxed, though not enough to let go of her hand.

"You haven't been back in Chicago for very long and I get the sense you ate Polish for most of your childhood. Not to mention you're a Southsider, rooting for the White Sox and all. You won't have made it up to Clark for breakfast. These are the best in the city. They have other stuff you should order, but the cinnamon rolls are the reason people go."

She laughed, a sound as warm and colorful as her personality. "You're trying to sell me on goods I've already purchased. Let's go eat."

THE HOSTESS SAT THEM at a table in the back and Dan immediately ordered cinnamon rolls and coffee.

A waiter came back with coffee and Tilly stirred cream into hers. Dan drank his black.

"I have to ask, why the blue hair?"

She absently ran her fingers through her hair and the movement of the strands mesmerized him. "It's stupid, really."

"A bad bet." It wasn't a guess. She'd told him at the Taste.

"You remembered."

"You say you're the one giving me a chance, but my life would also be easier if I could forget about you." Dull, but easier.

Tilly's answering smile said she understood. Their relationship had been loaded with complications before he'd bought her a hot dog.

"But now you're in my head and I won't ever be able to get you out."

"You have entirely too much charm," she said, but she was smiling and Dan decided he could eat Polish food—and nothing else—for the rest of his life.

"The first week of culinary school, I got drunk with my new friends. I had some Polish honey vodka I'd snuck from my mom and everyone wanted to try it."

"Tsk, tsk, drinking underage."

"I was one of the youngest students, since I'd fulfilled the requirement of working in a professional kitchen by the time I was sixteen. Most of the other students were old enough to drink, but curious about my honey vodka. And as you will hear, I learned my lesson several times over, and not just from the hangover the next day."

Dan nodded, remembering several occasions in college where he had "learned his lesson," until the next time the shots came out.

"We were drunk and talking about our dreams, how we

were going to get famous. I would own a haute Polish restaurant, another woman wanted to be the next caterer to the stars and this one guy wanted to be the next James Beard, with his own food foundation and food awards." She paused for a sip of coffee. "We all laughed that the first person to achieve their dreams would have to do something drastic. I said I would dye my hair blue for a year."

The waiter returned with their cinnamon rolls and to take their order.

"Mother Mary! How am I supposed to eat one of these *and* brunch?"

"Don't try to eat it all. Anything you don't finish we can drop off at my house later. Have you had a chance to look at the menu?"

"No, but I know what I want." Tilly turned to the waiter. "I'll have an omelet with tomatoes, mushrooms and Swiss cheese."

Dan ordered Southern Decadence eggs benedict and the waiter left. When Tilly opened her mouth to finish her story, Dan pulled a piece of cinnamon roll off and put it in her mouth.

"You couldn't finish the story without trying one of these rolls," he said. The tip of her tongue darting out of her mouth to lick frosting off her lips was as arousing as he'd hoped and feared. Everything she ate should involve frosting or a sauce of some kind. *Or salt,* he thought, remembering the sight of Tilly licking celery salt off her lips at the Taste.

"I don't think I've ever had a cinnamon roll so decadent. My teeth are going to rot just thinking about them." She took another piece and popped it into her mouth. "Cinnamon courage, to finish my story.

"Where was I? Oh yes, I agreed to dye my hair blue. With my grandmother's inheritance, I had the start-up money to start my own restaurant, so I moved back to Chicago and began hunting for space. A friend of mine reminded me of the old bet."

"And you didn't try to get out of it?" Honoring a bet was important.

"Sure, a little. But, drunk or not, I'd made the bet and I was the first to achieve my dream. I'm determined to make a success out of it, even if I have to work every station myself all day, every day on the way to excellence for each and every person who comes in the door. If that doesn't happen, I will invite a Russian restaurant to invade." She nodded hard and her bobbed blue hair bounced. Dan was struck by a desire to have Tilly with frosting on a beach in the Caribbean, even if the sand would grit his teeth.

The corners of her lips rose, but her expression wasn't a smile. It was an unhappy realization of the indisputable facts of their relationship. "I don't know where that leaves us."

"With a chance," he reminded her.

"Right." She blinked and the loss in her eyes dimmed. "The day before opening I went to a salon, near here, actually, and got my hair dyed blue. The hairdresser recommended the turquoise. She said it would go better with my skin tone.

"Anyway, I've talked a lot about me. How did you get into writing?" She took a bite of her omelet. Her part of the conversation was over. She said she wasn't certain she could trust him, so he'd tell the truth to whatever she asked. Then she'd see why he couldn't retract the review, and that it didn't have to define their relationship, if they didn't let it.

"I got my degree in journalism, specializing in magazines, planning to write about sports. I wrestled in college, so I traveled a lot. One day I wrote a review of some nasty diner in Ann Arbor, just as a joke, but it got passed around the teams. Everyone thought it was funny and so I wrote more. Eventually I stopped writing them as a gag and slogged my way through the freelance trenches until I could make a living."

"I always assumed you lived in New York. I know your work, of course. The article on noodles was in *Food & Wine* and the other one on the international trade of women was in *The Atlantic*. How did I not put two and two together at the Taste?" She looked at him with wide, astounded eyes. "I knew the chef who was thrown in prison from my externship. He was the nicest, most supportive person I worked with. I was surprised by the news of the child slavery ring, but I suppose you can never really know a person. I remember being so impressed with the dedication of the writer." She cocked her head and her mouth opened in a smile. "With you."

"Thanks." Pride lifted his shoulders at the respect in her eyes. "I like my job and am proud of that article."

More than liking his job, he loved it. He got to eat and travel for a living and, much to his father's surprise, made money doing it. He was well respected in his field, invited to speak at events and sought after for magazines and newspapers. When he'd been struggling to make a name for himself, the promise of family money (and finally actual money) had kept him alive, but now he lived solely on what he earned. Writing gave him a freedom hard to find in any job. He never had to worry about someone standing over him, berating him for minor mistakes and trying to control his every moment.

When his father called, Dan could hang up the phone.

But the independence his job afforded him was nothing when compared to the admiration in Tilly's voice as she talked about his work.

"Chicago's an easy city to travel from. Plus, I like it here.

I went to Northwestern and Chicago feels like home. My family lives close. I don't see them often, but I can't seem to leave them."

Dan couldn't seem to leave his sister. While he had successfully edged himself out from under his father's manipulative thumb, Beth hadn't been so lucky. She still strove to please a man who could not be pleased and he couldn't abandon her while she tried to do it. So he stayed a drive away from Meier Dairy's headquarters in Wisconsin for whenever she needed a break. It was the only thing he could offer her.

TILLY ATE HER BRUNCH as she and Dan talked about first-date things: jobs, sports and favorite hangouts in the city. She had promised to give him a chance, but today was also about giving herself a chance. No question she was attracted to him; if it wasn't for the review, she'd pursue a relationship despite her work life. Babunia had trusted her enough to leave her the money for Babka. Did Tilly trust herself to make a good decision about Dan? She wouldn't know unless she tried and she couldn't try halfheartedly. This was a date, as innocent and as complicated as two people exploring a relationship. If she shortchanged the day, she'd always wonder.

People afraid of risk didn't own their own businesses or work as chefs. She wasn't planning to fail, but she wasn't afraid of it, either. Dan, and the attraction she felt for him, was a risk she had to take.

Dan listened and understood her connection to food and family, how the two interacted and how she couldn't separate one from the other. He was smart and charming and warm. And sure of himself. She was sick to death of worrying about her restaurant and how risky the business was. It was nice to talk with a man who seemed not to worry about anything. He was confident about everything he had done in his life and who he was. When she forgot he was The Eater, Tilly relaxed into the feeling that the world was the way it should be, and, if she kept plugging away, everything would work out.

The waiter took their plates away and returned with cinnamon rolls packed tightly in foil. They got in Dan's car and drove the leftovers to his place.

She let the exotic, buttery spiciness of the cinnamon rolls filling the car overwhelm her reluctance about Dan and, for the first time in months, felt free of all her burdens. Her anxieties flapped in the wind with her hair and eventually blew out the window. She imagined them flying past the mansions on north Lake Shore Drive and over Lake Michigan, past the B'Hai temple, and far away.

CHAPTER SEVENTEEN

DAN'S TOWNHOME WAS tidier than it had been when she'd come here for an emergency shower, but it still had all the personality of a furniture-store window. His kitchen, on the other hand, was a dream.

"This is magnificent. Can I cook you dinner sometime in this kitchen?" Tilly ran her hand over the butcher block countertop next to the six-burner gas range. The butcher block was near the stove while the area around the sink was stainless steel. The island in the middle had a third type of surface, a large square of marble. To some, the kitchen would seem a hodgepodge of oversize appliances and mismatched countertops. To Tilly, it was heaven. Every surface had its purpose and every task had its own surface. She put her hand on the cool marble and imagined making chocolates and pies, the stone keeping the butter cold until her culinary masterpiece was finished.

Like a restaurant kitchen, nothing was hidden from view. Open shelving allowed easy access to all the pots and pans while utensils hung on racks within easy reach of the stove. And, while the rest of the apartment looked barely lived in, every shiny surface of the kitchen gleamed with life.

"My Realtor didn't believe when I bought this place that I did so for the kitchen," Dan said with obvious pride in the room. "The previous kitchen was a bland disaster of poor planning and even worse materials, but it was huge and I could imagine what it would become. I didn't feel any guilt when the first cabinet was ripped from the walls." He held out his hand and she took it. "Come see the pantry."

Tilly followed Dan into his pantry, which was bigger than her kitchen and filled with well-organized and interesting dry goods. She picked up a bag of organically grown beans from Idaho. "I thought you would be too busy eating at exotic locations to cook."

"I test recipes and I like to collect local and interesting foods as I travel, especially by small producers. I give a lot of it away to my friends, but—" he gestured to the pantry full of packages, cans and jars "—I can't seem to give it all away."

Dan smiled as he wrapped an arm around her waist and pulled her close. The plastic bean packaging crinkled between them. He took the bag from her hands and placed it back on the shelf, never once taking his eyes off hers.

Tilly's knees turned to softened butter. *Why this man, knees?*

"I've dreamed about you standing in your fridge at Babka, surrounded by all that cream and cheese." He tucked a strand of her hair behind her ear and ran a finger along the side of her chin.

The intensity of his blue eyes trapped her, and her breasts felt heavy with desire. She questioned the wisdom of her breasts, too, but she didn't pull away. Now was not the time to think about the intelligence of her actions. She just wanted to feel.

He leaned his head down until his lips brushed hers. "Just the thought of kissing my hot chef surrounded by all this food was enough to distract me from work, not to mention what I pictured every time I made my toast in the morning."

The soft touch of his lips sent hot shivers down her spine

until the butter in her knees melted into a pool on the floor. "Are you going to kiss me or just talk about it?"

Dan's phone sang in his pocket.

"Damn," he said as he pulled away to dig in his pockets. "It's my sister. She never calls unless it's important." He dropped a peck on her lips. "Stay like this, thinking the same thoughts, for a minute. I won't be long."

Tilly resumed peeking through Dan's collection of dry goods as she kept the same dirty, delicious thoughts in her head. She was examining a small jar of zucchini relish from some store in Iowa when Dan came back into the pantry, his face a tight mix of lust and frustration.

"Is your sister okay?"

"She apparently gave her boss the finger and is nearly in Chicago, looking for a place to sleep."

"Oh. Is that good or bad?"

"Good, because her boss is an asshole who will never see how wonderful she is for the company." Dan's near permanent smile withered away. "Bad, because her boss is also our father."

Mother Mary, the blessed virgin. "Do we need to cancel our date?"

Dan scowled. "No, she has a key. I told her I was on a date and wasn't going to be home. She said she didn't mind."

"Did she say it like she really didn't mind or like you would be the most awful person in the world if you weren't home?"

Dan chuckled, bringing back a bit of the twinkle to his eyes, though the sound was hollow. "I think the latter, but I'm going to risk it. If she did quit, I'm going to be busy with family problems all week. I'm not even sure I'll make it into Babka for a beer. I want to spend as much time with you as possible before any shit hitting the family fan splashes back on me. If we pack our dinner now, we can be gone before Beth gets here."

"Are you sure you don't need to be here for her?"

Dan grabbed her face tightly in his hands and kissed her, hard, as though he had to pack a week's worth of kissing into one brief second. "I'm sure. My dad will follow my sister to Chicago and I don't know when I'll see you again. Plus—" his smile was a little sad "—I promised I'd have you home early so you could work. Beth's arrival guarantees I do that."

DAN WAS DRIVING A BEAUTIFUL, vibrant woman up to one of his favorite Chicagoland destinations with a picnic basket of delicious food in the car and he couldn't think of a single thing to say. His only coherent thoughts alternated between joy that his sister was finally stepping out on her own and annoyance with her for doing it *today*. Couldn't she at least have waited until next week when she was coming down for a wedding?

But she had to choose the moment right before he was going to kiss Tilly. And having no place other than his townhome to escape to. And needing to escape in the first place.

He circled his jaw to loosen the tension in his face. This was a date, dammit. With a woman he wanted to spend time with. He needed to think of clever things to say, to get Tilly to look past the review. Instead, he was thinking about Beth.

"Tell me about your family," Tilly said quietly.

Dan looked over to see Tilly watching him with compassion etched on her face.

"You're obviously thinking of them," she said. "Talk to me."

"You know Meier Dairy." It wasn't a question. Everyone knew Meier Dairy.

"'Meier Means Dairy.'" She quoted the slogan from the packing on everything Meier made. "I grew up eating Meier grilled cheese at my best friend's house. Never at my house, because my grandmother didn't make such things."

"Meier does mean dairy." He smiled wryly at her. "It's a sad fact that not a single person in my family deals with cows anymore. My great-grandfather was a dairyman in Germany when he decided to move to the States. My family ran a small dairy farm until my father had the good fortune to marry a woman with money. He bought out the neighboring farms, sometimes through hostile takeovers worthy of a Hollywood movie, until he had enough head of cattle to stop selling his milk to distributors and cheese makers and to start making his own product."

To Dan Sr., food was a product. No love for the food, no heart, went into Meier cheese and dairy products. He could have as easily started a lumber company or a coal mine. His father had seen the future painted in cow shit on some whitewashed dairy wall and stepped into it until his entire world was colored brown.

"He foresaw Americans drinking less milk and bet my mother's money on dairy products. Cheese, yogurt, sour cream, etc." He shrugged. He could never decide if his father had been a genius or lucky. "He was right and it wasn't long before a Meier cheese sandwich was in every little kid's lunch box."

"And your sister worked for your father."

"More than worked for him, she's been running the company for at least five years." Dan couldn't keep the anger out of his voice at the injustice of it all. Beth was wonderful for Meier Dairy. She was as firm as their father in business negotiations, but had a better vision for the future.

Dan Sr. was still stuck in a world with only agribusiness; he couldn't see opportunity in the new world of farmer's markets and organic everything. "But he doesn't want to pass the family farm, such as it is, on to his daughter. He wants me to work for him. Has for years."

Beth slaved away for the man, even though every year Dan Sr. called his son and asked him if he was ready to take over. Every year Dan told his father to pass the company on to Beth and every year his father said the business needed a man's hand.

Before he had given up on the company forever, Dan had wanted nothing more than to run Meier Dairy. He had dreamed of being a part of steering his heritage into the future. He might still be interested in working for the family company, so long as his father wasn't breathing down his neck. It had occurred to Dan, if not to Beth, that the real reason their father wanted Dan to work for the company was not because he believed the company should be passed down the male line, but it was Dan Sr.'s excuse to keep his son where he felt he could control him.

"Why didn't you go work for your father?"

"You think I should?" he asked, surprised.

"Not now. You have a career you enjoy. I mean, after college, before you had made a name for yourself."

In a tiny apartment, before he'd either made money writing or reached the age of maturity for his trust fund, when he'd been eating ramen noodles for every meal so he would have enough money to pay for dinner at Chicago's finest restaurants for his articles, he'd thought about it. For about one minute. He was poor and alternating between feast and famine, but his father no longer loomed over him.

"My father's a hard man to please. He's hard on Beth and harder on me. My senior year of high school, I snapped and decided I didn't care anymore."

"What happened?"

Dan's hands gripped the steering wheel tightly, his knuckles turning white, as he thought about the day he told his father to go screw himself. He hoped Beth would be able to look back on her break with the family more calmly than he ever could.

"It seems so minor now, but I was seventeen years old when it happened. My dad wanted me to go to Iowa for college. They have the best wrestling program in the Big Ten, if not the country. I didn't make it. I did, however, get a scholarship for wrestling at Northwestern, which has a decent program and, more importantly to me, has a school of journalism. Instead of being proud at my acceptance into Medill and a scholarship, my father told me how disappointed he was because I didn't have what it took to be a Hawkeye."

Tilly's hand was warm as she squeezed his leg. Dan's hands relaxed on the wheel. "I told him he could wed and bed a Hawkeye himself if it mattered that much to him, but I didn't care any longer." Actually, he'd said something more foul, but he wasn't going to tell Tilly that.

"I'm sorry," she said simply, comfort and concern in her tone and in the pressure of her hand on his leg. "I would never want my family to fail me."

Dan lifted Tilly's hand and kissed it, before placing it back on his knee. "What's worse is that the way I wrestled in college would have easily gotten me a scholarship to Iowa. Without my father pointing out my every last fault, I wrestled because I enjoyed it and I was damn good at it. But I wasn't wrestling for Iowa and he never came to a single one of my matches."

Dan exited the freeway and followed the road to the Ravinia Festival parking lot among all the other cars of people with picnic baskets excited to sit on the lawn and listen to the Chicago Symphony Orchestra. As he looked to his right before turning, he saw a self-satisfied, Cheshire-cat grin on Tilly's face.

"You look like a cat in the cream."

"When we met at the Taste, I thought you had to be a wrestler. You looked—look—so much like Midwestern-farm-boy goodness. With your build…" Short is what she meant, wrestlers were on the shorter side of the athlete scale. "…and rolling, confident gait, I decided you had to be a wrestler."

"I still have my singlet," he said, waggling his eyebrows. "We can play dress-up and I can wrestle you to the ground."

"Probably not until your sister leaves."

"We can play dress-up at your house and I can seduce the hot chef out of her chef's uniform. We can probably find a naughty chef's uniform on the internet if we search hard enough. A chef's jacket and those red polka-dot undies would be costume enough for me," he said, gratified when she blushed.

The car bumped along the parking lot and Dan found a spot.

"Will your dad try to talk your sister into coming back to Meier Dairy?"

"No more discussion of my family and their upcoming implosion while we're here. Let's enjoy the music."

CHAPTER EIGHTEEN

DAN AND TILLY carried their baskets through the gates and onto the lawn, where they found a place for their blanket between a group of retirees with an extravagant picnic—the full Ravinia spread—and a group of college students with what smelled like Harold's Chicken Shack. The older group had set roasted chicken, ham, salads and a tier of cupcakes on their rollup table in a bag while they toasted someone's birthday with champagne in flutes.

Dan laughed as he looked from the retirees to the college students with their greasy sacks of fried chicken, fries and white bread, all covered in sweet barbecue sauce. "I think between these two is right where we belong."

The smaller basket held plates, napkins, cups, a heavy loaf of crusty bread, a bottle of *cava* wrapped in an ice pack and towels to keep it chilled, and one bottle of sherry. The second basket was brimming with small containers filled with many different kinds of food.

"Tapas," Dan explained as he placed container after container on the blanket. "Tangerine-marinated olives and Romesco sauce." Two more containers were added to the blanket. "*Bacalao* hash and marinated sardines. Tortilla, cantaloupe wrapped in Serrano ham, dates stuffed with Marcona almonds and, lastly…" Dan pulled the last container out of the basket and set it on the blanket. "…a selection of Spanish cheese and chorizo."

"I'm going to be so full I'll sleep through the concert."

"You packed me delicious lunches every day for two weeks, the least I could do was plan a picnic. Besides," he said, popping a date into his mouth. "I have a hot chef to impress. Here." He speared a piece of juicy, orange cantaloupe wrapped in the salty cured ham and offered it to her. "I won't bother you if you sleep through Brahms, but I'm waking you up for Beethoven."

Tilly closed her eyes as she edged the cantaloupe off the fork with her tongue and teeth. She chewed, pure bliss on her face, and Dan desperately wished his sister hadn't called. Standing in his pantry, he could have put that expression on her face. Had dreamed of putting that expression on her face.

The strategic part of him knew sex too early would be a bad idea. Tilly was already skittish about their relationship and she wasn't the type to believe sex cemented them together. She was more likely to see it as a ploy to win her trust. The strategic part of him was relieved his sister had called and provided an excuse to break apart. The rest of him needed release.

Loud laughter came from the retirees. They'd drunk too much champagne for four in the afternoon and were telling dirty jokes. The college students who had previously been looking longingly at the cupcakes were now a part of the rowdy crowd and providing their own jokes in exchange for glasses of champagne.

"Scoot closer to me and we can talk a little more privately while we finish our dinner."

Tilly crawled on the blanket over to Dan and he put his arms around her. They sat silently, the noises of other symphony goers in the background as they fed each other bits and bites of tapas.

Warm from the sherry and the sun, Dan asked the question he had been pondering since brunch. "You said your grandmother left you money to open the restaurant when she died. Where did it come from?"

Her hair brushed against his bare biceps, stirring the warmth from his stomach to his toes as she lifted her puzzled face up to his.

"It's a personal question, I know, but opening a restaurant is an expensive endeavor and I don't imagine Healthy Food made your grandparents wealthy."

"You don't know?" Tilly asked softly, her brows still furrowed. "Everyone knows."

"Knows what?"

"Twenty-two years ago, the driver of a brewing-company truck was drunk when he slammed into the back of my dad, grandfather and brother on the Kennedy." Her voice was flat and her body tense against him as she talked. "They were coming home from Leon's hockey game."

Dan remembered. Not the accident, though it had probably made the news in Wisconsin, but the fallout. The driver had a history of DWIs and had still managed to renew his license after a hefty bribe made by the trucking company. Years later, Dan's first year of college, the scandal was still creeping up the political hierarchy until several key state government employees were resigning in handcuffs. The Mileks weren't the only family struck by tragedy as a result of the bribe scheme. A family in Wisconsin lost all six of their children in another horrible accident. Pundits and writers could joke about corruption in the great state of Illinois, but those involved had cost a family the lives of their children and the Mileks nearly half their family.

"Babunia never touched a penny of the insurance money. 'Blood money,' she called it. She set it aside for each one of her grandchildren to use so we could live a life Leon never could. She wanted us to live our dreams. Babka is my dream."

Dan kissed the top of Tilly's silky hair while her story flooded over him and with it came the surging realization that he'd made a grievous error. For him, the review had been a mild release after his mother's terrible birthday dinner and the fiasco that passed for family bonding to the Meiers. So what if he was supposed to visit a restaurant at least three times before he wrote anything? One review, one restaurant, in the course of his career was nothing. A blip, soon to be buried amid the other content on *CarpeChicago*.

Babka was Tilly's life and her connection to her grandmother, while also being a legacy for three lost family members. He'd made that legacy the laughingstock of Chicago and, when she'd questioned him about it, had given her some stupid lecture on separating business and personal. In her professionalism, she'd never once questioned the fact of the negative review, only that he'd written the review after eating at Babka once, and on a night that was clearly out of the ordinary.

In response, Dan had applied a lesson learned from eighteen years living under his father's roof. Instead of admitting he was wrong and accepting the fallout, Dan had tried to manipulate Tilly's emotions until she was willing to risk a relationship without his having to face his culpability. He'd had the ability to help fix the damage he'd caused and he'd let his experience with his father control his actions, even as he pretended to be free of the man.

He'd marveled at the generosity of women when wondering how Shane and his inane humor had a girlfriend—but why was Tilly even sitting next to him? She couldn't have forgiven him, because he'd been too stupid to notice he'd done anything that needed forgiveness and too selfish to apologize even if he had noticed. He'd credited her willingness to see him again to his smile and charm, but that was bullshit. Their connection went deeper than charm. Their strengths complemented each other and they understood each other's passions, but was that enough for her to share more than a meal with him?

At least he hoped she'd said yes to the date because of an emotional link binding the two of them together. When he'd asked her on a date, he'd been afraid she'd say no. Now he had no idea why she said yes. If her presence on his blanket, drinking his sherry, was due to his successful manipulations rather than an actual connection she felt for him, he would never forgive himself.

He had to fix the mistake he had made with the review. The bullshit he had been telling himself about the power of a reviewer's voice being deadened by a correction was just that—bullshit. He wasn't ten years old and needing his father's approval anymore. Tilly's good opinion was worth far more, if he was lucky enough to keep it.

Whether or not she forgave him, or even acknowledged his existence, he owed her the power of his voice to get people back in her restaurant. Tilly didn't deserve a corrected review because of her story, but because he'd violated all the rules of critiquing he'd previously held dear. Chicago *wanted* to eat in her restaurant. All they needed was a push.

He wasn't God or the fates, but he was a big name in the food business. The Eater could drive people to an unknown restaurant or dissuade people from a well-known one. His words, written in anger at the situation and not even at Tilly, had extended a tragedy in her life. Authenticity of The Eater or not, Dan had a moral obligation to repair the damage he'd done.

"I'm sorry," Dan whispered, though the powerful stringed opening of Brahms's "Hungarian Dance Number 5" drowned out his words.

CHAPTER NINETEEN

DAN PULLED HIS car into a space in front of Tilly's apartment building and she stirred slightly in her sleep. He got out of the car and walked around to open the passenger door.

"Wake up, sleepyhead," he said, unbuckling her seat belt.

"Are we back already?" She yawned and stretched.

"Already?"

Tilly had fallen asleep the instant they pulled out of the parking lot, her head flopped over against the window and soft snores coming from her mouth. With the traffic from Ravinia, she had been asleep for almost an hour.

She rubbed her eyes. "I love sleeping in the car." She laughed softly. "I'm like a baby, the slightest bit of movement and I'm out like a light."

He reached down and scooped Tilly up into his arms, swinging her out of the car and slamming the door behind them with his foot. "I will drive you around Chicago every night so you can fall asleep. I won't even wake you up when we get home." He spoke the words as if they were living together, as if saying such things could make them true. "And I'll carry you to bed. Now, where are your keys? I have to get back to my sister but I'll provide door-to-bed service for you."

"Don't be silly." She squirmed and Dan let her down. She stuck her key in the door and turned to face him. "Thank you for everything today. I had a wonderful time."

"We're not saying goodbye yet. I said door-to-bed service and, even if you don't take me up on that, I'd rather not kiss you on the stoop."

Her smile was answer enough.

DAN TOOK HER HAND as he followed her up the stairs to her apartment. His thumb traced small circles on her palm and anticipation shivered up her arm. The desire she felt pushed away the last of her sleepiness. She fumbled with her key in the lock, distracted by Dan's hand, which was burning her skin as he traced a line up her arm to her neck.

"Blue hair makes your skin glow and I think of every sandy beach that ever warmed my skin and cool ocean wave I've ever wanted to plunge myself into," he whispered against her neck before lightly kissing the sensitive area beneath her ear. Tilly twitched with a burst of sensation and the lock popped open. Dan reached around, his body hard against her, and opened the door. As soon as the door shut behind them, Dan's mouth came down on Tilly's, awakening a hunger she'd previously associated only with food.

His lips were soft and still tasted subtly of cinnamon and sherry, but there was nothing soft about the kiss. His body molded to her, one arm around her waist, the other holding her face as though she might escape at any moment. She slid her hands along the smooth skin of his abdomen under his shirt and around to the strength of his back. She deepened the kiss, exploring the ridges of his teeth with her tongue and pushing her hips against his, his desire for her unmistakable.

"Tilly…" He pulled his mouth away from hers, his eyes half-closed with desire. "How did I manage to find you in the crowds at the Taste?"

Like a bucket of ice water, the reference jolted her back to reality. Wine, good food, sun and beautiful music had lulled her into a world where he was just Dan Meier, not also The Eater. She stepped back. "I'm sorry. I can't do this."

Heavens, but she wanted to.

He reached for her, his face stricken. "I can fix the review."

She stepped away from temptation and the fantasyland their relationship existed in to put her hand on the door. "It's too late. Even if you write a new review, I'll always wonder—did you fix it because you wanted to or because you wanted me?"

Her hand hit the doorknob. The door creaked as she opened it, but not loudly enough to hide the sound of her coming tears.

"A chance…" he protested.

She wouldn't cry. She worked in a man's business and there was no room for tears. "That's what today was. And you have your sister to comfort."

"Who'll comfort you?"

"I don't need comforting in my decision." She pulled the door open, firm in her resolve.

"I'm going to keep coming by Babka."

"I won't bar you." He reached out for her again, but she sidestepped the risk of his touch and pulled the door wide open. She didn't look at him. "But I think you need to leave now."

The last thing she saw before she shut the door was Dan standing on the building's stairs, his bright blue eyes wet with tears. She closed the door before she could change her mind.

DAN'S CURSING AND the heavy thump of his footsteps reverberated around his mind as he went quickly down the flights of stairs to the street. He'd been so certain he was right about sticking to his opinion, but something in his feelings for Tilly had changed when she'd talked about the insurance money and living her dreams. He'd stopped thinking about a relationship with Tilly as a "what-if" and started thinking about her has a "had-to-be." It wasn't fair. Just as he was ready to beg her to let him make it up to her, in bed, on the blog, shouting from the Willis Tower, if that's what it took, she decided he wasn't worth it.

I'll always wonder. Did you fix the review because you wanted to or because you wanted me?

He stopped, his hand on the inside door of the apartment foyer. He could turn around. She still wanted him. The thin cotton of her dress hadn't been enough to hide her hard nipples, even as she was holding the door open and telling him to leave. He could push his case, touch her, force her body to overcome the objections of her mind. Manipulation was in his blood. He was his father's son.

But despite what Mike insinuated, he wasn't that much of a scumbag. He was close, but close only counted in horseshoes and hand grenades. Fortunately for him, this was neither.

He wasn't looking for a night of sex. One night was no good, unless she kept wanting to have sex with him, again and again. Forever. With food involved. Long walks on the beach. Sunset drives, walks on the beach and every other sappy relationship thing he could think of.

Showing up at her door empty-handed would win him a short-term goal, but she would wake up the next morning and question his motivations. He needed to convince her mind, body and soul that he understood her hurt and accepted responsibility.

He depressed the door handle and exited the apartment building. The outside door slammed with a bang.

Dan grimaced as he closed his car door. He needed to

figure out how to keep Tilly talking to him. She wouldn't have sex with him if she wasn't talking to him. And, if he had to choose, he'd rather the talking than the sex. He wanted both, but he'd put himself in a position where he might not get either.

Meiers don't make mistakes. Meiers make cheese. Mike's mocking voice bounced around the inside of the car, giving him a headache. He'd scoffed at the comment but it was true. Dan Sr. was unforgiving of mistakes, no matter how small. A single dropped ice cream cone made a five-year-old a klutz, and Dan Sr. had punished his son by not attending a year's worth of wrestling matches after one serious goof when Dan was twelve.

Daniel Jacob Meier Sr. was an ass of historical proportions. Dan's car started in agreement before he sped down the side streets back to his house. His parents' relationship had been daily proof of what a relationship based on judgmental comments and emotional manipulation looked like. He'd told himself repeatedly that he wasn't like his father and, when the chips were all out on the table, he wasn't. It hadn't been luck that Dan Sr. had married a woman with money; he'd seduced and impregnated her as an investment opportunity, not a moral in sight. If his wife and family had suffered from it, well, Dan Sr. didn't consider anything he did to be a mistake. Dan Jr. at least knew when he'd messed up, even if he was late to the parade.

And what he'd done to Tilly was the single biggest mistake of his life.

With Beth's phone call that afternoon, Dan had been able to put two and two together and realize why he had been so hard on Babka. At Babka, his dinner with his mom ruined, he'd seen red. But he hadn't been angry at Babka, he'd been angry at what his mother had been telling him. Beth had offered to get married and start having kids. Surely she'd have a boy sometime and Dan Sr. could pass the company on to his grandson. Dan Sr. had said he'd think about it. While his mother had been telling him all of this, his father had sent him a text message offering him the company again.

His old man couldn't be thinking too hard about Beth's offer if he'd texted his son a job offer. While his mom complained about her ruined dress and the fight between her daughter and husband, Dan had heard his father's voice booming in his head. The part of Dan that was just like his father, the part he tried to pretend didn't exist, had taken over and written a nasty review. Even without the family problems, his first dinner at Babka would've been horrible, but he would've gone back at least twice before writing the review.

After the one night, he should've written about how Tilly and her staff had handled a ridiculous situation quickly and efficiently. A cat had gotten in her restaurant. Unusual, but not unheard of. Cats were sneaky creatures with amazing abilities to worm themselves in where they weren't welcome.

A customer had brought a dog in. Bad form on the part of the customer, but the dog had been tiny and Tilly was in the kitchen. It would have been impossible for Tilly to know about the dog and hard for her staff to notice. And when disaster struck, Tilly had handled the restaurant, her customers and her staff like a pro. Even the salty food was understandable, if Dan was right about someone purposely wrecking Tilly's plumbing. If she had a saboteur and he had been recognized… He didn't even have to be recognized as The Eater for a saboteur to oversalt his food. That person only had to recognize him as Dan Meier, food writer.

No, the glaring mistake in this entire episode was that Dan Meier, part of the no-mistake Meier family, had made a mistake. He could continue to insist that dining was an experience and that the bad time he'd had at Babka meant Tilly deserved the bad review, but his reasoning was worth a pound of manure to a city boy. Not once since that fateful night had he seen anything about Babka to give him doubts about the restaurant and Tilly's capability. And worse, he'd probably have seen his mistake earlier, if he hadn't had a conversation with Dan Sr. about a reporter retracting a story. Either he or Beth completely escaping his father was a fantasy.

Even if he removed his desire for Tilly from the equation, had he returned to Babka at least twice more before writing the review—the way he should have—and been served the kind of food he'd been eating for lunch and the kind of service he had seen provided, he would have written a glowing review. He might have mentioned the cat incident in his review, but mostly to laugh the scene off as an amusing story highlighting what a professional Tila Milek was.

Dan parked his car behind his sister's impractical MINI.

Inside, every light in his townhome was on and the TV was blaring a Brewers/Cubs game, but Beth was sound asleep on the couch. Whatever fight Beth had had with their father had to have been terrible.

But family problems weren't what occupied his mind. Instead of thinking about Beth and his father, Dan was hoping to God Tilly would forgive him.

CHAPTER TWENTY

TILLY'S BUTT HAD just hit the seat of an armchair and she had set her tea on an end table next to a box of tissues when the buzzer to her apartment rang. She looked hard at the intercom, wondering who it was and if she should answer it. She should sleep. Or work. Or something other than sit on a chair with a cup of tea and cry.

But nothing else was going to happen. She was too keyed up with emotion to sleep and too exhausted to work. The worst of both worlds. At least she wouldn't have to worry about Dan's presence interfering with her concentration at work anymore.

The buzzer rang again and Imbir stuck his head out of the bathroom, where he liked to sleep in the sink, to see what noise was disturbing his beauty rest. After her cat gave both her and the buzzer a dirty look, Tilly struggled out of her chair and depressed the call button.

With her luck stuck on bad, Tilly wasn't certain what to expect. It would be fitting if the person ringing the bell was a burglar making sure no one was home before they tore apart her apartment looking for jewelry she didn't have. A robbery would certainly give her something other than Dan to think about. Or maybe her luck was changing and it was Publishers Clearing House with her millions. An oversize check would also give her something other than Dan to think about.

Who was she kidding? Today wasn't going to end her

nonstop thoughts about Dan; it was only going to make them sadder.

"Who is it?"

"It's me. I saw your light was on." Renia's voice crackled through the intercom. "I've had a rotten day, let me up."

Tilly pushed the door buzzer to let Renia through. How rotten could her day have been? Her business was successful and she hadn't just dumped the only man she'd ever really been interested in. Or had to worry about a saboteur, if Tilly's theories about the ongoing problems at Babka were right.

Cracking the door open for her sister, Tilly went back into her kitchen to pour another cup of tea. She was adding sugar and milk when Renia walked in, looking as fresh and snug as a well-made bed in her pearl-gray pantsuit with her hair up in a tight bun, not a wisp in sight. Tilly sighed. After a long day outside, her hair was stringy and matted and she had a spot of red Romesco sauce on her yellow dress she hadn't noticed until after Dan left. It probably matched her bloodshot eyes and she could pretend she was color coordinated.

Renia walked into her single room and they sank in unison into Tilly's armchairs.

"So, why was your day so bad?" Maybe it would make her feel better to know her perfect sister had problems, too.

She let her mind kick her brain for even thinking such a thing. She didn't want her sister to have a bad day, but she'd had so many recently it was hard to remember other people had them, too.

"No wedding." Renia put her cup on the end table to rub the bridge of her nose.

"What do you mean no wedding? If there wasn't a wedding, why are you still in your work clothes?"

Renia sank back into the cushions, her words buried in

the hands over her face. "Well, first the groom showed up drunk. Not hungover—drunk. Pissed. Pickled. Wasted. If I could think of more terms I would. He was as drunk as a skunk."

"That doesn't sound so bad."

An eye peered out at her from Renia's manicured hand, a perfectly done French manicure without a chip in sight. *How does she do it?*

"I mean it doesn't sound great, but it could be worse." Tilly tried to sound helpful.

"I'm not done." Renia dragged her hands over her face, stretching her skin down the otherwise perfect facade. "The best man was too drunk to hold him up. Then the bride was late walking down the aisle. I would love to say she looked like a dream, but she was more of a nightmare. Her eyes were puffy and red, her hair had fallen out of its updo and she had hot-pink lipstick stains on her dress."

"How'd the lipstick get on her dress?" The rest of it was mostly understandable given a drunk groom, but the dress?

"Ah, yes." Renia squeezed the bridge of her nose again. "Well, the groom had taken her dress to his bachelor party and the lipstick stains were from the call girl his best man paid for. Later I heard something from her maid of honor about the bride wanting the groom to face his crime."

"Okay. That's bad."

"Oh, I'm not done." Renia collapsed against the back of the chair in an elegant sprawl. "The bride walked down the aisle with the lipstick all over her dress, the groom at the altar swaying to and fro, with the rabbi having to stabilize him every few swerves. It was completely ridiculous."

"And everyone was going to go through with this?" What rabbi would let a couple get married when one of them was obviously drunk?

"I was wondering the same thing, trying to decide if I

should take photos or not, when the bride got a whiff of her groom at the altar. She got so mad she tossed her bouquet at him and then ran back down the aisle."

"I'm still wondering why you didn't get off work until now. When did the wedding start?"

"Five. It was supposed to be a beautiful afternoon ceremony outside. The bride was about an hour late getting down the aisle before this mess broke loose. Not only did she run off but the best man took off after her calling, 'I told you he would hurt you like this. I would never do this to you.' I was stuck with the groom, who alternated between crying and trying to kiss me." Renia leaned her head back against the chair and talked to the ceiling. "He smelled like Chanel No. 5."

And she still looked perfect after her horrible night. Tilly couldn't look perfect ten seconds after she dressed and put on her makeup. "Where was his family when he needed to be consoled?"

"They were yelling at the bride's parents over who was going to pay for the fiasco. The bride's parents said it was the groom's fault since the groom slept with someone the night before and the groom's parents said it was the bride's fault since she ran off."

"Why did you come over here, then? I would've gone straight to bed."

"I knew you would make me feel better. You'd still be up, probably having a cup of tea, and you might even have news that would remind me my day could have been worse."

Any other night Tilly could've shrugged off her sister's comments, but tonight she just held back tears.

"Oh, Tills, I didn't mean that the way it sounded. I meant, at least my career setbacks are private, not splashed all over the papers and posted on Twitter. I'm here—why don't you tell me about your day?"

"There's nothing to talk about." *Liar. You're still mad about Renia's comment.*

"Then why are your eyes bloodshot?"

"I've decided work and romance don't mix after all."

Renia squeezed into the chair with Tilly and put an arm around her. "I think there's something you're not telling me, but I won't push you. Why don't we sit here and drink our tea. We can wallow in our own bad moods together." Renia let her sister go and sat in her own chair.

They sat together, silent except for the slurps of tea before Tilly spoke up. "I had a date today."

"What?" Renia's full attention had turned now to Tilly. "With The Eater?" She looked intently at Tilly, shock mixed with curiosity on her face.

"You don't have to look so surprised he would ask me out."

"Oh, Tills, I'm not surprised a man wants to date you. I'm surprised you said yes. He was clearly interested in you at the demo. I watched him and he didn't take his eyes off you, not once. Your food looked good, but I think he wanted *you* served up on a platter, not the pierogi. Is he going to write another, fairer review?"

"Even if he did, what would it matter?" The tears she had been saving to enjoy alone came through in a flood. "How would I know he was being truthful and not just writing it because he liked my underwear?"

"When did he see your underwear? No, never mind. Tell me everything. Don't leave anything out this time."

Tilly began to talk because she needed to and because sisters were there to listen. At the end of her long story about men, cats, restaurant reviewers and toupees, Tilly held out her hand for her sister to take. Renia gave it a squeeze and didn't let go.

"My life was fine until Imbir nearly ruined my restaurant. I know I'm often a klutz and I seem out of control, especially when compared to you, but I knew where I was at Babka." She sniffed and tried to get control of her voice. "My food was excellent. My staff, kitchen and front-of-house worked together like a team. We had regular customers. I was busy. Now I'm a bit lost at Babka. A restaurant fails when its chef begins to doubt. It's like throwing chum in shark-infested waters. The food is still excellent and the staff are still working together, but the customers aren't as regular. I'm still busy, but a lot of it is being busy with worry, and I wish Dan was a different person. No, I wish he was the same person—I just wish he hadn't written a review I can't get past."

Renia's thumb stroked the back of Tilly's hand and she sighed with release. She needed to get all this emotion and pent-up anxiety out to someone who would listen and care.

"The worst part is that I worry I'm betraying Babunia when I wish Dan could be in my life. She was the only person who believed in my dream. What does it mean about my respect for her legacy if part of me wants to throw it all away for a man who might not believe in me?"

"Tills, Babunia wasn't the only person who believed in you. Mom was, well, she had her own problems after Dad, Leon and Dziadunio died." Neither of them mentioned the years after the accident that Renia had spent trying to be the wildest teenager in Chicago and her eventual exile to Cincinnati, though the thought of them weighed heavily on both their minds. Renia never allowed talk of her past mistakes. The moment of silence and Renia's stopped hand on Tilly's spoke for itself. "Maybe Dan can do something to show you that he's for real. But if he can't, you've given a relationship and a job a try together. Maybe it'll work next time, with someone else."

Tilly wanted it to be this time, with Dan, but she only said, "When did you get to be so smart?"

"I spent an afternoon fending off a drunk groom's advances at the remains of his own wedding. Those who can, do. Those who can't, lecture their sisters."

They both laughed and Tilly sat up, strengthened by her sister's faith in her.

"You liked him a lot," Renia said with a long look at Tilly.

"I did. When I'm with him and I can forget he's The Eater, I feel as if the romance, the restaurant and anything else I want to do are within my reach. I'm superwoman when I'm with him. He looks at me and I feel powerful." Tilly bit her lip, unable to put all of her feelings into words. Her heart swelled when she saw him until she wasn't certain if it would fit into her chest and her body grew tingly at the thought of seeing him.

Was it love?

Then she thought about the unwarranted review and Dan's stupid argument about business and personal and she wanted to throw something. Love wasn't supposed to betray her.

She humphed when Imbir jumped onto her lap. He did a couple of circles and tested her thighs for comfort before lying down. The ginger tabby knew he was loved. She'd been prepared to make cat stew out of him after she'd caught him at Babka, but when she'd gotten to the vet's to pay the bill, he was cleaned up, fed and purring as he rubbed his face against the cage. Now she didn't know how she'd lived without him. He was company, always willing to hear her complaints and ideas, and he never argued if she kept the apartment cold. He bit her if she didn't feed him quickly enough, but she understood the importance of food and eating. Sadly, so did Dan.

CHAPTER TWENTY-ONE

By the time Dan woke up, Beth was gone. She'd left a note saying she was looking for an apartment and expected him to take her to a great place for dinner. She was always a reliable dinner date for a review. He knew people who shared his love of food, and there were others whose company he enjoyed for long hours over dinner, but not many enjoyed eating dinner with him the way Beth did. Some enjoyed the experience, but he couldn't always avoid the coward who looked around the Chinese restaurant at the exquisite dishes of glazed pork belly, smoked duck tongue, whole fish glistening with ginger, and plates of barely cooked Chinese vegetables and wondered where the chow mein was.

His sister would try anything and he valued her opinion. If she was moving to Chicago permanently, Beth could be his Tuesday to Saturday date and he'd save some of the special places for Tilly on Sunday and Monday nights.

After a cup of coffee and toast with a ginger-peach jam, Dan turned on the hot water in his guest bathroom and stepped under the spray. Stupid, but he wanted to shower where he knew Tilly had been.

The water washed over him and with it a new thought. Rich might fire him from writing for *CarpeChicago* over this. It was unlikely, but possible. Rich valued integrity and journalistic ethics—both traits Dan had stepped on since his aborted dinner at Babka—but he also valued the popularity of the blog. The review post had triggered enough discussion that Rich had closed comments, and the one with his dish of crow was certain to get more hits. Rich might forgive his mistake if the hits were high enough.

Out of the shower, water dripping onto the bath mat, Dan dried off and wondered if he cared more about the *CarpeChicago* gig or freelance writing. He enjoyed the freedom from schedule and the adventure of his job, but the constant pressure to be critical might have turned him into a faultfinding jerk.

He didn't need the money. Meiers might make cheese, but they made a lot of cheese. "Meier Means Dairy" was stamped on bricks of cheddar from coast to coast and he also had the money he'd inherited from his grandparents.

Dan Sr. might be a father figure only a psychopath could look up to, but he wasn't stupid. He'd been the son of a small-time dairy farmer who'd married into money, turning it into a fortune of dairy products from cheese to ice cream. The man was even talking about sponsoring a stock car racer, although Dan didn't see how the sponsorship would last past the driver's first wreck. Dan Sr. would never understand wrecks were part of the sport.

But the man could make money and Dan had benefited from it. Neither he nor his sister had to work if they didn't want to. It wasn't as heartwarming as a dad cheering proudly in the crowds, but it was reliable and useful. The money would hold him until he discovered what else he wanted to do with his life besides traveling, eating and critiquing other people's lifework.

Have I already decided to quit, even if Rich doesn't fire me?

This was something to talk over with his sister when they met for dinner. Especially since Beth had recently changed jobs herself. Dan wasn't sure what he would do if he wasn't writing about food, but he sure as hell didn't want to take over the family business.

"WELL, DAN, THIS will be a first for me. I've never had Korean food," Beth said as she snapped open the menu. "I don't know why I'm even looking at this. I'm sure you'll tell me what to order."

"I've never been here before, so order whatever you want. If I want you to order more, I'll tell you. They have Korean barbecue we can make tableside, but I want to wait until we have at least a group of four."

Bath set her menu down on the table, closed her eyes and let her finger fall. "Looks like I'm having 'classic bibimbop.' It's hot outside, but I'm curious about the hot stone pot."

"That's what I was going to have, but I won't argue with fate. My second option was kimchi stew."

His sister raised a brow. "Adventurous food critic staying in safe territory?"

"It will give me a chance to try the Korean classics people know before venturing into the more unusual dishes."

When the waitress stopped at their table, Dan ordered the stew, along with kimchi dumplings and sesame noodles to share. The waitress collected their menus and returned with their *banchan,* small Korean side dishes including kimchi, sprouts, cucumber and a couple of things Dan didn't recognize immediately.

"What's this?" Beth asked, holding up a small, dried fish in her chopsticks.

"A piece of dried fish."

"Not helpful." The fish wiggled as she shook it at him in admonishment. "Before I put this in my mouth, what should I know about Korean food?"

"It's spicy, garlicky and makes heavy use of fermentation in traditional dishes like kimchi."

Beth looked the bite-size fish in the eye, shrugged, then popped it in her mouth. Dan smiled. Fearlessness was one of his favorite things about his older sister.

"Spicy and crunchy. This would be good with beer."

"Order some, then." Dan put a strip of something white into his mouth and chewed. "Potatoes." He pointed at the small bowl with his chopsticks. "Cooked with garlic, onion and sesame oil."

Beth poked through the kimchi before finding the piece she wanted. "This is interesting. I wasn't sure I'd like anything you described as 'fermented,' but it's pretty tasty." She took another piece. "And addictive."

"Of course it's tasty. Do I take you to bad restaurants?"

"Yes. Mike and I are your guinea pigs. I've been to some terrible places with you." Dan smiled apologetically and Beth laughed. "Don't try that smile on me. I'm your sister and immune to your charms."

"It was worth a shot." Dan plucked a piece of shiny cucumber with his chopsticks and stuck it in his mouth. A sharp, vinegary bite, with a little sesame oil. "Find a new job or apartment yet?"

"I'm not even looking."

Dan raised his eyebrow.

"For a job. I'm looking for an apartment. I won't be camped out at your townhome forever, I promise. Living with your younger brother sounds even lamer than working for your father. Oh, and when I move I'm taking those towels in your guest bathroom with me. I don't think you appreciate them. Or the potpourri."

"Why no new job?"

"Well…" Beth put another piece of kimchi in her mouth—a stalling tactic if Dan had ever seen one. If his fearless sister was hesitating, she wanted something from him. She chewed and swallowed, then looked at the small dishes scattered across the table. "I'm thinking of starting my own company."

Dan raised the other eyebrow but didn't say anything. The waitress brought out their appetizers and Beth took the opportunity to sample a mouthful of sesame noodles. Another stall. She must want something big.

"I know a lot about the food business. Not only about dairy products, but about the business in general," she said.

He nodded in agreement.

"And you know a lot about food, so…I was thinking maybe we could go into business together."

"Doing what?" Dan speared a dumpling and dunked it into the dipping sauce before sticking it in his mouth. The salty flavor of the soy sauce exploded in his mouth, followed by the spicy garlic of kimchi all wrapped in a chewy dough fried crisp on the bottom. He filed through his memories of tastes, comparing it to other Asian dumplings he'd had as well as past experiences with Korean food. The dough was maybe a little soggy and the crisp bottom seemed more like a pot sticker than a traditional Korean dumpling, but he couldn't fault the taste.

"I don't know how you find them, but you always discover small, family-run food companies making, growing or producing something amazing. Things you can't find in the grocery store and won't find in Williams-Sonoma for another ten years. Like those beans grown in Idaho or those pork-fat fried potato chips from Pennsylvania."

Dan paused to swallow his bite of sesame noodles before he answered his sister. "What's your point?" he asked, more curious now than suspicious.

"Where do you find those companies?"

He shrugged. "I meet a lot of people when I'm traveling and I hand out a lot of business cards. People mail me things. I troll online food message boards and read newspaper food sections. I stop in every mom-and-pop store I see. Occasionally, I write about a product or an ingredient and I want to know all the available options, either from a larger company or a smaller one."

"How would you like to sell those finds?"

Their waitress removed the appetizer dishes. She returned shortly with steaming stone bowls for each of them. Dan leaned over his bowl, taking a deep breath full of the rich, peppery vapor. Chunks of tofu, slivers of beef and slices of kimchi floated in a fiery beef broth. He shivered. It may be summer outside but the restaurant was over-air-conditioned and he was looking forward to his first warming bite.

Beth looked down at her bowl. "How do I eat it?"

"With chopsticks."

"Are you twelve?"

Dan chuckled. She was so easy to annoy. He pushed a bowl of brick red chili sauce toward her. "Add as much of that as you want. If you break up the egg yolk, it will make a sauce to coat the beef and vegetables. The stone pot makes the rice at the bottom crunchy. If you don't like it, I'll eat it."

She wrapped her arms around her bowl, leaving plenty of space between the hot stone and her bare skin, and glared at him. "This smells delicious and I'm not letting you have any of it. If you want to some, you will have to come back and order it yourself."

They enjoyed their meals in silence. Beth's idea had merit. She wanted to use her knowledge of the food business and his knowledge of food to create an online store selling specialty items from small producers and growers.

Dan did make a lot of food finds and many of the small producers were interested in finding a larger market for their products but didn't have the inclination, time or money to do more than run a small website and peddle their products at a local grocery store.

"What about the competition? There are already online stores like you're talking about."

"I don't want us to be the first. I want us to be the best."

"Okay. Why would some local beef farmer trust two Meier kids with their product? Dad remembers the buyouts of the eighties with fondness because he managed to build a dairy empire out of the mess, but many people in the beef industry think we're little better than carpetbaggers. Dad may think Meier means dairy, but to lots of smaller producers, Meier mostly means industrial food business and the death of the family farm."

"This is where I think we could succeed." She pointed a chopstick at him with a bit of pickled carrot clinging to the tip. "I know local producers are suspicious of large food companies, but large food companies like Meier Dairy are profitable because they've developed efficiencies over time to keep their prices low. Some of those efficiencies are because of the scale of the company, but some of them could be adopted by smaller producers. If they sell online exclusively with us, they get the benefit of my business knowledge to help them lower the cost of their goods. As they lower the cost of their goods, both the producer and my company can share in the profits."

Dan let a big piece of silky tofu smooth over his tongue and cool the wallop of garlic from the kimchi while he mulled over her proposal. Beth's pitch was fate. He had been thinking about what he would do if he didn't write and he liked the idea of an online store. He loved traveling, eating and discovering interesting people and businesses more than he liked the writing. While there were many articles he was proud of, most of them were just a way to pay the bills.

Even reviewing wasn't as interesting anymore. He had written his share of bad reviews, including the one of Babka, but he preferred to write positive reviews. A negative review carried a sick rush, but no satisfaction. For satisfaction, he needed to write a glowing review of a restaurant he couldn't wait for the city to discover. Finding a small restaurant, maybe a hole-in-the-wall ethnic place or a chef starting out, and introducing them to Chicago was why he had agreed to write for *CarpeChicago*.

Bad reviews were part of the business. When he wrote for *CarpeChicago,* it was his responsibility to spend money at a restaurant so their readers didn't waste theirs. For some restaurants he had even savored typing in *CarpeChicago*'s web address and seeing a deserving dump skewered in cyberspace. Hell, he had enjoyed Babka's terrible review until Tilly had spilled a beer on his shirt.

Knowing Tilly had soured him on bad reviews. She was one-of-a-kind, but how many of those restaurants he'd burned had deserved one more chance? Not all of them, surely, but just as surely some of them had. He couldn't review without writing bad ones. They were a necessary part of the business. No one trusted a perpetually pleased critic. If he couldn't stomach the bad reviews anymore, or alternatively, enjoyed them too much, maybe it was time to get out of the business.

Beth's online store would give him the opportunity to write only glowing reviews. His job would be to find those producers he couldn't wait to present to the world. Instead of contributing to the downfall of a dream, he could help hundreds of dreams succeed. He'd also spend less time looking for mistakes, which meant the side of him that tended toward his father's faultfinding would be given less exposure to the world.

"I know why I'd be interested, but what made you think of this?"

"I quit Meier Dairy because Dad refused to consider leaving the company to me, even if I agreed to find a husband and start popping out babies, but I've been soured on the company for a while. Meier Dairy stopped feeling like a family business. When he sold the actual family farm to a developer, it hit me. I'm sick of working for the big guys. I want to work for the small ones. I don't want to make sure Meier butter is on every table in America, but I want those families who would appreciate Farmer John's hand-churned butter to have a place to buy it. You help me find Farmer John and I'll make the company a success."

"You fell asleep with the lights on and the TV blaring last night. Crying."

Beth glared at him. Any mention of her weaknesses tended to get him a glare. Or a punch.

"Today you're looking for an apartment and have an idea for a new company. This seems like a fast turnaround."

For the first time that night Beth looked uncertain. She'd eaten a dried fish without blinking, but admitting to crying was harder. "I took Dad's phone by accident. We have the same model and I grabbed his instead of my own. I saw the text he sent you, offering you the business again, not five minutes after I offered to sacrifice my love life and womb to a child if that's what it would take for him to leave me the business."

He didn't say anything. Beth wouldn't want him to. She was so tough, so hard on the outside, but inside her was a little girl still hoping for Daddy's approval. They both knew it was there and neither talked about it. Beth wouldn't have cried last night had he been home. Crying was admitting to being a little girl. Dan stopped feeling even the least bit guilty that he hadn't been home last night for his sister. She'd needed the time alone.

Beth continued, "When I confronted him about it, he was surprised I would even be angry. Like I should've known my offer wouldn't be acceptable. I was still the girl in the family and girls don't get to run the family farm. Asshole," she said with sharp vehemence. "I've been thinking about the website for years, not certain how I could start my own business while running Meier Dairy. Now I don't run Meier Dairy anymore."

Dan looked hard at his sister. They both looked like their father. Strong jaw, well-defined cheekbones, bright blue eyes and blond hair. Those traits made his sister handsome, rather than pretty, but also gave her a determined look her personality enhanced. If she said she would make a success of the operation, she wouldn't stop until she did it.

A part of him doubted her desire to help Farmer John. For as long as he could remember Beth had wanted to run Meier Dairy. She'd done everything she could to impress their father with her competence and interest, right down to always showing off Meier Holsteins for 4-H. If he knew his sister, she had her Best-in-Show ribbons from the state fair packed away in the suitcase in the guest bedroom. But circumstances changed people. If Farmer John was what pulled her away from being Dan Sr.'s whipping girl, pit bull and industry slave, Dan wouldn't argue. As long as Beth believed in Farmer John, he would believe in her.

"All right, Beth, what's your timeline?"

Beth pumped her hand in the air. "I'd hoped you'd be interested." Then she outlined her full plan.

It was a solid business plan. She'd spent a lot of time researching the market and her competition. She'd found a web designer and a warehouse. All she had needed was an interested foodie—Dan—and a backer. Dan didn't doubt she would find a backer. Beth was like an overgrown terrier, fearless and stubborn. Plus, according to her plan, Dan would keep his writing job for the foreseeable future. He could live without the money he earned, but even rich kids needed something to do and Dan liked working.

The waitress returned to collect their empty bowls and Dan ordered cooling persimmon punch for dessert. She returned with two bowls of coral-colored liquid with a dried persimmon sitting at the bottom and pine nuts floating on the top. The scent of cinnamon danced over the table, cutting through the cloying smell of sugary persimmon.

Beth sipped her punch and looked over the bowl at Dan.

"Something's up with you. You have the job you say you've wanted since college. Why are you willing to give it up?"

He let the cold liquid wash over his tongue, warmed by the cinnamon and the heat in the ginger, before he crunched on a pine nut and answered his sister.

"I'm tired of bad reviews."

"Does this have anything to do with the cute, blue-haired woman from the Taste?"

"What do you know about Tilly?"

"Just because you hate social networking doesn't mean it doesn't exist. I saw the picture posted to Twitter." She looked at him sympathetically over her bowl of punch. "You looked really into her. I'm sorry."

"She dumped me yesterday."

"What!" She choked and coughed before she succeeded in swallowing her drink. "You were dating her?"

"I was trying to. One date was all she would give me."

"I'm not surprised."

"Thank for the support, sis."

Beth shrugged and didn't look the least bit abashed. "If

I were her, I'd knee you in the nuts and leave you for the wolves."

"When your employees said you were a ballbuster, I didn't think they meant it literally." Dan smiled at his sister. "Fortunately for me, Tilly is nicer than you. I'm hoping she's also more forgiving."

"Don't quit reviewing because of one bad experience. I want your help, but not if you're going to be dissatisfied with the work in three years and leave me. I'd rather find another foodie."

"I don't think this will be a temporary career change." Dan pictured Tilly's wild hair and expressive face. What would she look like in twenty years? Thirty? Forty? He wanted to know and she wouldn't be a part of the future he envisioned if he kept reviewing. "I'm feeling pretty permanent about it."

"You have a stupid, puppy-love look on your face. It's a good thing I'm the businessman in this relationship."

Dan laughed loudly enough for heads in the restaurant to turn and stare at them. "We'll be good cop/bad cop. And, sis?"

Beth raised an eyebrow at him.

"I'm going to love working with you."

CHAPTER TWENTY-TWO

TILLY LOOKED OVER the carefully designed menu for the rehearsal dinner. After talking with the bride, she'd prepared three choices for each course and added a meat option to the "something vegetarian and something chicken." Appetizers were cabbage pierogi served with sour cream and mustard, duck sausage with warm sauerkraut, or cold *barszcz*. Entrées were rolled steak with fresh mushrooms served with mashed potatoes and green beans, chicken legs braised in sour cream with handmade egg noodles and carrots, or crisp fried leeks with a hot tomato sauce served with a beer and buckwheat pancake. Dessert was apricot compote served with fresh farmer's cheese, rum babka, or chocolate cheesecake. Each diner also got the choice of three cocktails before dinner (two planned to match the bride's colors of butter-yellow and a vibrant beet-red), wine or beer with dinner, and coffee with dessert. Guests who wanted more to drink could go up to the bar and buy from Candace.

All this *and* she had managed to be cheaper than the original restaurant. Of course, she was only charging enough to cover the ingredients, decorations and staff. She would barely make a cent from tonight's dinner, but she hoped word of mouth would get Babka more customers. And the reason her costs were low enough to talk the groom's father into adding a meat dish was that she had struggled to plan a menu that sounded elegant, would taste delicious and used cheaper cuts of meat; the only splurge was the duck for the sausage. With the tougher cuts, she could still purchase good quality meat from her regular suppliers while keeping costs low. Polish cooking at its best and most wholesome. She was gambling on some of the guests being from Chicago, remembering Babka and returning later with friends and credit cards.

Renia had come in before the rehearsal and helped Tilly decorate the dining room. Small bud vases on the tables held either a deep pink or a yellow rose. Babka's white napkins had been replaced with matching yellow or pink and her dark wooden tables were covered in crisp white linens. Large arrangements of roses adorned the bar and hostess station. Tilly even had the menus printed on a heavy-weight butter-yellow paper with one beet-red rose across the page. She thought the restaurant looked elegant, especially for little more than a week's notice.

She helped the waitstaff lay the menus on the tables and check the spacing between the place settings. Her work in the kitchen was done. The dishes were prepped and waiting for the guests to choose their meals. Candace had briefed the staff on the best beer or wine pairings with each dish choice. Even the tea candles floating in glass bowls on each table were already lit.

She had nothing to do but wait and fret.

Before opening Babka, Tilly had never been a fretter. Even the first few weeks after Babka's opening had been fret-free. She'd had steady enough business due to the respect Chicagoans had for Healthy Food and the general curiosity people had for "fancy Polish." Her menu was delicious, her staff hardworking and committed to her vision, and her dream a reality. Even her dishwasher seemed unlikely to toss his apron in the sink and walk out during a busy dinner service.

There had been nothing to fret about.

Then Imbir and that dog had overturned her restaurant. Someone had upset the careful arrangement of ingredients for the line cooks. The toupee clogged her pipes. Paychecks were left lying around. The rat was planted in her kitchen. Thinking about the rat, at least, had taken her mind off Dan. He hadn't been to Babka at all in the past week, and she was disappointed.

And disappointed in herself for being disappointed.

At least now her free moments could be spent trying desperately to imagine her saboteur's next move, while feeling instantly ridiculous for thinking she even had a saboteur. A restaurant was an accident waiting to happen, but she wasn't fighting cuts and burns. The saboteur was the only explanation for the rat and the toupee, but it was still too incredible to believe. Why would one of her employees want to sabotage Babka? She didn't think any of them had a personal vendetta against her, but the alternative was one of them ruining her dream because someone paid them, which begged another absurd question—who would want to hire someone to sabotage a Polish restaurant? Was there some mad Prussian chef intent on widening his domain to include her little slice of Poland?

Ridiculous. Forcing her to close Babka was the only result anyone would get out of the damage they caused and who would want to close her restaurant? All an employee would get was no job. If one of her employees didn't want to work there so badly, they could quit. If she kept with her theory about someone hiring an employee to close Babka… that didn't make any more sense.

Babka didn't have any competition, other than Healthy Food and a smattering of other Polish restaurants, but she was different enough from those places not to be a direct competitor. Babka was not a casual family restaurant. Tilly expected—and got—a fancier class of customer. If she got the Polish cops coming into Babka for a taste of their mothers' cooking, she got them when they were taking their wives out for a nice meal and dressed up in a tie, not when they were in uniform.

There were a few other nicer Slavic or German restaurants in Chicago, but Tilly had planned carefully to slip into the niche they left open. Her food was neither Russian nor German, but distinctly and authentically Polish. Pierogi might be similar to Russian *pirozhki,* and she served sauerkraut, but Babka served the characteristically tangy and spiced food of Poland. And, like the aristocratic Poles of old, she served it plated in a fancy French style rather than more casually served food of Germany.

Even if she were competition for the other Eastern European restaurants, casual, fancy or somewhere in between, Babka was certainly not doing well enough to be poaching a significant number of their regulars. If those other restaurants were suffering a loss of business, her empty tables were evidence that those customers were not coming to Babka.

Not that it mattered. Tilly couldn't imagine her saboteur's motive, but her saboteur hadn't stopped acting. Various new catastrophes jumped around in her head like cumin seeds frying and popping in oil—all of them terrible and all of them probably not the saboteur's next move.

And that was the worst part. No matter what jumped out at her, the saboteur had something nastier to burn her with. The devil was waiting in the wings of her imagination, taunting her as he poked his pitchfork into her brain before jumping out of sight. She wouldn't know him and the damage he caused until he struck.

So she fretted. She paced her restaurant, rolling her hands together and checking in every hiding place for the next surprise while both hoping the bridal party would come and the night would be over soon and dreading the moment they walked through the doors. The wedding rehearsal that could save Babka would be the perfect time for the saboteur to strike.

A taxi pulled up and four people poured out. Tilly yanked her hands apart and forced them to her sides as Karen threw the front door open for the first guests.

"Welcome to Babka," Tilly said as she smiled and shook hands. Wedding rehearsal or not, she was the hostess of tonight's party and she was going to greet each and every guest. They were going to remember the delicious food, the gracious service and the individual attention of the chef. More importantly, they were going to tell their friends and return with money and appetites. She gestured to the dining room. "Please have a seat. Miss Carter requested open seating and menus are on the tables. I will be around until all the guests are seated to answer any questions about the food. My waitstaff also knows the menu and has tried every dish should you want to ask them for suggestions."

Tilly shook hands and smiled at more guests, answering questions about some of the dishes and hearing compliments from people who loved Healthy Food and asked after her mother. Renia snapped pictures—the bride's family had paid for her sister to cover the entire wedding weekend—and some guests commented on how alike they looked. One guest, whom Tilly recognized from his editorial photo in the *Sun-Times,* asked her about Karl and the inspector general's office. Tilly answered honestly. Karl never talked with her or the rest of the family about his work. She just made him pierogi whenever he asked.

"Tilly…" Steve's hands were shaking badly as he pulled her away from the editorialist. "…there's a woman who needs to know what she can eat that is gluten-free."

Tilly resisted wrinkling her nose. The bride had mentioned the vegetarians, but could have warned her about the gluten-free. Instead of being able to plan a special dish for the woman, Tilly would have to piece together bits of other dishes. The result would be tasty, but wouldn't have the polish she preferred. She sought the woman out and they talked about what she could eat and what she couldn't. All the appetizers had bread or flour in them, so Tilly agreed to make a stacked beet salad with the same cheese used in the apricot dessert. The roasted chicken leg would be good with the mashed potatoes and the apricot compote was gluten-free, as long as the kitchen didn't include the butter cookies in the presentation.

As she hurried to the kitchen to let them know about the special order, a strong hand rested on her shoulder.

"Hey, Tilly." Dan's familiar voice stopped her heart. "I'd like you to meet my sister, Beth."

"I didn't know you would be here." Tilly robotically shook hands with a woman who looked remarkably like Dan, cheekbones, strong jaw and all. The woman gave her a hard stare before her face softened into a smile.

"My brother has mentioned you a lot. He raves about your food."

"Um…" Not knowing how else to react, Tilly decided on nonchalance. If Dan could pretend they were friendly strangers, so could she. They were both adults and wishing that Sunday's ending of their relationship had hurt him more than it apparently had wasn't a good enough excuse to not be pleasant to his sister. "It is a pleasure to meet you. I hope you enjoy your meal here at Babka. Please let me know if there is anything I can do to make it a better experience for you."

Dan had described his sister as a hard-as-nails businesswoman. The smile softened Beth's face, but her penetrating eyes evaluated Tilly's every move. She was the serious older sister to the lighthearted younger brother, almost the reverse of the Mileks, without Renia in between.

"Dan," Beth said in a no-nonsense voice, "let's find a seat and leave Tilly to her business."

As Tilly walked off, a female voice said, "Dan, I'll bet you never expected to see your personal life covered on a gossip blog."

Before Tilly could think too much about that statement, the kitchen door opened and she remembered the gluten-free woman and her errand. The night would definitely be a disaster if she made one of the guests sick.

DAN CRINGED WHEN HE HEARD one of Beth's sorority sisters—he didn't remember her name and didn't care—say, "Dan, I'll bet you never expected to see your personal life covered on a gossip blog."

Given Tilly's bland greeting of Beth, she hadn't yet read the embellished report of their relationship on one of Chicago's gossip blogs. Rich had forwarded the post to him two days ago, and it had been like a figurative punch to the gut. If Tilly had read the post, she probably would've given him a literal punch. He wasn't responsible for the post—Rich was pulling strings to figure out who the "anonymous source" was—but Tilly seemed to trust a dead bug on the side of the highway more than she trusted him. She'd hit first and ask questions later—and he wasn't sure he would blame her for it.

Tilly was a busy woman, and probably didn't spend her rare moments of free time reading gossip blogs.

But Beth's sorority sister had read it. The chances that she or someone else at the party who'd read it would mention the post to Tilly seemed pretty high. Any chance was too high. He never should've come.

Beth had called him in a panic on Thursday morning, seeking a date for the rehearsal dinner and wedding of a sorority sister. "Certain disaster" is what he'd said in return. He had plans to win Tilly back, but they didn't include surprising her at her restaurant. Again. The gossip post had gone live and he'd refused. Again.

Beth had persisted—she always persisted—and eventually he'd given in. Especially after she threatened to show Tilly the post herself.

Dan didn't think she'd do it. Beth was ruthless, but she valued family over everything. Enough niggling doubt had poked at his mind that he'd agreed to the dinner after offering up every single man he knew as an alternative. Beth had been willing to take Mike. Mike, however, had been unsympathetic to Dan's problem. Like Beth, Mike thought the discomfort of the night was "cosmic justice for being a total douchebag" and Dan shouldn't have ever gotten himself in this position. Neither of them had seemed too concerned that Tilly would also be uncomfortable with his presence.

And so Dan was here, sliding his seat under one of Babka's tables, glancing at a yellow menu and keeping his attention focused on how he'd lost the best thing to ever happen to him. And how everyone in Chicago knew it.

Dread clenched at his gut. No way would he be able to enjoy his food tonight. He'd eat. He could always eat and not eating his meal would draw more attention to himself, but he wouldn't taste a single bite. He didn't even know what he ordered, just pointed at menu items and hoped for the best. The other guests chatted cheerfully around him. Dan answered when questions were addressed to him, but didn't allow himself to be drawn into conversation. Plastering a smile on his face, he tried to appear like every other wedding guest, here to have a good time and some drinks on another person's tab.

If this had happened to someone else, he would've said it was funny. Wrecked by his hubris. Hoisted with his own petard. Even the idiom attached to his current problem was funny, though Hamlet, from whom the saying originated, probably hadn't found it so.

Dan smiled and laughed at the comment of the woman across the table from him, something from *The Daily Show*. He didn't have to know what Jon Stewart said. It was probably funny. So many things were probably funny. Even his current problem was probably funny, if it were to have happened to someone else.

TILLY KEPT BUSY in the kitchen and had little time to think about Dan's presence in her restaurant. Every seat, with the exception of those at the bar, was full. Besides being—*hopefully!*—good advertising for Babka, the rehearsal dinner was a nice test of her restaurant. This was the first time the kitchen and waitstaff had experienced a full house. The full house came with a limited menu so the kitchen had less chance to mess up a dish, but the pressure to keep in sync was the same. Greater perhaps, because all the diners had been seated at the same time and would want their food to come out at about the same time.

Everyone, from the dishwasher to Karen and Steve, was working their asses off, and all of them with a smile. Not only did they need to coordinate the service, but the guests all knew each other. They were standing up, going over to talk with their friends, getting more drinks at the bar, and generally making it difficult for the waitstaff to keep track of who was where and what they'd ordered. Several people even switched seats to be closer to their friends.

Waitstaff kept track and managed to find their diners, deliver the correct dish and barter dishes with one another so all the dishes for one table were served at the same time—even if two people at the table had been seated somewhere else when dinner began.

None of the diners noticed, of course. Which was how it should be. A restaurant should run smoothly, with all bumps and burps covered by the competency of the staff. The diner's job was to enjoy the food and drink.

And they were doing their job just fine. Plates came back to the kitchen all but licked clean. Steve passed on every compliment about the food, which meant he passed on a lot of compliments.

No sign of her saboteur. Babka was closed to the public. He or she wouldn't strike tonight.

DAN WAS FEELING more relaxed. One surprisingly earthy and spicy cocktail—some beet and ginger ale combination Candace had mixed up—and a refreshing pilsner that cut the richness of his braised chicken dish was all it took for him to stop worrying that one of the guests would make a crack about the gossip column. Well, he corrected himself, two drinks and the fact that no one had done it yet.

If someone was going to ask Tilly about their supposed sexual escapades on the bar, they would have done it before everyone sat down to eat. Now, with Tilly's delicious food in front of them, everyone was too busy eating to worry about talking to anyone not sitting next to them. With the sounds of flatware scraping across plates echoing through the restaurant, many people weren't bothering to talk.

He was miserable. She was so close and, when she passed him by after the entrées were served, he couldn't even reach his hand out to touch her.

Steve collected empty plates and another staff member brought around coffee cups, French presses and coffee timers for the tables. Dessert would be coming out soon; they would eat and leave. After the dinner, he would say goodbye to his sister and try to talk to Tilly. Dreams of her welcoming him into Babka with open arms were shot. His current prayer involved her letting him stay long enough to talk with him and build a foundation for forgiveness.

Don't lie to yourself, Danny. You hope she invites you back to her place; you're just not stupid enough to believe she actually will.

He took a cookie from his plate and used his spoon to nudge some of the crumbly farmer's cheese and coral apricot compote onto it. As usual, Tilly's food was exquisite. Part of her culinary magic was her ability to take the humblest ingredients and infuse them with family and history. The cheese tasted of fresh spring grasses and the apricots of the summer sun. Together with his crumbly butter cookie, they tasted like a perfect summer's day spent outside on a picnic blanket with the sun on your feet and the shade from an old oak tree over your head. Maybe there were some kids playing Red Rover and butterflies dancing in the flowers. The bees buzzed, but didn't intrude. A simple summer day that existed in paintings, but never in real life.

She had to forgive him. For all the attraction her body held for his, more than anything Dan wanted to be a part of the passion that created her food. He wanted to know the history of every dish she had learned from her grandmother—Babunia, he corrected—and to be a part of the future she imagined when she tweaked a dish to make it her own. When she stood in the kitchen, rolling out pierogi dough with her children, he wanted those children to be his.

"Dan." His sister leaned into him, her plate of chocolate cheesecake scraped clean. "When you said the food was good, I had no idea."

"Most people don't," he replied. Not a single plate on the table had food left on it. Even the woman across from him who had been "appalled when Michelle said we were eating at a Polish restaurant, she knows I'm on a strict diet" had eaten every last crumb of her babka.

"It makes what I wrote even worse. I was wrong about so many things. I have to hope time does heal all wounds."

"You marry your blue-haired chef and every person in our family will gain twenty pounds. I might gain thirty," Beth said with a mournful glance at her empty plate.

"Mom could use it. She looks more and more like a skeleton every day."

"I'm not certain she would eat Polish food again. Dad hasn't let her last experience here go." They shared raised eyebrows about their parents and their father's disrespect for his own wife's feelings. "Seriously, Dan, I like Tilly. I would like her because you like her, but her food is delicious and one night in her restaurant has told me enough about her work ethic that I have a healthy respect for her."

"No pressure, though, right, Beth?"

"Don't scowl at me. I'm not the one who screwed up. If you'd done the right thing the first time you came here, you probably would have written a glowing review *and* gotten the girl."

"Meiers don't make mistakes. Meiers make cheese." He didn't believe the stupid family saying anymore. He probably never had, but he said it out of habit. The lie was comforting, especially as he confronted the biggest mistake of his life.

Beth rolled her eyes. "Meiers make both mistakes and cheese. Good on ya for being man enough to admit it."

Dan knew the instant Tilly walked into the dining room. His body felt her trajectory through the tables until she stopped at the table next to him. "How was everything?" she asked the father of the groom.

"Great," the man replied with the enthusiasm of someone who'd given up drinking beer and had settled for doing a taste test of Tilly's excellent selection of Polish *wódka*. "But I expected a butter, uh, better, a better show."

"Bill…" His wife had grasped his dress shirt. "We're here to celebrate the upcoming wedding, remember?"

Tilly gave a smile Dan recognized as the one waitresses around the world gave drunken men acting weird, but not yet completely crazy. "It is a happy occasion…"

"No one can tell he screwed you," the father of the groom said in a voice only an inebriated fool would think was a whisper.

"Bill!"

"It's fine, Margaret." The drunk pried his wife's fingers off his shirt, the wrinkles left clinging to his sleeve evidence it wasn't *fine*. "The lovely chef is profess…a prosess, a professional. She knows how to handle her private life on a blog."

"Shut up, Dad," the groom said as his mom again tried to silence her husband.

"Is he talking about…?" Beth asked.

Dan got up from his table and slid into a chair. "Bill, congratulations on your son's marriage. He is a lucky man."

His decision to intervene was a mistake. For the first time that night, Tilly looked directly at him, her brown eyes disgusted by what they thought they saw. "Do you know what he's talking about?"

The goddamned drunk wouldn't be distracted by his son's happiness—or his wife's increasingly fervent urgings to be quiet. "I thought this guy—" the drunk jammed his thumb in Dan's shoulder "—was the one who spilled details of your hush-hush relationship, but maybe it was you. Good publicity. Good strategy." His nods looked more like a headbanger at a rock concert than indications of approval. Watching him gave Dan a headache.

Or maybe it was the dawning sense of understanding

in Tilly's eyes that was giving him a headache. "Did you write another blog post?"

"It wasn't me." His protestations were as useful as a cheap handheld fan trying to blow a tornado in the other direction.

"Strange, but I don't believe you're as innocent as you're trying to look."

"Tilly, would you listen to me for a minute?"

WHAT WAS SHE GOING to listen to? How he hadn't gotten enough internet hits from trashing her restaurant and now had to boost his name recognition by crowing about how he'd almost managed to get her in bed without apologizing? She could see the headlines in *ChicagoScoops* now: "Reviewer Screws Chef Twice."

"Oh, God." She put her hands over her mouth to block out the scream desperate to escape. She had read that headline; it had been on Karen's iPad screen yesterday. Only, Tilly hadn't imagined the article was about her. She wasn't a celebrity, so there was no reason for *ChicagoScoops* to write about her love life. Or lack of love life. Or lying like a dirty bath mat lack of love life. "Get out."

"Tilly, I didn't…"

She managed to keep her voice modulated, but her control couldn't last forever. Soon the humiliation of having her stupidity posted for all Chicago to read and laugh at would overtake her and she'd have a mental breakdown. If she could only get him out of Babka, she could postpone the collapse until all the guests had left. She pointed to the front door, since he seemed to be both stupid and a scumbag. "Get out."

Movement out the front window caught her attention. Outside her restaurant, on a busy Friday sidewalk, stood her runner. His arm was raised above his head, reminding

Tilly through her grief-clouded brain of a baseball pitcher, though shakier. Then, like a baseball pitcher, Steve released whatever he held in his hand and the large plate-glass window at the front of Babka shattered.

All her dreams and aspirations exploded in sharp, shiny pieces.

CHAPTER TWENTY-THREE

DAN RAN AFTER Steve at a full sprint. Shattered glass crunched under the soles of his dress shoes as he raced out the door and down the street.

Steve was younger, but Dan was more fit and any onlookers quickly got out of his way. With one final push of speed, Dan was able to tackle him from behind and pin him to the concrete. It was a Tight Waist Far Ankle into a Half Nelson his college coach would have been proud of. Steve *oofed* as Dan pushed his head down onto the sidewalk and twisted his arm up and his shoulder down. Steve struggled, but a well-executed Half Nelson was hard for even an experienced wrestler to muscle his way out of and Steve was a skinny, spindly thing.

By the time Dan had dragged the man to his feet and marched him back to Babka, the police were there. He looked at the man struggling against his hold, then to the two uniformed officers speaking Polish to each other. "Just your luck to piss off a beloved member of the Polish community in a city with a large number of Polish cops," he said to the squirming man. "I'll bet half the force has eaten at Tilly's mother's restaurant."

The two officers talking with Tilly noticed Dan with his prisoner and walked over, but Dan wasn't paying them any attention. Tilly's cold stare pierced through him. She blinked and her eyes focused on him, but she still didn't acknowledge him. By the time the officers reached him, Tilly was gone from sight.

"Who do we have here?" the shorter cop asked.

"Tilly's runner, Steve. Everyone in the restaurant saw him throw something through her window and run off."

"Officer Czaja will take your statement, and you," the older one said as he took the runner from Dan's grip, "can come with me." Steve struggled until one of the cops jingled some handcuffs. Steve stopped struggling when the cuffs were clicked on and meekly ducked his head as the older officer pushed him into the back of the patrol car.

When the door slammed on the dishwasher, Officer Czaja turned to Dan and took out his notepad. "All right, Mr. Meier, tell me what you know," the younger man said with a glare. "No hiding behind a blog."

Dan sighed. He wasn't in the back of a cop car, but clearly Officer Czaja wished he was. Apparently everyone in the city of Chicago thought he'd blabbed to the gossip blog.

"Can I talk to Tilly first?"

The officer laughed a hard, unforgiving noise. "I hope Tilly won't talk to you ever again."

Dan looked over at the runner now safely in the back of the cruiser. At least he was in official custody and the cops had rules about how they could treat him. Dan was out on the street, having betrayed and humiliated the daughter, granddaughter and sister of prominent members of the Polish community in a city with a lot of Poles.

He was surprised he'd made it from the posting of his original review of Babka to today without getting noise violation tickets for breathing too loudly. Unexplained boots on his car. Jaywalking tickets. Tilly must've been holding them off. If the cops thought he was responsible for the gossipy blog post, the tickets would bankrupt him.

The guests from the rehearsal spilled out of the restaurant, buzzing like bees released from a hive and their faces alternating blue and red in the flashing patrol car lights. An ambulance pulled up. Some of the guests had been cut by broken glass.

Tilly didn't come out. He could see her through the broken window, sitting at the bar with her head in her hands. Candace and Renia sat on either side of her, one stroking her hair, the other rubbing her back. Renia caught his glance, held it for a moment, then looked away, giving him no more notice than she would give a dead opossum on the side of the road.

He wanted to scream out, "But I didn't do it!" Instead, he turned to find Beth and go home, wondering why he was the villain when Steve had been the saboteur.

TILLY SPENT THE REST of the night with Candace and Renia. After talking to the cops and explaining the series of events, the trio cleaned up the glass and boarded up the window while they waited for Tilly's insurance agent to assess the damage. Dan was nowhere to be seen. For all Tilly knew, he'd been taken away by the police—arrested for crimes against her sanity.

Renia and Candace had tried to talk to her about Dan and Steve, but Tilly ignored them. She had no interest in Dan, Steve, Babka, reviews, anything. Thinking about the big picture caused too much heartache right now. Instead, she concentrated on each small piece of glass she swept into the dustpan and the tearing noise of duct tape as she pulled silver strips from the roll. The rough edges of the scrap wood from a neighboring bar bit into her fingers as she held the piece against the window for Renia to tape.

Details. She could think about details today. The big picture—her failure—could wait until tomorrow.

"Tilly." Renia came toward her, her camera bags strapped across her body, followed by Candace, who held Tilly's purse. "I don't think you should stay at your apartment alone tonight."

Tilly looked around for something else, anything else to do. The window had been boarded, taped and nailed to the best of her ability. She'd talked with the insurance agent and found out how much the company would cover and, oh joy, her deductible would go up.

"But your rates will probably go down because of it," he had said—as if a lower monthly rate made the entire episode worth it.

The cops left, after promising not to call either her mother or her brother. A couple of officers who'd grown up in her neighborhood looked shifty while promising, so she'd gotten her rosary from the office and made them swear on the cross, after reminding them she'd gotten the rosary at World Youth Day and it had been blessed—by a Polish pope. Their final promise included a time limit, but Tilly ignored the hedge. She was planning on telling the rest of her family tomorrow.

Her other employees had already left, not knowing when they would be able to return to work. Tuesday at the earliest. Tomorrow—no, Tilly corrected herself after checking the clock on the wall—today was Saturday. Babka had to be closed today and was closed Sunday and Monday. Hopefully the window could be repaired on Monday and they could reopen Tuesday.

Reopen to whom, she didn't know. Tonight's episode would make the papers. She could hope Chicagoans would be drawn to Babka like paparazzi to Britney Spears, but notoriety was a finicky business. She needed customers to show up and buy dinner, not just take pictures and tell their friends.

Like Scarlett O'Hara, she would worry about that tomorrow. After she had a good night's sleep. Tilly would have a good night's sleep, even if she needed chemical help. She had some antihistamines and cold medicine at home. Either one was guaranteed to knock her out, and keep her out for at least eight dreamless hours. She could wake to her personal nightmare rested and ready to pretend it had never happened. At least until her first cup of coffee.

"I'll be fine," she assured Renia. "I'll be in my own bed, at my own home, with my own cat and I'll be fine. I'll even take something to help me sleep."

"No, you won't," Renia said with a shake of her head. "You'll sit on your couch with your medicine on the table, petting your cat, thinking about every single moment and how one step to the left or the right would have meant tonight never happened. And you won't stop at Imbir's dramatic entry into your life or believing Steve when he said he wasn't using. You'll go all the way back to some ridiculous memory of Babunia teaching you to make pierogi as where your life went wrong."

Tilly bristled. "None of my memories of Babunia are ridiculous and she could never be responsible for my life going wrong."

"Some other memory, then. You know what I mean."

Tilly scowled, but Candace spoke before she could respond. "She's right, you know. You mean to go straight to sleep, you know you need to, but the temptation to pick at all your open wounds will be too overwhelming. Go home with Renia, or come home with me. We'll make sure you sleep. Hakim might even have something for you to take." Candace's boyfriend was an E.R. doc.

"I need to take care of Imbir."

"A lame excuse and you know it." Renia rolled her eyes. "Even if your cat wasn't fat and spoiled, he can survive one night on his own. You don't know how long he lived on the streets and he seemed to do fine for himself there."

"But…"

"I have a key," Renia said with a voice that didn't allow for argument. "Candace or I can take care of Imbir. I don't think you should stay by yourself."

"If you don't want to stay at our house, I can go home with you," Candace offered. "I'll need to call Hakim and let him know."

Tilly wrinkled her nose at this idea. "I'll go to Mom's."

As soon as she said the words, Tilly knew it was what she wanted. She wanted more than sympathy. She wanted a mother hen to cluck over her. Mom may have wanted her to take over Healthy Food, but once her mother accepted her children's decisions, she supported them one hundred percent. Sometimes her mother just took her time deciding she didn't always know better.

Her mother would hover, tell her what a wonderful person she was and what a horrible person Steve was while feeding her Polish comfort food. She wouldn't pressure Tilly to make any decisions just yet, would even caution her against making them, and give her a shoulder to cry on.

And a shoulder to cry on was all Tilly wanted. Tomorrow, she would want Karl's push for answers and Renia's supportive anger but right now her mom was all she wanted.

Candace took Renia's key to Tilly's apartment and promised to check on her cat. Renia called their mom, then drove Tilly home.

CHAPTER TWENTY-FOUR

HER EYES OPENED, but it took a few more seconds for reality to register. The antihistamines had worked a little too well. Tilly blinked several times, but her brain was still foggy.

She squinted and tried to peer through the mist clouding up her mind. All she saw was Steve throwing a brick and a drunk man congratulating her for a marketing ploy. Dan's face as he tried to deny responsibility. For all her doubts, for all that she thought she must be crazy for considering that an employee could be sabotaging her restaurant, she had been dead-on, even if she still didn't understand why. Being right didn't feel so good. The wound of ending any hope of a relationship with Dan hadn't scabbed over yet and her heart wasn't ready for the betrayal of a trusted employee.

She'd given Steve a job and trusted his sobriety when no one else would. Stupid.

She closed her eyes at the memories marching in toward her in the haze and reached for her cat. Instead of soft orange fur, Tilly's outstretched hand hit a wall and the shock forced her eyes open. She wasn't at home, in her apartment. She was at home, in her old room, in her mother's house, off Archer. She'd trusted Steve and that had exploded in her face right at the moment Dan had been telling her he hadn't publicly humiliated her. Again. Surely that was a sign from God.

Does returning home make me a failure?

Not yet. Babka would reopen and she wasn't running Healthy Food with her mother yet.

When I can't say "yet" anymore, then I will have failed.

The smell of coffee wafted past her nose. Coffee and— she sniffed—yeasty, fresh-baked bread. Breakfast. The smell woke up her stomach and her stomach woke up her brain. She looked over at the clock on the windowsill. Ten in the morning. She'd managed to sleep in and was more rested than she had been for months. It was nice to have your mom take care of you and give you a slightly ratty nightgown, when you were too tired, too stressed and too brokenhearted to do anything more than show up on her doorstep asking for a bed and some sleeping pills.

Knowing she could get out of bed and her mother would take care of her eased some of the tension in Tilly's neck. She could go to the kitchen, sit down, and her mother would feed her and rub her back, never questioning her. Her mom would allow her to heal, and comfort her with hot coffee and sweet *kołaczyki* with apricot filling.

The green shag carpeting in the hallway was soft and warm under her feet as she padded into the kitchen. There, at the round yellow laminate table, her mother and Renia sat drinking coffee and talking.

Their sudden silence when Renia noticed her presence was a dead giveaway. Of course they were talking about her. She had showed up on her mom's doorstep at two in the morning, tears in her eyes. They probably thought she was going to fall apart on them.

She wasn't. Her business was in shambles, parts of it literally in a trash can. Her personal life—sex life, relationship, whatever it was she had outside of Babka—was exposed for public humiliation. But she had managed to get out of bed this morning. She was wearing her mom's ratty old nightgown, but she planned to get dressed, which was the first step to putting Babka, her life, back together.

No, if she was going to collapse and stop functioning, she would have fainted last night the moment the rock hit her window. She was up and out of bed today. She would be up and out of bed tomorrow. And the next day and the next. Babka would survive.

Without Dan, Tilly didn't have anything to distract her from making her restaurant a success.

"Don't worry about me," Tilly told her mother and sister. "A broken window was no more of a disaster than rotten tomatoes from one of the farms at the height of tomato season, and I survived that just fine." Even if it still ticked her off.

What had the farmer thought she was going to do with those tomatoes? Green tomatoes, sure, those had a use, but rotten ones? Did he think that because she was, as Dan had nicely put it in his review, "better suited to the chaotic mediocrity of a suburban family restaurant," she would accept the produce she was given without complaint? Did the farmer, and seemingly everyone else on the planet, think she was going to give up her dream because he thought she was too nice to complain?

What if the tomatoes had also been part of the sabotage?

The thought closed in on her heart and she grabbed the back of a chair. How could Steve betray her like that? She'd given him a job when no one else would. He'd been fresh out of rehab, broke, and she'd stuck her neck out for him.

She stopped herself before she imagined her head rolling around on the floor. She'd kept herself together last night and she was going to keep herself together now—no matter how much sympathy her mother and sister put in their eyes. She wasn't going to cry. They couldn't make her cry.

"Oh, honey." Her mother put down her coffee cup, got up and wrapped Tilly in her arms. "It's okay."

She cried.

Kołaczyki and a cup of coffee shoved at her she could have handled, but her mother's hug broke her.

"You should cry, honey. You've had a stressful week and you need to get it all out of you." Her mom stroked her hair. "Plus, my food is perfectly salted and I don't want you messing up the seasoning with your tears."

Tilly giggled the type of wet, snorty giggle that came with a good, hard cry.

Her mother pulled away from her and looked into her eyes. "There, there. Don't you feel better now that you've had a cry and a laugh?" She steered her to the table. "Sit down and I'll get you a cup of coffee. Breakfast will be ready soon."

As her mother rushed off to get a cup of coffee, Tilly leaned over to her sister. "You rat fink," she whispered. "You told her what happened."

"Of course I did," Renia whispered back, a bit too primly for Tilly's liking. "I expected you to at least tell her why you showed up at her door at two in the morning asking for pajamas and Benadryl. You went to bed without a word as to what's wrong. She called me at six this morning in a panic. Didn't you want her to know?"

"I wanted to tell her myself," Tilly hissed back under her breath. "I made Jan promise not to tell her—made him swear on a rosary—so why would I want you to?"

"Little Janny Czaja's had a crush on you since kindergarten. Right now, he's probably planning his appearance as a white knight saving you from an evil restaurant reviewer, slaying a drug-addled runner and taking you home to his castle." Renia snorted. "Anything to stop having to eat his mother's pierogi."

"Renia Agata Milek, what a terrible thing to say!" their mother called from the counter.

"Dorothy Czaja's pierogi are like eating a Frisbee she's cut in half, stuffed and fried, and everyone knows it. I don't think she's been allowed to make anything other than coffee at St. Bruno's since before I was born."

"I've told her time and again she overworks the dough, but she doesn't listen to me. She would listen to your grandmother, but I'm not expert enough for her to believe me."

"See," Renia said, triumph on her face. "You even agree with me."

Their mom's mouth flapped open and shut like a fish before she gave up. "It still wasn't a nice thing to say, even if it is true."

Tilly looked across the table at her sister. The instant their eyes met, snickers escaped and quickly became full-fledged laughter. Their mother managed to look stern for about thirty seconds before she, too, burst out laughing.

When they were all wiping tears from their eyes, Tilly told them more about her conversation with little Janny Czaja. "He wanted to call Karl, but I made him swear he wouldn't."

"Karl will find out soon enough—he always does." Her mom set a steaming, milky cup of coffee in front of her. Then she eased herself into a kitchen chair with a sigh. "Drink it. It'll make you feel better and then you can tell me all the news you have, both good and bad."

"Why should I tell you? You already know," Tilly snapped, then immediately regretted her tone. She was frustrated with a lot of things, but neither her mother nor Renia deserved her spite. Well, maybe Renia with her loose lips. Tilly didn't apologize, though. It might not be fair, but if you couldn't snap at your mother and sister at times like this, who could you snap at?

"I considered waking you and asking you why you showed up at home in the middle of the night, but, being your mother and therefore the most saintly person on earth, I decided to call your sister instead." She reached across the table and grabbed Tilly's hand. "Tilly, please, Renia and I want to help. No matter how old you are, I'm still your mother and I still care about you. I'm going to feed you and, when you're ready, try to help you solve your problems."

"What is there to be done, Mom? There's this man I think I could love, only he publicly humiliated me. And then he did it again. He must think I'm an idiot and a flake who should be running tables rather than owning my own restaurant." She sipped her coffee, letting the bitter brew rest on her tongue before she swallowed. She'd said the word *love* aloud. That was more serious than thinking it privately. She'd said it to her sister and her mother. Saying it made it real.

"And then there's Steve," she said, more to turn her heart to a different hurt. Steve's betrayal was no less personal, but at least she didn't wonder if she loved him.

"In Dan's defense, Tilly, you don't know he was the source of the gossip." Renia stirred her coffee, the spoon clinking against the sides of the Christmas mug. "Since the Taste, he's constantly said how good a chef you are, how original and inspiring. You said he understood what food meant to you, that it was more than not feeling hungry anymore."

"You knew about the *ChicagoScoops* post." Tilly had to work hard to keep from shouting. Her own sister had known her personal life was splattered all over the internet and hadn't told her. God, everyone knew. Karen, Candace, they'd both known and not told her. Did they expect she wouldn't find out?

The gossip article was a blessing in disguise. It was a

hammer dropping on the floor and making the cake fall into a flat, hard mess when she'd forgotten to grease the pan and it would've been ruined anyway. She could banish Dan from her thoughts completely and focus on Babka. When she looked at her situation from this angle, last night was almost a good thing. She could get back to making Babunia proud.

Then why did she still feel so bad?

"I knew." Renia stopped stirring her coffee and turned her attention to Tilly. "Karen saw it first. Some of us didn't want to tell you because we didn't want it to hurt you. Some of us didn't want to tell you because Dan might not have been the source and…"

"You thought I was too weak to handle the news and you thought I would never get another man if I didn't eventually forgive Dan?" Tilly tried to keep her voice hard, but she wasn't able to keep it under control.

"Stop twisting my words around."

"You're defending him!"

"Maybe I said 'in his defense,' but you did like him. Maybe you still do. You just said you might love him, for Pete's sake. He's the first guy you've wanted to spend any amount of time with in years and that was all while you *knew* he was The Eater."

Renia paused for a sip of coffee. "So he made a major mistake. But we don't know if he made this one. He still hasn't apologized for the review, but don't compound his sins without reason. I'm not saying you should talk to him. Ignore the bastard's phone calls for the rest of your life, but think about what he meant to you. For the past couple of weeks, you've been a bigger, better Tilly. A stronger Tilly. A Tilly who can have her restaurant and her personal life, too."

"I don't need a man in my life to be happy."

"I don't think Renia is saying you do," her mother said. Great, now they were ganging up on her. "You were so focused on your career you wouldn't think about a love life. But Dan proved it was possible for you to have both. And you both want it and like it. Just because Dan's not the right man for you, doesn't mean the right man doesn't exist somewhere. You don't have to search for him, but don't let your experience with Dan convince you to actively pretend the right man might not exist."

But Dan proved it was possible for you to have both. Her mom's words echoed between her ears. And, loudly and clearly, came the response from her subconscious she'd been ignoring. "But..." She hesitated. "What if Dan was right?"

"What if he was right about what?"

"What if I shouldn't own a nice restaurant? What if I should move back home and run the family business? What if Healthy Food is all I'm cut out for? What if I *am* too much of a flake for greatness? I mean, how could I not have known about Steve?"

If Dan Meier was right about her restaurant, then she didn't need the time and mental energy to worry about Steve and bad reviews. She could work at her mother's restaurant and date Jan Czaja. Even if he wasn't the man of her dreams, he would fill her new life, which wouldn't have her dream restaurant.

Why reach for the golden ring at all?

Either way, working too much or helping her mother, Dan didn't fit into the picture. He wasn't boring enough for her life without Babka and was too wonderful for her life with it.

"Oh, honey." Her mom squeezed her hand. "Is this what you're afraid of? That you're not good enough for your dreams?"

"Is it ridiculous?" Tilly's tears were fighting their way back into her eyes. She sniffled. "You may not remember how many times my teachers called you into a conference because I wasn't doing well in school, but I do. And the teachers were always saying how great a student Karl was. Owning your own business is hard and it requires a lot of smarts. I never had much smarts."

Renia broke in angrily before their mom could start talking. "Tilly, they told me the same thing all the time, too. We couldn't compete with Karl. I run my own business and we can both agree I had a worse time in school than you did. You had to find a reason to work hard, and you did. Your reason is you like to work in the kitchen." Renia took a deep breath. "I'm perfectly happy to hold a pity party for you, but you only get pity for things you deserve." She threw her hands in the air, forgetting about the coffee cup she held. The remains of Renia's coffee dribbled out of the cup and onto the table. "Your high school grades don't deserve our pity and they have nothing to do with the situation you've found yourself in. I don't know if I'm angrier at Steve for his sabotage, or at you for doubting your abilities."

"And, Tilly…" It was her mother's turn to disagree with Tilly's version of the past. At least her mother spoke in a voice meant to calm, rather than Renia's loud frustration. "The teachers called me into school all the time, but not for the reasons you think. They didn't call me in to tell me you were a bad student, only a misdirected one. They knew, as well as your grandmother and I did, that you didn't put any effort into school. Perhaps you have forgotten that part of the story. Your grades were mediocre, but you never did your homework, either."

Renia started talking again—it was like tag-team wrestling, the older Milek women versus Tilly. "You of all people should know when you put your mind to it, you can do anything. Perhaps you've forgotten your seven attempts to make a soufflé when you were twelve. I would have been happy with any of the middle five, but you wanted it to be better than Julia Child's and you did it."

Tilly did remember those cheese soufflés, seven in one weekend. By the time she was finished, even the dog was sick of eating soufflé, but the last one had been beautiful— high, light and airy. The memory still made her proud.

But her soufflés from more than fifteen years ago were not the point. The point was the present, not the past. Or not the past her mother remembered. "You're saying I should close Babka and open six more restaurants before I get it right."

"Don't be purposely obtuse." Renia spit out the words. "Babunia left you the money for a reason. She knew you'd use it to make her proud and you have. One stupid review and one scummy employee wouldn't have changed her opinion of you so easily. Give our grandmother's memory more credit."

"Listen to me." Tilly looked up from the yellow laminate into her mother's soft eyes. "Whether or not you decide to forgive Dan or let another man into your heart, I'll let you fight that out with Renia and your own thoughts. But don't let any of this make you think you don't deserve your dreams and you can't have them. You will make your dreams come true. It's a fact everyone has known since you were a little girl."

"Why didn't you ever tell me anything like this before?" Her mother had always been kind and supportive, but distant with her support. She had been so involved in Karl's choice of colleges and finding Renia a life after she got kicked out of high school that she'd been in the background for Tilly. It was Babunia who had been supportive.

The only time her mother had even expressed an opinion about Tilly's choice of career was when she realized Tilly would never run Healthy Food.

"I'm sorry. Maybe I should have, but I never thought you needed it. Karl needed someone to help him learn what it meant to be a man without his father, and Renia needed someone to keep her out of jail, but you were always so quiet, cooking in the kitchen with Babunia. I didn't think you needed me to tell you what I thought you already knew."

The timer dinged and her mother stood up. "The bread should be cool enough to eat and Renia still has a wedding to work." She sliced the bread and laid it on the table with cold ham, butter, jams and sliced cucumbers and tomatoes. "Let's eat while your sister is still here and we can talk about this as much as you like later. You don't have to be back at work until Tuesday and you're welcome to stay here the whole time. I'll even put you to work in my kitchen."

CHAPTER TWENTY-FIVE

TILLY WAS WAITING tables during dinner at Healthy Food when Karl came in. He waved at some of the old men playing cards in the back and stopped to talk to Father Ramirez and Father Szymkiewicz. After he'd made his rounds and shaken hands, Karl sat at an empty table in her section.

"Why don't you answer your phone?" he asked by way of greeting.

"I'm working," she said, pulling at the pink flowered apron tied around her waist.

"You didn't answer your phone earlier today, either, and you weren't working for Mom then."

Earlier today Tilly had been working for herself. After Renia left, Tilly had called the glass company her insurance had recommended. She'd met them at Babka, arguing with them about how long it would take to fix her window. They couldn't fix her window on Monday. Babka couldn't reopen until Wednesday. She would lose another day's business.

"I didn't hear the ring." She hadn't heard it because she'd turned the ringer off. Each time Dan's phone number popped up on the screen she had to sit on her hands—or smack herself upside the head—to keep from answering.

"The phone only rings if you turn the sound on." Tilly smiled innocently at her brother, but he wasn't finished with his lecture. "You didn't turn the phone off completely, because you didn't want calls to go straight to voice mail. It would be too obvious you were hiding."

"Fine." Why was it so hard to lie to family? "I turned the ringer off. But waiting on tables is hardly hiding."

Karl looked at her apron and short green uniform. "Why are you out here anyway? Why aren't you in the kitchen with Mom?"

"She kicked me out," Tilly answered under her breath.

"Why?"

Tilly rolled her eyes. "I kept correcting her technique."

Karl sighed and Tilly took sick pleasure in knowing she could get a rise out of her perfect sibling. "When you want something, you have to strategize and plan. You can't just say whatever comes to your mind. Correcting Mom's technique," he said with a tsk and a head shake. "She's been cooking for longer than you've been alive. No wonder she kicked you out of the kitchen. Planning, Tilly. Planning and a good filter to prevent stupid comments from coming out of your mouth. Both those things would go a long way to helping you with your goals."

"Thanks, *Dad*. Any other life lessons you need to impart to me before you succumb to old age and senility?"

Karl opened his mouth and Tilly worried he was going to launch into another reprimand. Given their family's history, it might not have been the most sensitive way of teasing him. Instead, he laughed. "You're right. I deserve that. Neither you nor Renia need me to be a father to you."

"No." She smiled to soften the blow. "We like you fine as a brother."

With eight years between them, and their father and brother dying when she was eight, Renia twelve and Karl sixteen, he had tried hard to be two brothers and a father figure to them. He'd stopped, for the most part, when Renia was sixteen and moved to Cincinnati. Tilly had wondered if he'd given up, until his wife left him. After his divorce, Tilly realized Jessica had been insistent that Tilly and Renia didn't need Karl to be a father to them. Without Jessica around he occasionally retreated into his old ways.

"As your brother, I'm telling you to start answering your phone."

"If Dan's been calling you, I'm sorry. I'll text him and tell him to stop."

"Dan?" Karl looked at her quizzically. "Oh, Dan Meier. No, he's not been calling me. Ed Davis, from the *Sun-Times,* called me. He was at Babka last night."

Tilly looked around the restaurant and saw only the first rush of Healthy Food diners, and older Polonia with no kids living nearby, who came in for an early dinner on Saturday. They wouldn't get the cops or college kids in until later. She sat down at the table. "I remember him. He wanted information about your office." She closed her eyes and pictured the tables. "He was seated with a gluten-free woman."

"His daughter." Karl knew everyone in Chicago. Not just in the Polish neighborhoods, both the thriving ones, like Archer Heights where Healthy Food was, and the historic ones, like the nearby Back of the Yards that were now more Hispanic than Polish, but across the city. Maybe he'd even known about Steve's drug habit.

"Was he calling you because of my unsatisfactory answer?"

"No, and thank you for not revealing anything. He was calling me because one of the *Sun-Times* writers has been working on a feature story about starting a business during hard times. After Ed told him about both the calamity of last night and the graciousness with which you made sure his daughter got dinner, he wants to make you the centerpiece of the story. It's scheduled to run on Wednesday, making your troubles perfectly timed."

"Really?"

"Yes, really," Karl said, exasperated. "Ed's been trying to call you all day and finally gave up right before the Carter wedding started. He called me in desperation."

"Should I do it?"

"Now you want fatherly advice?"

"I want *your* advice. You know the impact of media stories better than I do. I can't do the interview if the story will make me an object of pity and hurt Babka's chance of survival. I still want Babka to succeed."

"It'll help. After last night, Ed admires you. He wouldn't have suggested this if he didn't think it would help. And Ed may harass me some in the papers, but I trust him."

"What do I do?"

"Just call the man and do what he says." Karl pushed a piece of paper across the table. "And answer your phone. It might be someone important."

Karl slid out of the booth and smoothed the wrinkle out of his slacks. Tilly called out to him before he reached the door, "Aren't you going to stay for dinner? Mom will be heartbroken if you leave."

He shook hands with four people coming in the door before he answered her. "I have a charity fundraiser I'm late for. Tell her I'll eat her food another time."

AFTER THE WEDDING, which had been as horrible as he'd expected, Dan got to take a woman home. Only it wasn't the woman he'd hoped to spend the weekend with. Tilly wasn't answering her phone and Dan wouldn't be surprised if she never answered another phone call from him in her life. She couldn't overlook his review and she blamed him for the gossip column.

No, instead of delicious Tilly, Dan was seated in his living room with his sister. His unsympathetic sister. The sister who insisted she needed a date to the wedding, even when everyone now knew about his failed relationship with

Tilly. And his role, however unintended, in helping Steve sabotage Babka. He'd given Beth every argument he could think of.

When he'd said how unpleasant the experience would be, especially after last night, she'd said, "Oh, will everyone be mean to Danny?" in the obnoxious voice he remembered from childhood. Then she'd told him he deserved whatever ill treatment he got.

Beth had raised an eyebrow at his attempt, halfhearted at best, to paint her as an accomplice. She hadn't gotten the father of the groom drunk and, even if he hadn't contributed to the gossip column, he'd written a stupid review and was being punished for it. His ballbusting sister could keep her brow raised longer than he could look offended. In any case, she was right. He deserved the old-fashioned tar-and-feather treatment. No one would be in this situation if he'd followed his personal standards when reviewing Babka.

He'd tried another argument. "My presence will just be a distraction from the blessed event."

"Better you be there to be the villain than Michelle's future father-in-law. You missed his drunken exhibition while you were chasing down that skinny druggie." Beth had never given an inch, not once in her life. Except when she had given a mile to their father.

"I'm never going to another wedding with you again." He put his feet up on the coffee table and took a drink from his beer. "This has been the worst weekend I've ever spent. It's not even over."

"You have…" Beth began.

"…no one but myself to blame," Dan finished for her. "I know. Strangely, the knowledge I screwed myself over doesn't make me feel any better. Do you think it will help me sleep tonight, knowing I'm the agent of my own destruction?" Or that he'd been a stubborn fool because he was still afraid to disappoint his father.

Beth shook her head and they sat together in silence for several minutes. Beth hadn't had a fun weekend, either. As Dan had been frantically calling and texting Tilly, Beth had gotten a call from their father. Some leak in the grapevine had alerted their old man to their business plans and he was trying to convince Beth to come back to Meier Dairy. But he was their father, so he wasn't trying to convince her by promising to leave the company in her hands after he retired. Dan Sr. still insisted Dan would wake up one day and want to be a cheese maker to the masses. No, Dan Sr.'s way of convincing his daughter to return to the fold was to tell her what a failure she would be on her own, which proved how little Dan Sr. knew about his daughter.

Beth wasn't a ballbuster because she needed bluster to cover her own fears, but because she knew her own worth and liked to smash people who weren't smart enough to figure it out. The phone call pissed Beth off and made her more determined to make a success out of their new venture.

Dan Sr.'s voice hadn't made the wedding any more pleasant. Dan had heard his father's closing remarks loudly and clearly, despite Beth trying to tuck the phone away. "The man you were dating left you because he needed someone a little more womanly. No one wants to marry a bitch. Everyone at the wedding will take one look at you, on a date with your brother, and know you can't hang on to a man. Your offer to give me a grandson was a joke."

Asshole. Dan Sr. had been trying to call him all night, a ring Dan ignored. He checked his phone every time it vibrated—in case Tilly called—and enjoyed the childish burst of spite he felt every time he sent his father to voice mail.

"Aren't we a fun pair?" Beth spoke first.

"Dad's a douchebag."

Beth snorted halfheartedly, but didn't smile.

"I'm a douchebag, too, so trust me—I can recognize one from a thousand paces."

Silence.

A dog barked and a car drove down the street. Beth's beer bottle clinked as she set it on his coffee table.

"What are you going to do about Tilly? I like her."

"I like her, too, but she's not talking to me right now."

"And you're going to let her ignore you?"

"I've been at a wedding all day. It's hard to pursue one woman when you're at a wedding with a different woman."

Beth shrugged. "If you want her back, you have to fight for her. You need something big. Positive marketing of some sort."

"I'll take any suggestions you've got."

"A new review. I think you owe her that much."

"It's written. Stupidly, I was going to talk with her first—I didn't want to blindside her again—then have the new review published. I didn't want her to think I published the review to manipulate her into forgiving me. I wanted her free to decide." Dan finished his beer in one long pull and set the bottle down next to his sister's. "I had a plan. This morning, instead of waking up feeling like something the dog barfed up, I was going to take you to the wedding. After the wedding, when I was feeling good and romantic, I was going to go to Babka and wait for her to get off work. Maybe after we talked, she'd want to come back here—and you'd want to go somewhere else."

A clattering sound came from next to the TV and both Meier siblings looked over to see Paulie spinning his wheel. The rat's movements mirrored Dan's feelings. He was a rat, stuck in a cage, on a wheel, and it was all of his own making.

"What's stopping you?"

"Babka's closed, so I can't go there. She's not answering her phone, nor did she answer when I stopped by her apartment. She thinks I was *ChicagoScoops*'s source for that damned gossip column."

"That column really screwed with your chances of sleeping with her. I mean, not more than you screwed with them, but it didn't help."

"Tell me something I don't know."

"And if the lady wasn't interested in your heartfelt apology?"

"Part of my 'heartfelt apology' was the new review. The piece is more than already written. I've submitted it to Rich. I have the email chain to prove it. Hell," he grunted, "I even won my weekly bet with Mike."

"You wrote the review to get into Tilly's pants?"

"I wrote the review because I was wrong and the restaurant deserved another chance. Not only for Tilly, but for every single employee in there, except Steve." Beth's look forced full honesty from him. "I wrote the review for noble reasons. I made sure I had the email chain as proof of my submission so she would forgive me and I could, as you so nicely put it, 'get into Tilly's pants.' And, while you and Mike both seem to have this obsession with Tilly's pants, what I want to have is for her to talk to me again. Let me take her out on another date. Meet her mom. You know, have a normal relationship that—God willing—will lead to something long-term and permanent."

"You need more than the review now. Dad may question my femininity, but I'm enough of a girl to know Tilly will need more before she'll even be willing to hear you out. Much more."

"I know." Dan slouched down into the couch. "Besides, the review is because Tilly the chef needs it. I owe a correction to her professionally. I need to give something else to Tilly personally. Something to prove that I know the depth of my mistake and that I'm sorry. Something without strings attached. It has to be hers, whether she takes me back or not."

She wanted proof that Dan wasn't correcting his mistake because she wanted him to, but because *he* wanted to. He'd give it to her, if he only knew what it was.

Beth stood and walked to the kitchen. He heard the click of bottle caps being removed and she returned with two more beers. She pressed one into his hand, then sat next to him.

"Does anyone know why Steve was trying to ruin Babka?" Beth asked.

"If they do, they aren't telling me."

"Maybe there's an opportunity there we can exploit."

"Beth, why are you trying to help me?"

"You're my brother," she said without hesitation.

"I figured you would side with Tilly and cast me as the unforgivable villain."

"You screwed up pretty badly, but I don't think what you did is unforgivable. It's not like you actually were the gossip column's source. And…" She paused. "I don't think Tilly thinks what you did is unforgivable, either, nor does she really believe you would broadcast your relationship across Chicago. I just don't think she knows it yet."

"Are you going to tell her?"

Beth shook her head. "I saw how she looked at you and how you two interacted last night. She was busy and more than a little stressed, but she avoided looking in your direction too much for her to not care. You do something for her, something worth more than the pain she's feeling. She needs a reason to forgive you."

CHAPTER TWENTY-SIX

AFTER TILLY ARRANGED to meet the *Sun-Times* reporter, she spent an hour on her mom's computer looking up Frank O'Malley's old articles. Karl's advice, especially about reporters and the city of Chicago, was generally trustworthy, but she didn't completely trust anyone who had a byline right now.

She didn't trust herself, and her personal doubt was the real kicker. Just as she'd been beginning to have more faith in herself, to believe that she could make it no matter Dan's review, Steve had blindsided her. She'd been so confident in her employees, in the hiring she'd done in an industry where transitory workers were rampant. In one night her confidence had been pulled out from under her, as if she were Charlie Brown, Steve was Lucy, and her self-image was the football. And Dan and the entire city of Chicago were on the sidelines, laughing.

The *CarpeChicago* review had shaken her. She'd known she would get bad reviews once in a while. Someone would come to her restaurant and not like the food or find fault with the service. Some nights drinks ran late, reservations got lost or waiters tripped and spilled food. Such criticisms were to be expected. No restaurant, not the French Laundry, not the much-missed Charlie Trotters, not Alinea, had perfect success. She'd been prepared for the impossible-to-please person whose food was always too hot or too cold, or the reviewer who didn't like Polish cooking and never would.

She hadn't expected to fall in love with the reviewer. What did such poor judgment say about her? And then the gossip column...

Dan had impaled her passion before flinging her over a cliff. For the days between the review and the Taste she had taken small, mincing steps at Babka, questioning her dream and herself. Something about Dan's understanding of the difference between eating to live and living to eat had pushed her to embrace her dream again. At first, maybe, it had been a desire to prove him wrong. Then she'd seen how much joy he'd taken in her food and it wasn't about showing him up anymore, but about giving enjoyment and hearing his opinion, no strings attached.

Dan took such pleasure in eating her food—and she took pleasure in feeding him. He had reminded her of why she had wanted to run a restaurant in the first place. She wasn't simply striving for perfection, though no one wanted to be a chef without reaching for that far-off star. She was providing people with the simple indulgence of a delicious meal that they didn't have to cook themselves, brought to them by courteous servers. Dan reminded her that cooking for the ones you love was giving them a gift, not just keeping them alive. She could be a chef seeking perfection and also the family cook providing warmth.

When she'd been around him, she'd felt a sense of permanence. She hadn't known love would comfort and excite her at the same time, or that her heart would beat faster and her blood race, but her nerves would settle. More than permanence, comfort and excitement, when she was around Dan, she had believed a family and a dream job was within her grasp. It would be possible because they would be working toward it together.

Perhaps that was the most frustrating thing about Dan and his critiquing job. The two of them had faced disaster together and they'd worked well as a team. If she could believe in love, she could believe that they'd shared a subconscious communication. Even when Tilly was feeling humiliated as she learned about the gossip column, as soon as Steve had revealed himself, Dan had gone after him. He'd known his role that night, just as she'd known hers.

The past month had been a roller coaster. A bad review—new low, no faith in her dream. Meeting Dan—new high, nothing but faith in her dreams. He'd been at Babka, for her and with her, as she worked through the fallout from his bad review to keep old customers and gain new ones.

When he'd promised nothing about the rat would make his website, she'd trusted him and he hadn't let her down.

Then had come the boot off the cliff. She was no longer on a roller coaster, but one of those endless free-fall rides. She kept falling and falling and falling without any ground to break her bones when she hit, because her hole had no bottom.

She hadn't lost faith only in her dreams. It was worse. She no longer had faith in herself.

Tilly had trusted two men and both had betrayed her trust. What else was she wrong about?

Her mind was like the blades of a food processor. Around and around and around she went. Cutting and chopping and mixing, bits of memories flinging out against the acrylic bowl. Dan fixing her sink. Steve, her reliable kitchen messenger, bringing her news of Dan waiting for her. Dan bringing her a pot of chocolate mint. Steve swearing he was clean. Dan trapping a rat and saving Babka from closing.

A gigantic finger would hit the pulse button and all those emotions would stop and start and stop and start. Of course she could trust Dan. Of course she could trust her own judgment. Her dreams were cracked, but still fixable. But before she could latch on to these happy thoughts, the finger would hit Pulse and the memories would be sent flinging around the bowl again.

Round and round and round she goes. Where she stops, nobody knows.

Tilly was exhausted. Every last cell in her body was sick and tired of these mind games. She'd managed to finish the dinner service at Healthy Food without incident, but only because most of the people who came in knew why she was back home and not working at Babka. Even the Saturday-night college kids knew. The Twitter hashtag of her review had been revived and the conversation was active again.

Everyone was nice about it. The college kids looked ready to make some jokes, but there were enough uniformed police filling their plates at the buffet for them to keep any rude comments quiet. Renia was right about Jan's image of himself as a white knight. He was falling over himself to be kind, attentive and understanding.

"No Polonia would ever have done this to you, Tilly," he told her with wide, innocent eyes. "Meier, he's German, right? You can't trust him. You should stick with your own."

She smiled blankly and ignored him. Jan couldn't help it if his hope was misplaced.

Tilly collapsed into bed after service was over, but sleep was elusive. All she did was toss and turn. What if agreeing to the *Sun-Times* article was a mistake? The Cuisinart was up and running around in her brain again. Physically drained but too emotionally keyed up to sleep, Tilly wandered into her mother's kitchen and turned on the computer to look up Frank O'Malley. Again.

Imbir snubbed her when she returned home on Monday.

Candace had checked on him on Saturday and Sunday, but Imbir's huffy walk and refusal to sit anywhere but on the tile in the bathroom was a sign. Candace's periodic feeding hadn't been enough.

His indignation didn't last long. Imbir soon decided sitting on the cold, hard tile being angry was not nearly as pleasant as sitting on Tilly's warm lap being petted. His purr rumbled through her thighs and his nails pricked at her shorts. As he kneaded his happiness, Tilly wondered what it would be like to go from scowling to forgiving so quickly.

I'm sick of those stupid doubts. I'm sick of myself. I can decide to get on with my life and keep fighting for Babka, or I can sit and sulk.

Poof. The thoughts that had been tormenting her all weekend were gone. Not completely, but at least the food processor in her head was turned off. If she pushed, she could unplug the damn thing. Maybe not stick it back in the cabinet where it belonged, but at least silence it for the moment.

She would trust herself.

Frank O'Malley was an older Irishman with a wrinkled, grandfatherly face and bright blue eyes. They met at Babka on Tuesday, while the repairman fixed the restaurant's large window. Frank had an easy way about him. Rather than jumping directly into the questions on his notepad, the kindly looking man with his only-in-Chicago nasally Irish accent talked with her about city neighborhoods, growing up with a strong cultural identity and shared funny stories of his immigration over forty years earlier.

By the time Frank started asking her questions, Tilly was treating him like a favorite uncle. She never completely forgot he was a reporter, but she allowed herself to be led into expressing her personal doubts and fears. She knew from her research that Frank liked David and Goliath stories. His favorite type of piece was one on a local businessman or nonprofit struggling against the odds to make good. By the time Tilly had read to the end of each piece, she was ready to drive out to Lamont, Oak Park, Clearing, Edison Park, Evanston and Forest Glen to support the little guy trying to hold steady in a shifting world. Frank's subjects never looked deluded for trying to hold on. The way he wrote about them, they were hardworking people striving for the American Dream.

Frank believed the people he wrote about were what made the city work. His articles wouldn't win any Pulitzer Prizes, but they captured Tilly's heart and reminded her why Chicago was such a great city.

His article wouldn't save Babka—only Tilly could do that—but it sure would help. Frank could help if she trusted him. Tilly could trust him if she trusted herself and, as of last night, Tilly trusted herself again.

After Frank turned off his tape recorder and put down his pencil, Tilly went to the bar and got them both a drink.

"It's not Guinness." She pushed the coffee-colored liquid with a creamy head across the table to him. "But I think this Polish stout will serve."

Frank took a long drink, finishing almost half the glass before setting the beer down and wiping off his foam mustache.

"I didn't know the Poles had it in them to make this kind of beer." He took another drink. "Not quite as roasted as I'd like and maybe a bit weak, but good enough."

She smiled. Frank had been eyeing the bar with its many bottles and taps since he'd walked in and sat down. "Come back for dinner sometime. Your meal will be on the house."

"You haven't read my article yet."

"I've read almost everything else by you I could find. I trust you."

"Hard words for a woman to say after being sucker punched like you were."

Tilly's answer was a sip of her beer.

"Do you know why your runner turned against you?" Frank asked.

"Karl sent me a text saying to call him and he'd tell me, but he's been in meetings all day. I haven't heard back from him."

Frank pushed his empty glass at her. "I'll trade you another beer for some information."

Tilly raised her eyebrow. "I thought it was a little weak."

He shrugged. "It's a Polish restaurant, not an Irish pub. My expectations are different."

She rose from the table with a chuckle and poured Frank another glass. "This one's from Finland."

"I thought you only served Polish here."

"I like having beers on the menu most people are unfamiliar with. They think they know what they're getting, coming into a Polish restaurant in Chicago. I like to surprise them."

He took a drink. "I hate to insult my host's heritage, but this one's better."

"From your comments, I thought you'd enjoy it." She took another sip of her beer and waited for Frank to tell her another story.

"Your runner is the nephew of the man who owns this building. He's worked in restaurants before, and been reliable when he wasn't using or hustling."

Tilly knew all of this. The other chefs she'd talked to had said Steve was great, if he could keep off drugs.

"Of course, users are hard to control and the boy sold out his uncle the moment he was confronted with an interrogation room." Frank chuckled. His grandfatherly air hadn't gone away completely, but now Frank seemed like a favorite uncle because instead of giving you candy, he told you things your parents didn't want you to know. "Maybe the Chicago P.D. doesn't deserve its reputation as thugs, but it sure must come in handy sometimes. A friend of mine down at the station said all it took was Detective Parker pounding his fist on the table for that boy to start talking."

"Why?"

"Why did he talk?" Frank looked puzzled for a moment as he took another drink. "Oh, you mean why did your landlord screw you over?"

Frank took a deep breath and settled in for his story. "Like all good screwings, this one was about sex. Your landlord has an expensive wife and an even more expensive girlfriend. He needed money and has been looking for new tenants for some of his buildings. He found one for yours and they wanted the building in December. Steve was supposed to find a way to get you out fast, without costing him extra money." Frank looked at her approvingly. "You had a pretty smart lease, cheap rent and a high penalty if he broke it. Good job."

Tilly gave a half smile. "It was a bad real estate market and one of Karl's friends helped me negotiate." Since Frank seemed to know everything, she asked him the one question that had been burning in her brain—was Dan's review coincidence or planned? "The cat and dog?"

"A prank pulled by the runner, who swore he didn't know Dan was going to be here. The animals were released on purpose, but the review was accidental. Steve knew Dan was a food writer, which is why he salted the food, but he didn't realize Dan was The Eater."

"What's going to happen to my building?" She could recover her sanity and her livelihood only to lose her building.

"Since the wife now knows about the girlfriend and

wants a divorce, your landlord has even bigger money troubles, but the tenant isn't interested in the building anymore. Your landlord found a buyer instead and I think you'll like him fine."

"Who is it?"

"I'm not sayin'." Frank crossed his arms over his chest and leaned back against the chair.

"Come on, Frank, it's my livelihood. We spent over an hour talking about supporting the little guy. I'm the little guy here."

Frank shook his head. "Tilly, I've been a reporter in Chicago for longer than you've been alive. I know when to keep my mouth shut and when to spill my guts."

Tilly humphed. "This is my restaurant and my life. I think I have a right to know."

"Karl may tell you. For all his glad-handing and public persona, he remains a trusted neutral in Chicago politics by being impossible to read. His only reaction when someone asked about you was to say, 'My sister can take care of herself,' with that wax-museum face of his." Frank leaned forward, his elbows thunking loudly on the table. "But I like you and I'll give you some unsolicited advice."

She gave him a long hard look before saying, "Okay."

"You've had a tough weekend and some people close to you have treated you pretty badly. Dan should probably have to sweat a little—the squirming will teach the boy a lesson—but he's a good man. You seem like you've got your head screwed on right. Whatever you decide to do about him, trust yourself and I think you'll come out fine."

"Is this the reporter talking?"

"I can't separate myself from my job. Not possible. But all of us in the dying print business know one another. And we know who to trust."

CHAPTER TWENTY-SEVEN

ON WEDNESDAY, Tilly couldn't escape the feeling of déjà vu dogging her steps. It had started in the morning as Imbir climbed on her bed, whining for food and nudging her head with his chin. The eerie sensation followed her as she drove through the streets of Chicago from her apartment to Babka in her old hatchback.

Sitting around the table with Candace, who had agreed to come early, the sense of déjà vu stopped following her and hit her on the head. They were waiting for Karen. On an earlier Wednesday, after an earlier disaster, she had been sitting around the table waiting for Karen when they got Dan's terrible review. Again, they were waiting for Karen to come in with a newspaper. Tilly hadn't trusted herself not to peek at the article. She wished she could have all her staff here for the reading of Frank's article, but she couldn't wait until family meal to see what he'd written. If the article was good, they needed to make sure the restaurant was prepared.

Babka was everything Tilly had ever wanted in a restaurant. Her staff made it possible, but it had been her dream and their livelihood. Over time, her staff had made Babka more than a paycheck; they had made her dream their dream. Their bar was interesting because Candace researched unusual Northern and Eastern European beers and wine, as well as creating unique cocktails with a Polish feel to them. Karen made the dining room function without a hitch. Karen, and the front-of-house staff, made sure all customers were welcomed and appreciated. They answered any questions about the food and always took the time to learn how to pronounce the Polish name for each dish. They wanted Babka to succeed as much as Tilly did, and not just because Babka was their job. They wanted it to succeed because they loved the restaurant, too.

They turned as Karen clattered into the kitchen and rushed through the doors into the dining room, the *Sun-Times* over her head. She slid into her seat, shoving the paper across the table at Tilly.

"Do we open the champagne yet?" She turned to Candace, her eyes wide with innocence.

First were the giggles, then a couple of snorts until finally the tension around the table disappeared in a fit of laughter. Déjà vu hadn't been dogging only Tilly. Her staff's mood had quivered like jelly. Karen's easy reference to the last time they had sat around the table waiting to read an article about Babka relaxed everyone.

"Well," Tilly said as she reached for the paper and flipped through it until she found the article. "Shall we see what it says?

"Oh, my!" Tilly laid the paper on the table. Accompanying the story was a picture. Tilly stood in Babka's kitchen in her chef's uniform, kneading dough, her hair under her white kerchief. Renia—according to the photo credit, Frank had gotten the shot from her sister—had caught her with a slight smile on her face and flour on her cheek. "Do you want to eat food prepared by that chef?"

Candace laughed. "You look hot in that picture."

"What?" She remembered the day the photo had been taken. Renia had been in the restaurant playing with a new camera lens. The kitchen was always hot, but it had been particularly hot that day and her face shimmered with perspiration.

"It's true. There are other ways to a man's heart besides his stomach and the I-dare-you look on your face appeals to all of them. I don't even care what the article says. The photo alone will get us some business."

"Thanks," Tilly said, pleased with Candace's compliment. The photo looked like another Tilly, the Tilly she had resolved to be. Candace saw something sexual in the picture, but Tilly saw a woman whose knowing smile meant she was confident in her success. Renia had taken the picture after Dan's review and the Taste, before Dan and his friend had come into the restaurant, when Tilly had been feeling pretty down about her chances of success.

But no one would know it from the picture. Renia's photographs always managed to capture some hidden truth. Tilly's hidden truth, so deeply buried she didn't even know it was there, was that Babka was going to succeed. The article in the *Sun-Times* didn't matter. Dan's review didn't matter. Steve didn't matter. Babka would succeed because the woman Renia had photographed would prevail. She would stick it out, day in and day out, until it happened.

"Are you going to read the article?" Karen interrupted Tilly's thoughts, pulling her back to the present.

"Yes, of course. 'Local chef battles for culinary success.'" Tilly read the entire article to her staff. Frank had started with the death of her father, brother and grandfather. "'After the tragedy, young Tila's grandmother took her under her wing in the kitchen. Tila Milek learned Polish cooking from one of the rocks of Chicago's Polish community.'" He breezed through her education and concentrated most of the article on the trials of the past couple of months, minus Paulie the Rat. "'Through it all, Tila has maintained a high sense of morale in her staff through her passion for cooking and her delicious food. While she is nervous about the new owner of her building, she is cautiously hopeful Babka will be another brick in the foundation of Chicago's Polonia.'"

Silence followed Tilly's reading of the article.

The phone rang. Karen left the table to answer it. "Yes," she said into the phone. "It was a nice article. Mmm-hmm, it has been a rough month, but we are confident in our restaurant and in our chef." Her voice faded as she walked through the kitchen into Tilly's office. "Let me pull up our calendar. Yes, we have a table for four at eight. The window has been fixed—you would never know it was broken. What's the name? Jorgenson? We'll see you at eight."

Karen raced back to the table with a happy squeal. "Tilly, you need to help prep. We have enough pending reservations through OpenTable to fill every seat all night. I might even have to turn some people down."

"Really?" Tilly got up and followed Karen into the office. While she looked over Karen's shoulder, her hostess accepted some reservations and sent responses to others, suggesting new times. If the online reservation system was to be believed, Babka wouldn't have an empty seat for dinner for two weeks.

She took a deep breath, but her relief couldn't be contained. She laughed. "I was optimistic when I placed some of my food orders this week. I'm glad I was, although I'm still worried we might run out of food. I'll have to call my farmers. All right, everyone, let's getting cracking." She clapped. "It will be a busy day." After that, Tilly didn't stop moving once. She wasn't the only exhausted person. After another warning from Karen about the number of phone calls they were getting, Tilly called her mom for extra help. Healthy Food sent her a second dishwasher, runner and another line cook. Everyone, from Tilly down to her new dishwasher, was busy getting Babka ready to reopen for dinner.

THE CHATTERING BUZZ of a busy restaurant fell completely silent when Dan walked through the door of Babka.

A month ago—hell, even yesterday—a handful of people in this room might have known his name, but had no idea what he looked like. Now, not only did everyone know his name and what he looked like, they knew of his largest failure.

Giving Babka a bad review had been a slipup, a professional error, but when he'd refused to consider a new review so his father could walk down the street with his head held high, he'd failed Tilly and his readers. And himself. He'd taken the coward's way out, justifying his decisions with ridiculous excuses. Maybe she could've forgiven him for the poor review, but his delay and the way he'd left her vulnerable to embarrassment from things like the gossip article were harder to forgive.

Dan was a betting man and only a fool would put any money on his chances tonight. Not only had he wagered money, but he'd wagered a lot of money. Fool or not, Dan had to try to win Tilly back.

Except for his usual seat at the bar, the restaurant was full. Candace raised her eyebrow at his approach, but she didn't tell him to leave or shoot him with the seltzer hose. He allowed his hopes to rise a little. Even if Tilly blamed him for the gossip article, maybe her staff didn't. His odds at success tonight were terrible, but they were marginally better if Candace and Karen didn't take a stand against him. He didn't expect them to take his side; he just needed them to be neutral. He could come back to Babka night after night after night, but he'd never get a foot in the door if they decided to ban him.

He slid onto the stool and put his papers on the bar.

Candace eyed the fat envelope. "Do you want a menu?"

"Yes, please," Dan said with relief. She was apparently neutral, and she might even be on his side.

Candace pulled a menu from behind her and told him the specials. He placed his order. When she returned with his beer and water, she nodded at the papers. "What's in the envelope?"

"You're being too nice to me not to have seen *Carpe-Chicago*. Has Tilly seen it?" He ignored her other question. An argument could be made that Candace had a right to know, but Dan wasn't going to be the one to make it.

Candace let his avoidance slide. "No. She hasn't mentioned your name to me since Friday night and has kept herself busy so she doesn't have to think about you. She couldn't avoid hearing us talk about your new review of Babka today, but I doubt she'll ever read it."

"No one told her what it said?"

"We're not going to make this easy for you," she said sternly. Then her voice softened and she shrugged. "We won't make it hard for you, either."

"Will you tell her I'm here?"

"She might not see you. Or she might kick you out before you can eat your dinner. Hell, she might even toss your food in your face."

"It's a risk, but I'm gambling tonight."

Tilly walked through the kitchen door and Dan's heart seized. Her jacket was splattered with flour, beet juice and something else Dan couldn't identify. Strands of blue hair had escaped her white kerchief and were plastered to her face, which had a fine sheen of sweat from work and the heat of the kitchen. Her face was tight with the stress of the full restaurant, and the shock of seeing him.

She had never looked more beautiful.

Dan had spent many hours imagining Tilly sweaty, mostly dreams involving them naked and in a bed, but his favorite way to imagine her was like this, passionately engaged in a job she loved.

Maybe second favorite.

She walked carefully toward him, the tension on her face turning to wariness as she realized each and every person in Babka was watching them closely. Not a single fork scraped a plate. Everyone wanted to hear what was going to be said. Tomorrow, the interaction between him and Tilly would be the talk of the neighborhood.

She stood in front of him, the bar between them, and the air in the room sizzled.

"Why are you here?" she asked in a low whisper.

"I embarrassed you publicly," he answered in a whisper. He raised his voice for what he said next so everyone in the silent restaurant heard him. "I am apologizing publicly. I'm sorry, Tilly."

She bit her lower lip and looked around the room. Not a single person in the room was hiding their interest in this conversation. Someone should hand out popcorn.

"I accept your apology. Enjoy your dinner."

She turned to go, but he jumped off the barstool and stopped her with a hand on her arm. "I didn't have anything to do with the *ChicagoScoops* article. Can we talk somewhere else?"

She gave his hand a look as if she considered it only slightly above a serpent, but Dan didn't let her go. He couldn't let her go, not yet.

"Please," he said.

"I have a full restaurant and don't have the time."

"Later?"

"I'll be sleeping."

Dan resisted sighing. He knew this wouldn't be easy, but

he'd hoped. Nothing worth fighting for was easy. Those words had seemed trite before, but were as real as love and death now. He removed his hand. "Before work tomorrow?"

"Babka's got a full house tomorrow. I'll be busy then, too."

"If you won't talk to me now, at least take this." Dan slid the envelope over the bar to her. "It's yours, whether or not you ever talk to me again."

"What is it?"

"My gift to you, free and clear."

She nodded, picked the packet up and walked away. Without looking back once.

Candace brought out his food. "You staying to eat?"

"Did you read what I said about her food in today's review?" He smiled, but he couldn't put his full heart into the grin. "Of course I'm staying to eat."

Dan reached for his fork, but Candace interrupted him again. "Are you going to be back?"

"Tomorrow night." He smiled again, this time with the warmth of faint hope. "And the next night and the next. At some point she will have to either hear me out or kick me out. I'd prefer the former, of course."

"I'll save you a seat."

TILLY COLLAPSED INTO the driver's seat when the night was over. Candace groaned as she eased her tired body into the passenger side. Tilly turned the car on and the air-conditioning to full blast, letting the cold air wash over them for a couple minutes before she backed out of her parking spot.

They could both hear the elephant in the car breathing in the backseat, even if they pretended not to see it. Candace spoke first.

"Did you read what he gave you?"

Tilly didn't pretend not to know who "he" was. "No."

"You didn't even open the envelope?"

"No. It's probably an apology and I'm not sure I want to read it."

"You didn't read the review, either."

"No." Too little, too late, she was sure. Did he think she'd fall over in gratitude because he'd fixed a mistake he shouldn't have made in the first place?

"Something else is in the envelope. The review was his big apology. You should read it. Half the people there tonight came because of the *Sun-Times* article, the other half because of Dan's review."

Candace spoke with her eyes closed. Tilly wished she wasn't driving, so she could follow suit.

"I suppose I shouldn't question *why* we have customers, but I wish they were coming for the food and not out of some voyeuristic desire for entertainment."

Candace smiled. "They'll come back for the food, at least. And Dan's article made it clear people should come for the food in the first place."

"Whose side are you on?"

"Yours, of course. You like Dan, and he's always been good company for me while he waited for you, without getting in the way of my job. The review was terrible, but his apology was pretty grand and I think you should hear him out. You don't owe it to him, but you do owe it to yourself."

Tilly *hmphed*. Candace's words made some sense, but she wasn't quite ready to hear them. She hadn't worked through her feelings for Dan yet. "Someone blabbed to that blog."

"Do you really think Dan was the source?"

"Maybe." That was a lie. "No. He didn't tell me he was The Eater at the Taste, but he hasn't lied to me since then." He'd even been painfully upfront about why he wouldn't write a new review. If he'd been the source for *ChicagoScoops,* he'd have been honest about it. The blog article was probably another of Steve's gifts to her business.

And she should match Dan's honesty with honesty of her own. She loved Dan, despite the hurt. The Dan who had come into Babka every night for a drink. The Dan who had taken her out for cinnamon rolls and to Ravinia. The Dan who had fixed her pot sink and rescued her from a rat. That Dan supported her. She still wasn't sure The Eater was the same Dan.

"Do you know anything about the new owner of the building?" Candace asked.

"No. He, or she, hasn't contacted me yet. Karl told me to go ahead and operate Babka like normal. It's weird, though. You would think they'd get in touch with me."

"No news is good news?"

"Let's hope so."

CHAPTER TWENTY-EIGHT

DAN CAME BACK to Babka every night. He sat in the same seat Thursday and Friday. Tilly always knew which dish was his because Candace would come back into the kitchen to get the plate and raise her eyebrow.

Tilly always ignored her.

She had plenty to do, and nowhere on her list was "talk with Dan Meier." Babka stayed full through the week and her staff kept up. While some of her customers were still people who wanted to witness Dan's vigil on the barstool, Chicago was quickly losing interest and moving its attention to the next local scandal.

Saturday was different.

Dan still sat on the same barstool and Candace raised her eyebrow at Tilly when she got his food from the kitchen. Only, he was still sitting there when Babka closed. Karen, Candace and her entire front-of-house staff—not one of those traitors kicked him out when the restaurant closed. They left him sitting there, as if he belonged.

Irritation welled up inside her stomach and burst out angrily. "Don't you have another restaurant to review?"

Dan's face was a mix of sadness and disappointment. "You didn't look at anything I gave you."

Disappointment? At her? She wasn't the one who'd written the stupid review in the first place. If she didn't want to look at the papers, she didn't have to look at the papers.

No matter what Candace (or Renia, who'd agreed with

Candace when Tilly had called her) said. Or Frank O'Malley, for that matter. If she didn't want to read his papers, that was her right.

"I've been busy," she answered testily.

"I'd hoped…" He stopped when she scowled at him. "Can we make a deal?"

Tilly stopped herself from responding with a childish "Why should I make a deal with you?" She was being prickly and she didn't like the feeling.

You owe it to yourself to hear him out.

"What's the deal?"

"I'll wait here while you read the papers. If you still want nothing to do with me when you're done, I'll respect your wishes. I'll leave without a word. But I'm not going anywhere until you've seen them."

"I'm supposed to give Candace a ride home."

"You don't need to," Candace said. Of course her entire staff was listening. "Hakim's picking me up tonight."

Very convenient.

Don't be bitchy, Tilly.

She had to hear Dan out. Her inner shrew was waving her finger and saying whiny, immature things because Tilly felt as if she were standing on gelatin. The only sure way to defeat the shrew was to have everything out in the open. If she kicked Dan out, the shrew wouldn't have him to attack. If she accepted Dan's apology and let him back into her life, the shrew wouldn't have anything to attack him about.

"Okay. The papers are in my office." Tilly stomped away, the shrew cackling with every childish stomp as the little bitch fought to stay alive and relevant.

DAN STARTED TO WORRY about Tilly when she didn't return in thirty minutes. He checked to make sure the front door was locked, then headed through the kitchen to find her.

She sat at the tiny desk in the closet she called an office, crying softly.

She looked up when he closed the door and sat in one of the other chairs. Her eyes were red and bright, but no longer angry.

"Is this real?" she asked, gesturing to the papers on her desk.

"Yes. Both the review and the promissory note."

"You've quit your job?"

"I'm no longer writing reviews for *CarpeChicago,* though I'll keep writing freelance for a while. Beth and I are officially business partners now."

"And the note?" She shook the paper at him.

"It's real, too. I, uh, well, I knew how to apologize to Tilly the chef for my poor review, but I didn't know how to apologize to Tilly the woman I love for the situation I put her in. Giving her ultimate control of her destiny seemed like the best I could do." The next words were harder to say, but no less required. "There's no price on your building. If you send me packing right now, the deed to the building will still be delivered to you. I don't want anything from you as a thank-you. I mean—" he hesitated "—I want a lot of things from you, just none of them as a thank-you."

"How much did this cost you?"

Dan coughed. "I'm not going to tell you, but I had the money. Now you have the building."

"So this—" she picked up the note that told her she would own the building as soon as the paperwork went through, and waved the paper in the air "—is nothing."

"I'm not going to be living off peanut butter and ramen noodles because of it, but it's not nothing. I need the business with Beth to succeed, or I'll be turning to my father for a job to make sure I can afford mortgage payments.

Does the money matter? I never imagined you to be interested in that."

"I'm not. I just…" She sniffled. "I don't know what to think of this. I don't know what to think of *you*." She wiped her eyes with the back of her hand, the note fluttering in her grasp as the paper moved across her face. She looked directly into his eyes. "I don't know if I can trust you."

Dan took a deep breath to still the pain in his heart as she said those words. If she didn't trust him, they were doomed.

"You cost me my certainty. I doubted myself because of you."

The break in her voice broke his heart. "I never meant to make you doubt yourself. I should never have written the review in the first place. I should have come back to eat at least two more meals. I should've written a new review earlier. I shouldn't have compromised both of us."

He leaned forward in his chair. He wanted to walk over to her and hold her in his arms, but he couldn't force her. She had to be willing to accept him. If he couldn't convince her to accept him, he was lost.

"These mistakes, they are all my responsibility. They are all things I did. In response to a terrible review and an employee being paid to close your restaurant, you worked harder. You take quality ingredients and make them better. You stood in front of the city and showed them I was wrong." He took another deep breath and willed her to hear him. Not just to listen to what he was saying, but to hear the importance of every word. "You faced all of this and stood strong. I am in awe of you."

A tear glistened on her face. "What am I supposed to do with you? With us?"

"You know what decision I hope you make. But no matter what you do tonight, I will always be thankful for my horrible dinner at Babka. Without that dinner, I wouldn't have gone to the Taste. And I wouldn't have met you. My life is better because I know you."

He gazed into her eyes, steadily and firmly, so she could see every emotion inside him. The bone-shaking fear that she would send him out of the restaurant forever and the hope she would open her arms and they could begin their life together. "Can you trust me for tonight?"

She nodded.

"Can you trust me for tomorrow?"

She nodded again.

Dan closed his eyes to collect his emotions before opening them and baring his soul to Tilly. "Trust me for tonight and tomorrow. In a month or so, you can start trusting me for weeks at a time instead of days at a time. We can work up to months, then years and then maybe for the rest of our lives. Would that be okay with you?"

Tilly sniffed a loud, shuddering sniff, and her answer came out in a shaky sob. "Yes."

Dan smiled, the pressure of his mistake sliding off his back, and, for the first time in weeks, he felt free. "That wasn't as forceful and joyous of a yes as I might have wanted, but you can't take it back now."

He looked at this beautiful, passionate and forgiving woman and knew what he wanted to do next. Actually, what he wanted to do next had never been a question; now he could actually do something about it.

Dan let one breath go in and out, thinking about what he had to say with a single-minded determination. "I want to kiss you, but if I kiss you now, I don't think I'll be able to stop until I make love to you." He didn't know what he would do if she turned him down. He wanted her with an intensity he'd never experienced before. "If you don't trust me enough tonight, let me know. Before I get out of this chair to kiss you, I want to make sure you know where this is headed and you're okay with it."

Tilly nodded one more time and Dan was out of his chair before her head finished moving.

He wanted to touch her everywhere at once, to haul her out of her chair and press the length of his body against her while running his hands along her sides. For a week, he hadn't been able to touch her and he wanted to make up for lost time in five seconds. Every muscle of his body tensed as he forced himself just to run his finger along her jaw before he leaned in to kiss her.

"God, Tilly, I want you," he whispered against her lips. "As much as I want to sit on the desk and lift you on top of me now, I intend to do this right." He looked at the dingy walls looming over the tiny, secondhand wooden desk and smiled. "As right as I can, not in a bed." He felt her smile against his lips. "Slowly and carefully."

The kiss began gently, lips against lips. Her lips melded perfectly to his mouth. Wanting, begging noises from the back of her throat inflamed his desire, but he concentrated on kissing this perfect woman. He only got to make love to her for the first time once, and Dan intended to make it last.

Tilly scooted forward in her office chair, her knees brushing past the insides of his intimately straddling thighs. She never broke their kiss as she inched closer to him and pulled his shirt out from his pants to rub her hands over his stomach. Calluses and scars nicked sensitive skin. Underneath the burning want was joy that Tilly was back in his life. The hands smoothing down his sides belonged to the woman he loved.

She pulled her hands away for a moment to unbutton his shirt. He shrugged, she pushed and when the shirt fell off his arms, he kicked it away with his foot.

They had to break apart when she pulled up his T-shirt,

which quickly followed his dress shirt to the floor. Tilly took advantage of the break to shift even closer to him in the chair and press her lips against his stomach. Heaven, her every touch was heaven. Her hands traced up and down his back as she kissed and licked.

He bunched his hands in her hair, holding her tight against him as he looked down at the woman he loved. Every rough spot on her beautiful hands prickled his skin as they explored his body. Those strong hands. He loved Tilly's hands. Her mind thought about her culinary heritage and she had extensive training, but her hands did the work. As she reached down into the waistband of his pants the rough calluses on her fingers tickled and when she grasped his butt he could feel the strength built from years of kneading dough.

Tilly crafted, made beautiful and delicious meals, with love and those hands. Those hands now caressing his body and those hands he hoped to have caressing his body for the rest of his life. Her hands weren't decorative, they worked. Tilly wasn't decorative. She had purpose.

Now the purpose was turned on him.

With a snap and a zip, his pants were undone and she slipped her hands into his waistband and down…

"I was trying to do this slowly and carefully," he said, breathing hard at the intense pleasure of Tilly's hands wrapped around him. He kept his tight hold on her head, his hands buried in her hair, afraid to move for fear he might explode.

She didn't move her hands away. "Think of tonight as a tasting menu and we're still having the predinner aperitif."

Oh, God.

"Tilly." He unwound her hair from his fingers, gently pulling her face so she looked up at him. Need stretched the skin of his face tight. "I want…I need to come inside you."

He backed up from between her thighs and drew her out of the chair. Hands under her arms, he lifted her so she sat on the edge of the desk and unbuttoned her jacket, which fell in a pool around her. She hungered for him. Her clogs fell with clunks on the floor as she kicked them off her feet.

"Beautiful," he said, running his hands across the tops of her camisole-covered breasts. He leaned over and kissed the slope of her breasts. She moaned, raising her breasts higher in offering. He didn't hesitate. He lifted the hem of her camisole up and pulled it over her head, leaving her in her cotton bra. The appetizers were over. She was dinner, laid out for him to enjoy.

"I have been dreaming of you," he said as he pushed the cup of her bra down. He caught her nipple in his lips and pulled gently. "Dreaming of this."

Tilly whimpered as he bit her nipple lightly. She scooted forward, pushing herself as close to him as possible, as if she needed to feel as though nothing could come between them. He obliged, kneading her breasts gently as though they were a delicate pastry.

He lifted her slightly off the desk and she shucked her pants and underwear. She scooted to the edge of the desk, leaning back into Dan's bracing arm. He supported her, would always support her. He wanted her to know that she could trust him to be there to lean on when she needed, and to let her stand on her own.

Her eyes were ablaze with desire and he suspected his were, too. They held nothing back from each other. Tonight, nothing existed between them but love.

"Condom," Dan groaned as he fumbled around in his pants pocket. He had one, several, in here. He just had to find them.

"Shit," Tilly said, struggling to sit up. "I don't have any in here."

Dan nudged her back against his bracing arm as he handed her the small package to open. "I've had some in my pocket since the Taste." He tilted his head down, nibbling her ear as he talked. "I've always been an optimist." He pulled her earlobe into his mouth and sucked, making her gasp and nearly lose her grip on the condom.

"Finally," Tilly said when the packet ripped, pushing him away from her enough to nudge his pants down and sheathe him.

Dan had never seen anything more erotic than Tilly, sitting on the edge of her desk, her chef's jacket in a puddle, naked except for her bra, as she rolled the condom over him. Her strong hands possessing and enjoying him, as he would soon possess and enjoy her.

He entered her, forcing himself to go slowly, savoring her softness as she enveloped him. His senses focused on the woman moving against him. Every small movement she made, every little wanting noise, claimed and sharpened his attention while the rest of the world fell behind in a mist. *This* woman, *this* moment, *this* place absorbed him completely.

Tilly was his fascination and his future.

She reached around to grasp his ass to pull him closer. Short, craving breaths came faster and faster as they moved in rhythm together. Tilly held him, moved against him, her head back baring her long neck, which he nibbled and licked. She was exposed, open to him, and Dan wouldn't be able to move slowly much longer.

She wrapped her legs around him and arched high, offering her breasts up to his mouth. As he savored the taste of her, she cried out and he knew she was close. He could wait for her. He would be happy to wait for her.

She tightened her legs around him as she bucked, moaned, then relaxed against his arm.

Dan pulled Tilly up to press against him as he released into her. They stayed joined, their breathing synchronized, their chests rising and falling together. Dan wished he could stay with her, skin-to-skin, forever. This was right. *She* was right.

Reality set in. The condom would be no good if he didn't remove it. Maybe someday he and Tilly would want to have children and he could enjoy her without this worry, but that day was in the future. Until then… He pulled out of her and disposed of the condom, then scooped Tilly off the desk and sat down in the chair, Tilly on his lap.

Her naked ass perched on him was enough to excite him again. "We should do this again. Soon, in a bed and…" He bent his head down to suck her nipple through her bra. "…fully naked the next time."

"Your place or mine?" she asked, wiggling against him while smiling with satisfaction.

"Ours." He looked Tilly in the eye as he said the words. "Maybe you're not ready now, but I want to be the person you come home to late each night. When you're high and jazzed up from a long day at work, I want to make slow, steady love to you until you're ready to fall asleep." He stroked the line of her jaw, almost unable to believe she— they—were actually here. "I want to be the person who tries your new dishes and the one to cook you breakfast in bed on Sunday." She rested her head and closed her eyes as he spoke. "I want it all now. But I'll take it whenever you say. I love you and I want to start our life together. Now. Tomorrow. Whenever you give me the okay. When you feel you can trust me."

Tilly looked so peaceful with her eyes closed. She was nearly naked and sitting on his naked lap. They'd had heart-stopping sex in her office. These were all positive signs but still he was nervous. Dan had never wanted anything so much. Not just sex—though he had wanted that—but Tilly. All of Tilly. He wanted to be in her life.

Sex didn't change the fact he'd used her poorly. He'd like to believe their lovemaking meant she wanted their relationship, too, but he didn't want to take anything about Tilly for granted. If he had to fight more for her heart and her commitment, he would fight. If he had to do more to prove his devotion and faithfulness, he would. Whatever she asked of him. He was hers.

She opened her warm brown eyes, the eyes he hoped his children would have, and looked at him. Then she smiled. "And Imbir? What will Paulie do with Imbir around?"

Dan exhaled quickly in relief. "Paulie has a cage and a wheel. He will be fine. They can start a club of animals used against and then saved by Tila Milek. We can even start a website. What's your middle name?"

"Marta. Martha, the patron saint of waitresses."

Dan laughed. "Really?"

Tilly grinned and shrugged. "Really. Babunia said my mom got so fat with me while pregnant that I had to be a cook of some sort. Lawrence is the patron saint of cooks and there is no good Polish female version. Marta was close enough."

"Our house will be the Tila Marta Milek-Meier animal rescue. We can even find that little dog and include him if you want."

"I never want to see that dog again."

"Fine. No dog."

He wrapped his arms around her and she laid her head against his chest. They sat in silence for several minutes until he noticed her shiver. When he rubbed her arm he felt goose bumps.

"Tilly?"

She murmured sleepily in response.

"Let's get you dressed and back to my house. You've had a long day."

"Okay," she said as she climbed off him and reached for her pants.

Dan helped her button her jacket and got her into her socks and clogs before dressing himself. While Tilly went to the bathroom to clean herself up, Dan dealt with the mess they'd made in her office, removing any evidence her staff might see. He also picked up the envelope with the promissory note and put it in her purse.

When Tilly came back, walking sleepily, Dan guided her through the kitchen to the back door. He set her down in the passenger seat of his Subaru and buckled her in. She was asleep before he started the car. He drove the few minutes back to his house through streets that were starting to empty of people. When he finally pulled up in front of his townhome and parked, he looked over at the woman snoring softly next to him. Quiet bursts of air puffed in and out of her mouth and Dan took a couple of minutes to listen to the music of the rest of his life.

TILLY WOKE UP ENOUGH to be aware when Dan picked her up out of his car and carried her into his house, but she didn't open her eyes. Opening her eyes sounded too hard. No, eyes didn't sound. They blinked. She stopped trying to think. Better to keep her eyes closed and fall back to sleep.

When awareness hit again, Tilly was in Dan's bedroom, in only her panties and an oversize T-shirt.

I must be tired to have slept through Dan undressing me.

She rolled over onto her side to find Dan's solid body next to her. When she pushed herself against him and laid her head on his chest, his arm encircled her. For the first time since she was a child, Tilly felt like home in a place that wasn't a kitchen.

"I love you, Dan," she murmured before giving in to sleep completely.

CHAPTER TWENTY-NINE

One year later

TILLY WAS CURLED UP on the couch enjoying her day off, the newest issue of *Lucky Peach* and air-conditioning when the doorbell rang. She put the magazine on the coffee table and padded over to the front door. Through the windows she saw the postman with a box in his hands. Dan was coming down the stairs in pajama bottoms and no shirt as she signed the slip. She quickly thanked the postman and closed the door in time to enjoy the show.

"Hey," he said, sliding his strong arms around her waist and bending his head down to give her a long kiss. "What's that?"

"I don't know." She turned the medium-sized box over and looked at the label. "It's addressed to me and I had to sign for it. Present from you?"

She turned away from him, but he pulled her close and kissed the side of her neck, sending tickling bursts down her spine and making her smile, before releasing her so she could go to the kitchen. The intimacy of living with someone was maddeningly wonderful. Or wonderfully maddening, she wasn't sure which. Just when she thought they'd established a rhythm to their lives, the postman would deliver a surprise.

She set the box on the counter and pulled out a utility

knife. Wrapped in tissue were two White Sox jerseys and an envelope.

"He's such an ass," Dan said, laughing.

"What? What is this?"

He pulled one of the jerseys out of the box and checked the tag. "This one's for you," he said as he handed her the jersey. "And this," he pulled the other jersey out of the box, "is for me."

"You're a Cubs fan," she said, looking at him with her brows furrowed. "Who would send us his-and-hers Sox jerseys?"

Dan glanced up from the jersey he was holding and laughed even harder.

"Why are you laughing? Shouldn't you be pissed off?"

Dan handed her the envelope that had come in the box. "Open this. I think it will answer your questions."

She took the envelope, still eyeing him suspiciously, and opened it. Packed inside were two tickets to the Crosstown Classic and a note.

Enjoy the game. Ask Dan to explain. He deserves it. Go Sox—Mike.

Tilly read the note to Dan, who chuckled wryly as he cursed his friend. "He really is a rat bastard."

"Are you going to explain?"

Dan looked uncomfortable and was silent long enough for Tilly to think he was going to ignore the note and her question entirely. Finally he relaxed his scrunched-up face and started talking.

"After the first review of Babka was posted, Mike gave both Rich and me shit for it."

Tilly nodded. She might have forgiven him, but she was still happy to know his friends had harassed him for it, too.

"I deserved the shit and he dished it out. We made this bet about whether or not the review would boomerang back

to me and bite me in the ass. If I won, Mike would have
to go to a Cubs/Cardinals game and sit in the bleachers
wearing a Cards uniform. If he won, I would have to go
to a Crosstown Classic game dressed up as a White Sox
fan. I always honor my bets, but I was hoping he'd forgotten about this one."

Tilly cocked her head and stared at the love of her life
until he flinched. "This—" she gestured to the townhome
they now shared, complete with Imbir's water dish on the
kitchen floor "—is the review coming back to bite you in
the ass?"

A cell phone bounced and vibrated on the counter. Tilly
picked up her phone and looked at the screen. Give him
hell, Tilly. Part of the bet was that he cheer for the Sox.
Make sure he cheers.

She peered back up at Dan, who squirmed under her
scrutiny. Talking about the review always made him uncomfortable. She'd forgiven him—was even grateful to the
fates because she wouldn't have met him otherwise—but
he was still sensitive about the part he'd played in one of
the worst episodes of her life.

That he was the best part of her life was something he
wasn't entirely used to.

She had to chomp down on the insides of her cheeks to
keep from laughing. He looked like a little boy waiting to
be yelled at by his mother. She felt sorry for him and part
of her said she should end his guilt-ridden squirming.

But not yet. Dan's easy smile and ready charm meant he
didn't often have to flounder around in nervous ignorance
and what was a girlfriend, if not the one person on whom
the easy charm didn't work so well.

She waited until he came up with an answer.

Dan eyed her up and down with a grin. "I don't think

you've bitten me on the ass yet, but we could fix that over-sight."

She folded her arms across her chest and waited.

He sighed. "Mike wins the bet. Not because anything I share with you constitutes a 'bite on the ass,' but because I expected my life to continue on as it had been before the review. And nothing about my life is the same. Everything is a thousand times better. While Mike didn't win the let-ter of the bet, he sure won the spirit of it."

Dan stopped talking long enough to put the jersey on. As he finished buttoning it over his stomach—still ribbed and flat despite a steady diet of Polish food—he spoke again. "I'm not sure I will ever be a White Sox fan, but if going to a game with you and rooting against the Cubs while wearing gray and black means I've won your trust, I'll be at U.S. Cellular Field every day. Beth can run the business by herself."

Tilly studied Dan carefully. He was still the best-looking man she'd ever seen, even if the jersey looked goofy on his solid wrestler's frame. They'd been living together for sev-eral months. Dan had asked her to trust him, if only for one day at a time, but it hadn't taken long for Tilly to realize she trusted him and, more important, she trusted herself. When she'd decided to pack up her things and move, Imbir and his litter box were packed up first.

Forgiveness had come surprisingly easily. The morn-ing after they'd first made love, they'd woken up together, his arms wrapped around her and her butt tucked against his erection. Tilly had rolled over to face him and offered up her forgiveness.

Trust had taken a little longer. Tilly had trusted him in pieces, daily for a little while, then weekly and finally she'd made the decision to trust him and she wouldn't take it back. But she'd never actually told him that. She'd just moved in, instead.

Tilly put her jersey on the counter next to the phone and tickets. Dan eyed her every move, wary of opening himself up and nervous about calling to mind bad memories. She reached up and flicked open the top button of his jersey.

"Hey, I just did that up."

She kissed the skin she had revealed.

He swallowed hard. "I changed my mind. You can unbutton anything you want."

"I—" she popped the second button open and kissed "—trust—" third button and third kiss "—you—" another button, another kiss.

He clutched her head in his hands and tilted her face up so they gazed into each other's eyes.

"No daily, weekly or monthly qualifications?"

"No qualifications. No jersey needed. You can go to the game in a Cubs jersey and I'll wear the White Sox jersey. I'll even protect you from Southside bullies."

He kissed her. Hard, possessively. His lips claimed hers, binding him to her, and his arms closed around her as he held her close. She parted her lips to let him in. He plunged his tongue into her mouth, tasting her. Enjoying her. Devouring her as she fully opened herself up to him for the first time.

He pulled her camisole up and his fingers trailed along her back, creating goose bumps in their wake. She pressed her hips up against him. Wanting. Needing. His erection was hard through the soft cotton of his pajama bottoms.

She pulled back enough to give her access to the silly White Sox jersey still covering most of his torso. When she reached up for another button, he stopped her.

"Upstairs," he panted. "I love sex with you in the

kitchen, but I want to make love to you in my bed. In our bed."

Tilly gave Dan a long, inviting smile before leading him upstairs.

* * * * *

Be sure to look for Jennifer Lohmann's next book, THE FIRST MOVE, available in April 2013 wherever Harlequin Superromance books are sold.

SPECIAL EXCERPT FROM

H HARLEQUIN

super romance

An Act of Persuasion

By **Stephanie Doyle**

One night, Ben Tyler broke his own rule about mixing business with pleasure. And it cost him, because Anna Summers quit. Now he's ready to do almost anything to get her back.
Read on for an exciting excerpt!

She was here. Ben Tyler felt a deep satisfaction watching her walk through the country club.

It had been twelve weeks since he'd last seen Anna Summers. Three months since he'd heard her voice. He preferred not to think too much about the fact that he knew down to the minute when she'd last spoken to him.

"Hello, Ben." Anna looked different to him. Softer maybe. Her red hair still shifted about her face, and her freckles were still scattered across her face, but there was a change. Or maybe he'd simply missed seeing her.

"You changed your cell-phone number." The words were out of Ben's mouth before he could stop them. He hadn't meant to start with accusations. He'd intended to be agreeable before asking her to come back to work.

She shrugged. "I guess I didn't want to talk then."

"But you do now?"

"Now I have no choice."

No choice? "Are you in some kind of trouble?"

"You could say."

"Whatever it is, I'll fix it," he said.

"Oh, you're going to fix it. Just like that. Snap and it's done." There was no mistaking the edge in her tone.

Ben sighed at his strategic misstep. "Can we go someplace more private to discuss this?"

She nodded. They left and were halfway to his house when she finally broke the silence.

"So what did you want to talk to me about?"

He'd hoped she would start. But that smacked a little bit of cowardice to him. He was a grown man who fully accepted his actions. "I wanted to apologize."

She shot him a look. "Exactly what are you sorry for?"

He struggled to find the speech he'd prepared, the one that recognized he should have taken her feelings into account, that admitted he'd been wrong to shut her out. But she spoke before he could say anything.

"I'm pregnant."

Will the baby bring Anna and Ben together?
Or will it drive them apart permanently?
Find out in AN ACT OF PERSUASION
by Stephanie Doyle, available March 2013
from Harlequin® Superromance®.

What if you desperately
wanted a family but had
given up hope it would
ever happen?

Award-winning author
Mary Sullivan
presents the follow up to
IN FROM THE COLD

Home to Laura

AVAILABLE IN MARCH

More Story...More Romance

HSR71837

REQUEST YOUR FREE BOOKS!
2 FREE NOVELS PLUS 2 FREE GIFTS!

HARLEQUIN
super romance

Exciting, emotional, unexpected!

HSR13